Doin' Me

Wanda B. Campbell

www.urbanchristianonline.com

Urban Books, LLC
78 East Industry Court
Deer Park, NY 11729

ISBN 13: 978-1-60162-756-8
ISBN 10: 1-60162-756-4

First Printing May 2013
Printed in the United States of America

10 9 8 7 6 5 4 3 2 1

This is a work of fiction. Any references or similarities to actual events, real people, living or dead, or to real locales are intended to give the novel a sense of reality. Any similarity in other names, characters, places, and incidents is entirely coincidental.

Distributed by Kensington Corp.
Submit Wholesale Orders to:
Kensington Publishing Corp.
C/O Penguin Group (USA) Inc.
Attention: Order Processing
405 Murray Hill Parkway
East Rutherford, NJ 07073-2316
Phone: 1-800-526-0275
Fax: 1-800-227-9604

Doin' Me

A novel by

Wanda B. Campbell

Dedication

For everyone who has ever experienced an identity crisis

"You are my father. You hold my future and destiny. You are my father. You are my father. In you I find my identity."
Words from the song "Identity" by Israel Houghton

Acknowledgments

First and always, I thank my Heavenly Father for entrusting me with the gift of speaking to His children through the written word. I stand in awe at the marvelous things He has done on this six-year journey. It is my sincere desire to continue writing the stories He gives me.

My life would be incomplete and the journey would be lonely without the companionship and friendship of my life partner, Craig Campbell, Sr. After twenty-four years of peaks and valleys, triumphs and failures, heartbreak and celebrations, your love for me hasn't faltered but has intensified to a level that leaves me breathless. I love you, Big Papa!

While writing this novel, I found myself experiencing what Bishop T. D. Jakes calls "a turn." This happens when life as we know it changes course and ventures into unfamiliar territory and causes an emotional unbalance. Turns aren't necessarily catastrophic events. Some turns are vital in catapulting us to the next level. My turn came in the form of my youngest child, Craig "Papa" Campbell, Jr., graduating high school and entering college, leaving me with an empty nest. Papa, while I will miss your daily presence and your smart mouth, I celebrate your future. Persevere and have fun while fulfilling the purpose God has ordained for your life.

Acknowledgments

During this same time period, God also performed a miracle by sparing my eldest son, Jonathan's life in a major car accident. Son, answer the line. The Lord is calling, and your purpose is closer than you think.

On Wednesday, April 5, 1989, I became a mother. I remember looking at my daughter and thinking, *What am going to do with her?* Twenty-three years later I still don't have an answer to that question. Chantel, just when I think I have you figured out, you surprise me with your spontaneity and courage. Keep working hard and being a good mother to your son. Remember, only God can give real peace.

Special thanks to fellow author Reverend Lawrence Gray Sr. and coworker Wanda Sanford. *Doin' Me* would not have its flavor without your expertise.

To all my faithful supporters and my publicity team at Alameda County Medical Center—Alaina, Amy, Denise, Mary, and Vincent, just to name a few—thank you so much for the encouragement.

Family and friends label me a fanatic, which I firmly disagree with. Just because I have at least three copies of every Israel & New Breed CD, DVD, and the book *A Deeper Level*, and have flown on multiple occasions to Israel & New Breed concerts, doesn't make me a fanatic. I'm simply blessed by their music ministry. Israel Houghton, thank you for writing songs that change lives.

Finally, but never least, thank you for spending your resources in purchasing this book and for taking the time to read it. Without you, the reader, there wouldn't be a journey.

"Come now, and let us reason together," saith the Lord: though your sins be as scarlet, they shall be as white as snow; though they be red like crimson, they shall be as wool.

-Isaiah 1:18

Chapter 1

Reyna Mills posed in the full-length mirror. She turned to the right, then to the left. She bent over at the waist and shook her shoulders. Unsatisfied with the results, she repositioned the bustier and performed the test again. Now pleased, she turned to view her backside. The snug eighteen-inch black skirt stopped below mid-thigh and just above the knee. She walked over to the closet and stepped into four-inch-heeled black pumps.

"Perfect!" she exclaimed at her reflection. Tyson, her unofficial date for the evening, was probably too anal to appreciate her newly waxed bare legs, but there was no way she'd ruin the black and red ensemble with nylons. Neither would she limit the display of her thirty-four C-size "girls." It had taken Reyna almost twenty years to appreciate her assets and not feel condemned to hell for showing them off.

For years she'd heard her mother and her former pastor, Rosalie Jennings, preach against everything from a woman cutting her hair to wearing makeup. "Modesty is best," the pastor had said. Pastor Jennings would probably have a coronary if she saw Reyna now. Not only had Reyna traded in her shoulder-length tresses for a tapered hairstyle with spikes, but she had also traded in clear lip gloss for a complete makeup kit loaded with color.

The new look was more than a metamorphosis. It signified her genesis. A rebirth. A coming-of-age. Why it took her so long to realize that inside her skull rested a brain capable of making sound decisions about her life, she'd never know. She chalked it up to being hoodwinked, bamboozled, or even voodooed. Whatever the verb, she would never allow anyone to control her again. From this day forward, decisions like where to go and what to wear would be based on what she wanted and liked, not the words of a self-serving dictator wearing a robe and toting a Bible.

Up until two short months ago, Reyna had considered disagreeing with Pastor Rosalie Jennings next to blasphemy on the sin scale. She'd grown up in the church, under the teachings of Pastor Jennings. Her mother and her beloved pastor were friends. Whereas Reyna's mother had been too occupied with church business to notice Reyna, Pastor Jennings had always had time for her. Reyna had spent many Sunday afternoons at the pastor's kitchen table. It was at that same table that Reyna had recited the sinner's prayer and had committed her life to Christ at the tender age of seventeen. Reyna couldn't pinpoint the date, but at some point the respect she held for Pastor Jennings had been transformed into idolization. That had left her with a busted lip, a blackened eye, and a night in jail for breaking into and entering a private residence.

Reyna turned to examine the tight layered curls on the back of her head. If she'd known she'd look this good, she would have made her hairstylist cut that mess off a long time ago. If she hadn't been so consumed with pleasing the woman of God, she might have been able to complete graduate school and land a husband. At Pastor Jennings's request, Reyna had put school on hold and had spent nearly five years chasing the pastor's son, Kevin. Her grand prize wasn't the great Dr. Kevin Jennings, but a badge of humiliation she doubted she'd ever live down. Reyna figured Pastor Jennings must have gotten the wires crossed with the prophetic word assuring her Kevin was her husband. Kevin reunited with his estranged wife, and they were now expecting their first child. All Reyna got out of the deal was a new job as property manager for a local real estate office, thanks to Tyson, who just happened to be Kevin's best friend.

Reyna moved to the dresser and sprayed on Halle Berry's new fragrance, hoping the fruity scent would make her more desirable, but not to Tyson. She hoped to meet a prospect at the charity benefit dinner tonight. Not that attorney Tyson Stokes wasn't a good catch. He owned his own home, his own firm, and had no baby mamas. But he was saved, sanctified, and filled to the brim with the Holy Ghost. Something she could do without. She'd been freed from the plantation—that was what she now called organized religion—and she was never going back. She'd give Tyson a superficial friendship, but never would she give anyone associated with God her heart. Pastor Jennings's manipulation and betrayal had annihilated her trust in God and anyone claiming to know Him. From now on Reyna controlled her destiny.

She'd accepted Tyson's invitation to the event only because despite growing up in the Bay Area, she'd never been inside the plush Claremont Hotel nestled in the Berkeley hills. Since the historic hotel didn't normally hold church functions, her once rigid religious beliefs didn't allow non-Christian social gatherings, and neither did her budget. Being friends with Tyson had its advantages.

She grabbed her clutch purse and sashayed downstairs and toward the front door. Out of habit, she opened the coat closet, then changed her mind. She looked too good to hide behind a lined wool coat.

"What street corner are you going to stand on dressed like that?"

The shrill voice, which always lacked affection, belonged to her mother. Reyna made the three strides to the front door before turning and addressing her mother. With each step she wondered why she hadn't she used the back door.

"You heard me, Jezebel. Where are you going?"

Reyna hated being compared to the evil biblical Queen Jezebel, mainly because up until a few months ago Reyna categorized a woman who went around with bare arms and bare legs and wore makeup as a loose Jezebel. Without knowing the woman's name or history, she passed judgment. Now she was one of them and didn't care what her mother or anyone else thought.

"Mother, I told you earlier, I'm meeting Tyson at the charity banquet for the youth center."

Jewel Mills, dressed in a floral-print muumuu, stood and stomped her left foot against the hardwood floor. "Have you lost your mind? You're going to a formal event with a prominent lawyer dressed like a two-dollar whore?" Jewel threw her hands up and shook her head. "I know Rosalie and I raised you better than that. You need to read what the Bible says about loose women."

The sound of her former pastor and mentor's name sent searing heat throughout Reyna's body. Her eyes burned. Her right fist involuntarily clenched. Her nostrils flared. Though her emotions raged, she remained calm as she scrutinized every inch of her mother as she stepped into her space.

The woman who'd birthed her yet failed to nurture her, opting instead to push her off on her best friend, had the audacity to criticize her. Jewel had sat back and plotted with Pastor Jennings and had encouraged Reyna to chase after a married man. Jewel had wanted her to marry Dr. Kevin Jennings and pastor the church. She'd even helped Reyna get dressed the night she attempted to seduce him. Now this holier-than-thou woman had the nerve to judge her?

"Why don't you read the Bible for yourself?" Reyna snarled through clenched teeth. "You might learn that your beloved Pastor Rosalie Jennings is the reason you couldn't keep Daddy around."

If Reyna's face wasn't so heavily coated with makeup, the slap would have hurt more. Jewel didn't like to be reminded that her husband had divorced her because she spent too much time on her knees at church and not enough time tending to his needs. Since her husband wasn't saved, Jewel had followed Pastor Jennings's advice and had rationed sex. Unfortunately for Jewel, her husband found a neighbor who was always open for business. He left Jewel and moved in with the woman and later fathered her three children.

Jewel's hand shook uncontrollably as she pointed at her daughter. "You better watch how you talk to me. I don't care how old you are. I'm still your mother! And what happened between me and your father is still none of your business!"

Reyna ceased massaging her cheek. "I'm almost thirty-one years old. How much older do I have to be to know you and Rosalie robbed me of my daddy's presence?"

"That's Pastor Jennings to you. And you got to see your daddy from time to time. It's not my fault he raised his other children and not you. And what's that got to do with you dressing like a streetwalker?"

It was useless; her mother would defend Pastor Jennings until her last breath. "Mother, I don't care what you think. This is how I dress now. If you don't like it, too bad." Reyna rolled her eyes and started for the door again.

"What about Tyson?" Jewel called. "What does he think about this *new* look?"

Reyna whirled around and glared at the woman she'd begun to despise. "Let me make myself perfectly clear. I don't care what you, Tyson, or even God Himself thinks about me. I'm a grown woman, and I'll do whatever I want." She slammed the wooden door and decided it was time to move out of her mother's plantation.

Chapter 2

"Man, why don't you just call her?" Kevin asked after Tyson returned from checking the lobby for the third time. "Maybe you should give her the speech about how much you detest tardiness and have no concept of CP time."

Without comment, Tyson reclaimed his seat and took a swig of sugarless iced tea. Reyna was late, and his best friend was correct with his assessment. Tyson's profession didn't tolerate tardiness, and socially, neither did he.

He'd offered to pick Reyna up, but she'd insisted on driving since this wasn't a real date from her perspective. He didn't completely agree but didn't bother to share his thoughts with her. In his opinion, they'd been in some sort of relationship for about four months. They'd never talked about their status, but Tyson's anal personality prevented him from wasting time on frivolous things, including relationships. After working together on projects at church for five years, Reyna knew that; therefore, having the "talk" was unnecessary. Tyson had spent countless days deprogramming Reyna from their former pastor's cultlike control and rebuilding her self-esteem.

He set the glass down and observed his friends. For the first time, he felt a tug of jealousy at the attention Kevin's wife, Marlissa, lavished on him. They constantly shared physical contact, everything from hand-holding to soft kisses. Tyson had served as best man in their wedding, then had represented Kevin three years later in their divorce proceedings, only to watch them reconcile and renew their vows. Now they were expecting their first child. Through all the drama, Tyson had never thought he'd missed much in the love department. The female acquaintances in college were sufficient in satisfying his physical needs but didn't come close to touching his soul. In graduate school, the law became his mistress, and up until recently, his law firm had left him fully sated.

At age thirty-six, he'd accomplished materially what most men dreamed about. Now he desired what Kevin and Marlissa shared. He wanted love, and he wanted it with Reyna. Slight tremors rocked him at the revelation.

Never in a million years did he think he'd be attracted to Reyna Mills, the church girl who had stalked his best friend. Then one day Reyna the square was transformed into Reyna the woman. Liking what he saw, Tyson dug deeper and pulled back the layers and found a woman he could love if given the chance.

"If you really want to get Reyna's attention, you should take lessons from your boy." Marlissa nodded toward Kevin. "He's the king of romance."

Tyson refused to admit he needed help in the romance department. If he could maintain a 95 percent win record in court, he'd figure out a way to woo Reyna. "You're right. He's so romantic that a few months ago you punched him at the altar," he said, referring to Marlissa's reaction to Kevin's confession of love during their surprise vow renewal ceremony.

"True. I had to whip him into shape, but now he's well trained." Both Kevin and Tyson laughed out loud.

"I'm serious," Marlissa said, patting her slightly extended belly. "If you want to get Reyna or any other woman, you're going to have to loosen up."

"Hey, guys." Starla approached the table, slightly winded, with Leon a half step behind.

"Great. Just what I need, more love floating around," Tyson grumbled at his friends. Like Kevin and Marlissa, Leon and Starla were madly in love and were expecting a baby.

"Man, don't be hatin'," Leon said as he pulled out Starla's chair. "It doesn't go well with your award-winning personality." He smiled and shook Tyson's hand.

Tyson's jaw twitched as he watched his friends greet one another as if they hadn't seen each other in years, when in actuality the couples shared Sunday dinner every week. He used to join them, until he began feeling like a fifth wheel. Reyna refused to join them, to sit around and listen to how good God was.

"Is Reyna coming?" Starla asked Tyson after getting settled. "I sure hope so. I don't want to spend the evening with your funky attitude."

Marlissa spoke before he could answer. "I was just telling him that he needs to loosen up. He needs to work on romancing Reyna."

"Tell me about it," Starla chimed in. "They've been hanging out for months, and I bet the girl doesn't even know he's interested."

"Girl, you know he hasn't even kissed her," Marlissa noted. Then she and Starla continued talking as if Tyson wasn't there, then with ease moved on to baby talk.

Tyson sipped more iced tea and faked interest in Kevin and Leon's conversation about Star Construction, Leon's company. Although he was an investor in the business, at the moment he could care less about its success. What Tyson needed was Reyna's presence, and he needed it now. He wanted someone special to share dinner conversation with, and when the music started, he didn't want to sit back and watch the other dancers. Tonight Tyson wanted to participate.

"I guess we'd better dig in," Kevin said after the waiter set salads in front of each of them, leaving one in the vacant space beside Tyson.

"I guess you're right. Wouldn't want to keep you lovebirds waiting on us lonely peons." Tyson mumbled a blessing over the food, then reached for the salt and pepper. It was then he realized his friends were staring at him. His jealousy had slipped through his lips.

He abandoned his quest for the salt and pepper and rested his elbows on the table. Seated at the table were the people he cared most about in the world, although he doubted if he'd told them that. Kevin understood him like a blood brother. He trusted Leon with his life. Marlissa and Starla, he loved them like sisters, but most of the time he treated them as emotional nuisances.

"Guys, I'm sorry. I didn't mean that." The group continued to stare. Apologizing was also new to Tyson. Normally, when he offended someone, he didn't care. He pushed his chair back and stood. "I'm going to get some air."

"Oh my," Starla gasped, looking past Tyson.

Marlissa's mouth hung open, but no words flowed. Both Leon's and Kevin's eyes bulged.

When Tyson turned and Reyna's frame came into focus, his mouth also dropped. His bright skin turned crimson, and his nostrils flared. Charcoal flecks appeared in his hazel-colored eyes. The need that had engulfed him only moments earlier vanished. Right now embarrassment clothed him. His anger rose a notch with every seductive step Reyna took toward him. She reached him, wearing a bright smile, and in his opinion, very little else.

"Hi, guys," Reyna greeted the group. "Sorry I'm late, but I ran into traffic. I hope I didn't miss much."

"H—hey, Reyna," Kevin stuttered. "You're right on time. The program hasn't started yet."

"Yeah . . ." Marlissa finally found her voice. "They just served the salad."

Leon and Starla stuffed baby spinach leaves into their mouths.

"Good. I'm starved." Reyna looked over at Tyson, who hadn't uttered one word, and gestured toward the empty chair. "Do I have to pull out my own chair?"

Tyson leaned close to her ear and said through clenched teeth, "I need to see you outside for a moment . . . right now."

Reyna waved him off and pulled out the chair and sat down. "Whatever you have to say can wait. I'm ready to eat."

Tyson continued standing until Kevin tapped his shoulder and visually communicated that people were staring and murmuring. Reluctantly, he sat down and glared at Reyna. Oblivious to his discomfort, Reyna poured on dressing and proceeded to devour the salad.

"Tyson." Starla's tone was softer than normal. "Eat your salad before it gets cold."

Tyson's face twisted, then relaxed, and he chuckled at Starla's attempt to calm him down. "Whatever you say, Mother Scott," he said in reference to Starla's mother-in-law, who was a member at his church and a noted prayer warrior.

Leon raised an eyebrow. "I think you could use my mother's help right about now."

"Don't I know it," Tyson mumbled before biting the dry leaves.

Forty-five minutes later, during dessert, Reyna finally turned and spoke to Tyson. "Now, what did you want to talk about?"

Tyson savored a bit of tiramisu before answering. He set his fork down and made eye contact with a gentleman two tables over. The same gentleman had been eyeing Reyna throughout dinner. He placed his arm around Reyna's bare shoulder, then nodded at the gentleman. With the unspoken communication, the stranger turned his attention elsewhere.

Tyson stood and held out his hand. "It's a little stuffy in here. Let's go outside." Reyna pushed back from the table and stood. Tyson felt his anger return. "Would you like to use my jacket?"

"Oh, no, I'm fine." Reyna strolled through the banquet hall with her head held high, unaware of the stares. When they reached the lobby, she sat down on the white leather sofa, with her legs crossed at the knee.

Tyson paced the Venetian carpet. This was new territory for him. If he were in the courtroom, he'd know exactly what to say to persuade the jury in his favor. But he wasn't in court, in front of a jury. He was in a historical five-star resort with a woman who looked like she'd do anything for fifty dollars.

He ceased pacing and stuffed his hands into his pants pockets. "Reyna, did I mention that this was a formal event?"

Reyna stopped brushing her nails on the hem of her skirt. "Of course you did. That's why I wore this black skirt and bought this new top."

Tyson closed his eyes and counted to ten. "Reyna, you're not this dense. What did you do? Leave the rest of the top on the rack? You would've done better showing up topless for the good that thing's doing." His eyes traveled to her legs. "And where's the rest of your skirt? My dinner napkin has more fabric than that thing. Take a look around you. Every man here has on a tuxedo, and the women are wearing evening gowns. I don't have a problem with the makeup and the haircut, but this attire is too much."

Reyna opened her purse and refreshed her lipstick.

Tyson ran his hand over his short hair. "Look, Reyna, I'm a prominent lawyer. I can't be seen socially with a woman who looks like a . . ." He didn't finish.

Reyna jumped to her feet. "Go on and say it, Tyson. Say how you really feel." She prodded until he gave in.

"Fine! I'll say it. You embarrassed me tonight. You're dressed like you don't respect yourself. You're displaying assets that should remain private. You look cheap."

For a slight second, he thought he saw hurt flash in her eyes. Then she spewed venom. "First of all, you invited me, not the other way around." Her forefinger wagged in his face. "I don't dress to please anyone but myself. I'm doin' me! I can show whatever I want to show. It's not like you're my man, anyway. If you don't like it, don't ask me out again. I only agreed to come in hopes of finding a real man." She left him standing in the empty lobby with his mouth open.

By the time Tyson had processed her words and returned to the table, Reyna was on the dance floor, bumping and grinding with the gentleman who'd been ogling her all evening.

Chapter 3

Reyna twisted her hips to the beat of the music and moved closer to her dance partner. She didn't know his name, but he'd been watching her all night, and for that alone she'd accepted his dance invitation when she returned from putting Tyson in his place. The tall Boris Kodjoe look-alike didn't have a problem keeping up with the wild moves she'd learned from watching MTV videos. Up until tonight the only dancing she'd done was a holy dance in church.

She turned and ground her backside against her partner's midsection. To her surprise, he squeezed her hips and pressed her even closer. The friction made her uncomfortable, and she opened her eyes to find Tyson glaring at her. To make sure she and Attorney Stokes had a clear understanding, Reyna leaned her head back and increased the pace, then dropped it like it was hot. The next time she checked, Tyson and the rest of his holy friends were gone.

After the third dance, her partner led her back to his table. "Since what we did out there could get us arrested in some states, I guess we should at least exchange names. I'm Chase." His grin revealed a set of perfectly white teeth and a right dimple.

Reyna's eyes traveled to his left hand. No ring. She returned his smile and accepted his extended hand. "I'm Reyna Mills."

"I didn't know girls were so formal these days."

Reyna hid her confusion by wiping sweat from her forehead with an unused decorative table napkin. She didn't have much experience in the dating department, but what was formal about using both first and last names?

Chase leaned in close. "I hope stealing you from that other guy doesn't cause you any problems later."

Reyna leaned closer and, without meaning to, gave Chase full view of her "girls." "You didn't steal me from anyone. That guy doesn't own me. We're only friends. At least we were before tonight."

Chase's eyes remained focused downward. "In that case, can I buy you a drink?"

Alcohol had never touched her lips, but tonight was a night of new beginnings, and Reyna wanted to try something new. Besides, it was okay to drink as long as she didn't get drunk. But what should she have? Discreetly, she looked around at the other tables and settled on what looked like a frozen fruit drink. "I'll have one of those." She pointed at a beverage on the table across from her.

Chase chuckled at her naïveté. "I see you're new at this." He stopped an approaching waiter. "Bring the lady a margarita."

"New at what?" Reyna didn't notice that Chase didn't order anything for himself.

"You know . . ." He raised an eyebrow. "Getting your swerve on."

Reyna assumed he meant dancing. "I may be new on the scene, but I can work you over."

Laughter poured from Chase as he leaned back in his chair. "We'll see about that."

The waiter returned with the margarita. Reyna thought to ask Chase if she should sip the drink or take a swig, but decided against it. This man was handsome and was interested in her. She still didn't know much about him, but she could tell by the Rolex that he had some money. No way was she going to reveal her inexperience with life. She took a chance and took little sips. She liked the salty lime taste and at some point little sips turned into swigs. Four margaritas later Reyna found herself inside Chase's suite, learning what the term *getting your swerve on* really meant.

Sunday morning arrived, and Reyna found herself too sore to move and was happy about it. After spending Friday night with Chase, he had talked her into staying over Saturday night. It only made sense, since she didn't wake up until three in the afternoon. From what she could remember, the man now in the shower had kept her up all night. She didn't remember much about Friday night, but she'd never forget Saturday.

Chase had introduced her to a whole new world, and she was the perfect student. She did everything he'd asked of her, no matter how painful. At Chase's coaxing, she'd even participated in acts she once considered disgusting and sinful. All because Chase told her she was beautiful and that he couldn't get enough of her.

During breaks, he'd fed her lobster and treated her to a hot bubble bath. She learned he was a stockbroker and had been invited to the charity dinner by his sister, who served on the youth center's board of directors. He had grown up in the Bay Area and loved to mentor youths.

The shower stopped, and Reyna stretched horizontally across the king-sized bed. She could love the man on the other side of that door. He certainly loved making love to her, and unlike Tyson, he wasn't embarrassed to be seen with her. She couldn't believe how easy it was to find a good man on her own, without God's help. All she had to do was conform to the "world's standards." No one waited for marriage to have sex anymore, and the ones that did didn't marry until they were much older. Reyna didn't have to worry about that now. She and Chase were sexually compatible. Now they could work on building a relationship. Since she planned to move out of her mother's house soon, maybe they could get a place together.

Since it was Sunday and the sun was shining, she planned to ask Chase to take her to brunch and then maybe to the beach. There were so many things she wanted to experience with him. She wanted to enjoy meals and watch movies. Take hot air balloon rides and romantic walks.

"I can't believe it. I finally have a man that wants me." She quickly wiped the tears that instantly pooled.

She heard the bathroom door open and sat up with her back against the pillows. Chase entered, fully dressed. Reyna glanced at the clock on the nightstand. Where was Chase going at 7:00 A.M.? She didn't have to wait long to find out.

"Good. You're up. Do you need my driver to drop you off somewhere on the way to the airport? Or do you have your own transportation? Either way, you need to be out of this room by noon."

Still lost in the euphoria of her first relationship, Reyna ignored his questions and reached for him. "What's the rush? I thought we could have brunch, then hang out at the beach." Chase stepped beyond her reach. That was when she noticed his luggage stacked near the door. She dismissed the sudden queasiness as hunger pangs.

He flashed the smile that had rendered her helpless all weekend. "You're kidding, right? I have to get back to my wife and kids. They're meeting me at LAX, and then we're going to church." Chase walked over to the dresser and tied his tie, as if he hadn't slapped her with his words.

This time the tears fell too fast for Reyna to stop them. Chase was married. But he didn't wear a ring. Reyna gathered the sheet around her and sat on the edge of the bed. It must be a loveless marriage if he'd spent the weekend making love to her, she reasoned as slight tremors shook her. Unlike a few hours ago, Chase was oblivious to her presence.

"Y-you're married and y—you're on your way to church?" Reyna stuttered after wiping her face. "I don't understand. I thought you lived in the Bay Area."

"I grew up in the Bay Area, but now I live in L.A.," Chase explained with ease. "It's simple. I married my college sweetheart, and we have two beautiful kids. I don't like to miss Sunday morning service, considering I'm a deacon." Before Reyna could probe further, Chase stood next to her. "I know you're wondering why I spent the weekend with you when I have a beautiful wife at home. Truth is, I love my wife, but she's saved and she won't do half the things in bed women like you do. So every now and then I enjoy a little extracurricular activity—but I always use a condom."

Reyna's head hung so low, her chin grazed her bosom. She was not going to let him see her cry. Then something he'd said registered, and her head snapped up. "What do you mean, 'women like you'?"

Chase pulled out his wallet. "You know, hookers. Or do you prefer the title lady of the evening?" He pulled out ten one-hundred dollar bills and offered them to her. "This should be enough to cover your service fee for the weekend."

Reyna's lower lip quivered uncontrollably as she stared at the money. She would not cry, not in front of him. She had thought this man cared. He had said he couldn't get enough of her, had said she felt good. It all made sense to her now. He hadn't asked her anything about her life, because all she was to him was a hooker. He hadn't kissed her on the mouth, either. She wouldn't give him the satisfaction of knowing that she wasn't a hooker but, in fact, had been a virgin.

"What gave it away?" she asked with what little pride she had left.

Chase's laughter filled the room. "You're kidding again, right? Trust me, you know how to dress for work." Chase dropped the money on the bed, then put on his jacket.

Bile collected at the back of Reyna's throat as she watched him remove a ring from his pocket and slide it on his left ring finger. Before he opened the suite door, he turned back. "You never did answer my question. Do you need a ride?"

Reyna dug her nails into the sheet. He would not see her cry. "No. I'm good."

"Okay. Remember, checkout is at noon." Then he was gone.

The time on the clock changed five times before Reyna whimpered. The whimpers transformed into sobs fueled by shame and regret. How could she have spent the weekend with a man she knew nothing about? And why had she thought for a second he cared for her? She loathed the fact that her mother and Tyson had been right. She looked like a whore and in turn had been treated as such.

In the recesses of her mind, she remembered the days when she judged Marlissa for being an alcoholic. Reyna had called her a heathen and unworthy of love. Today Marlissa was saved, sober, and loved to the point of obsession, by her husband. Reyna, on the other hand, had gotten drunk and had lost her virginity to a man whose last name she didn't even know.

Chapter 4

Praise service was always a spirited event at Restoration Ministries, but on first Sundays parishioners elevated the praise to another level, maybe because first Sunday was also Communion day. Tyson enjoyed the praise, but what had drawn him to Restoration Ministries was Pastor Drake's teaching. His method had catapulted Tyson from a place of stagnation and had ignited an internal thirst for the Word that Tyson couldn't quench. One service and Tyson could no longer sit under Pastor Rosalie Jennings's leadership.

Today, however, Tyson found it difficult to concentrate on Pastor Drake's sermon about unconditional love. Two days ago he'd thought he could one day love Reyna, but then she'd embarrassed him and bruised his ego in front of his friends. If the X-rated dance scene wasn't enough, she'd chosen to spend the night with a stranger, probably the man from the dance floor. He knew that because he had stopped by the Claremont Hotel Saturday morning to retrieve the Salvatore Ferragamo coat he'd left and had seen her car in the parking lot. It didn't take a genius to know they weren't dancing vertically all night.

Tyson wasn't blind, and naïveté wasn't his weakness. He and Reyna were traveling on a path, but not the same one. Perhaps he should have shared his feelings with her, but after Friday night he doubted it would have mattered. Reyna didn't want him, plain and simple. Besides, she couldn't fit into his life, harboring so much resentment toward God and church. He'd encouraged her to seek counseling from Pastor Drake, but she'd refused. He had even offered to pay for a private practice Christian therapist. To show her gratitude, she'd cursed him out. Thinking back now, he realized he should have ended his bland romantic pursuit then. But something in Reyna endeared her to him—something special that no one saw but him.

"Unconditional love doesn't dwell on what someone has done to us," Pastor Drake was saying. "It does not bring up someone's past when they wrong us. Unconditional love forgives even if the person never asks for forgiveness."

Pastor Drake's words helped Tyson understand that the feelings he held for Reyna weren't budding love. He cared for her, but after the stunt on Friday, he no longer liked her. At least that was what his head kept telling his heart. Until she apologized, he had nothing to say to her.

Show her unconditional love.

Tyson closed his Bible and ignored the still small voice. Even if he wanted to, he couldn't do that. Love, as he knew it, came with conditions. Love was a prize given for doing the right thing, all the time. When he was a child, his parents' love was predicated on his absolute adherence to their rules. If he scored the top in his class, Fredrick and Beverly Stokes showered him with time and attention, but when the grades slipped, they heaped coals of criticism and derogatory comments on him.

His father, a criminal judge, rationed affirmation in the same manner he rendered justice from the bench—

firm and precise. If a defendant was found guilty of breaking the law, sentencing came swiftly and without mercy. Now that Reyna had betrayed him, Tyson had sentenced her in the same manner.

Although Tyson was a no-nonsense lawyer, his rearing had made it easy for him to sit under Pastor Rosalie Jennings's controlling and condemning style of leadership for five years. Subconsciously, he'd simply traded one dictator for another.

"Love is patient. Love is kind . . ." Pastor Drake expounded on what church folks referred to as the love chapter: I Corinthians 13.

Love her like I love you.

"No." Tyson hadn't meant to speak the words audibly, but the voice pierced his eardrums. "I can't do that."

Kevin nudged him. "You can't do what?"

Tyson turned to the left and found not only Kevin and Marlissa, but also Leon and Starla, staring at him. When Tyson didn't respond, the group turned their attention back to Pastor Drake's sermon. Tyson closed his eyes and bowed his head. He remained that way until the benediction.

"Tyson, son, wait up." If he'd known Mother Scott would accost him after service, Tyson would have left during the altar call. Leon's mother, the prayer warrior, at times could be a little rough around the edges. She loved Jesus and could pray the kingdom down, but she hadn't perfected the scripture about studying to be quiet. She also had a gift for seeing deeper than the natural eye.

Tyson stopped, pasted on a smile, and turned around. "Hello, Mother Scott."

The walk from across the sanctuary had left the petite woman winded. She placed her hand on Tyson's shoulder for support. "How's my favorite free lawyer doing?"

"I'm fine, Mother."

Mother Scott cocked her head to the side. "Baby, stop lying in the house of the Lord."

"Mother—"

Mother Scott cut him off with a revelation of her own. "You tell that lie every time I ask you. You're not fine. You're in love, but you're too stubborn to *give* love."

Being lost for words wasn't a common occurrence for Tyson. He'd presented opening and closing arguments with ease, but Mother Scott left him tongue-tied.

She patted Tyson's stomach. "You need to push that plate back and pray until God delivers you. And a healing from your childhood wouldn't hurt, either."

"B—b—but, Mother," Tyson stuttered, "I never told you about my childhood."

The innocent smile that appeared would make one think Mother Scott was gentle as a dove, but Tyson knew better.

"Baby, don't you know I can see? Since Kevin fixed my natural eyesight, my spiritual discernment is double twenty-twenty. I see right through you. You love the Lord, but you need to practice what you read about in the big black Bible underneath your arm." Then Mother Scott served the benediction. "I'll see you later. I need to go lay hands on Marlissa's and Starla's stomachs. Those babies are future prayer warriors."

For the second time in three days, a woman left Tyson standing with his mouth hanging open.

Chapter 5

Shivering, cold, and more humiliated than the night she'd been arrested, Reyna stepped barefoot into the foyer at her mother's house. To add insult to injury, the unpredictable California October weather had dropped twenty degrees. If her arms weren't sore from the awkward positions Chase—if that was even his real name—had twisted her into, she would have slapped herself for not taking her coat. She wouldn't have minded the cold air as much if the disdainful stares she received as she walked through the Claremont Hotel hadn't reminded her of how foolish she'd been. The hotel's Sunday morning guests were more conservative than the Friday night private party crowd. During daylight hours people with her clothing attire weren't allowed. When a hotel employee approached her with a security officer in tow, Reyna had removed her shoes, had tucked them beneath her arm, and had run through the lobby, out of the hotel, and into the parking lot to her car. Once inside it, she'd leaned her head on the steering wheel and wept.

Hot tears had burned her cheeks as she sped down Ashby Avenue en route to her mother's house of judgment. While waiting at a stoplight on Martin Luther King Jr. Way, she stopped crying long enough to spit profanities at the church building on the corner. She'd never been inside of the stucco building; neither did she know anyone affiliated with the house of worship. None of that mattered. Her dysfunctional life was the result of a self-centered God. In her opinion, God was a controller and a user. He demanded all of your time and bombarded you with rules and regulations with no reward.

Her tires screeched as she entered the next intersection. She'd made a mistake this time around, but she would never step foot inside a church again. Not even a park service. She would continue on her self-discovery journey without the help of a narcissistic God.

Now, as she stood in the foyer with chattering teeth, Reyna had to figure out how to escape to the confines of her room without running into her mother. It was 8:00 A.M., and Jewel was probably in her prayer closet, interceding for Sunday worship service. If Reyna wanted to avoid a tongue-lashing for staying away all weekend, she'd have to hurry. With shoes in hand, she scurried across the hardwood floor.

Reyna hadn't made it halfway down the hall when Jewel yelled, "Where have you been?"

Reyna froze. She hadn't thought about how to answer that question without disclosing her weekend tryst.

"How dare you sneak into this house, wearing the same clothes you had on two days ago?" The creaking floor indicated Jewel was walking toward her. Before Reyna could turn around, Jewel's hot breath burned her neck. Jewel sniffed. "You whore! You had me worried sick about you, and you have the nerve to creep up in here smelling like sex!"

Reyna's shoulders slumped, and she cowered momentarily. Not wanting to spend a second longer at the hotel, she'd opted not to shower that morning.

Suddenly, an adrenaline rush of pride raged like hot coals through her veins. Her fists unclenched, and her stilettos made an echo when they clanged against the floor. Without warning, she spun around and glowered at her mother.

Jewel looked as if she'd aged. Her eyes were puffy and sunken. The usual red silk head scarf was gone. Instead her hair hung loosely. Jewel had said she slept in the red scarf to symbolize the blood of Jesus keeping her unconscious thoughts pure. For years Reyna had wanted to tell her to try some red lipstick to keep her mouth pure.

Reyna stepped forward and met Jewel's glare. Today she would finally set this woman straight. "If you'd had half the sex I had this weekend with Daddy, he wouldn't have left you." She braced herself for Jewel's right palm print across her face, but Jewel didn't utter a word or react. Reyna counted the silence as a victory and proceeded to pour alcohol on Jewel's wounds.

"I am sick and tired of you calling me names. If I'm a whore, then you and Rosalie Jennings made me one." She pointed at Jewel. "It's your fault I wasted my life trying to serve some imaginary God. I needed a mother and a friend, but all you've ever been to me is some sort of religious police. Where were your sanctimonious convictions when you agreed to send me after a married man?" Reyna paused for an answer. Still nothing. "You knew Kevin didn't want me, and if you'd been a better mother, you would have recognized that I didn't want him, either. I was just trying to please you and our beloved pastor." Reyna added several four-letter words for emphasis.

"No one warned me that what I was doing was wrong," Reyna lied. Tyson had warned Reyna several times, but Jewel didn't need to know that. The fact remained that Jewel had played a hand in her humiliation. "If my father was around, none of this would have happened. Like him, I can't wait to get away from you."

Jewel finally found her voice, although it sounded more timid than Reyna ever remembered. "I think that's a good idea. You're a grown woman—too grown to live with a controlling and callous mother." Jewel turned and started down the hall to her bedroom. Before turning the corner, she gave Reyna final instructions. "Leave your key and a forwarding address on the table when you leave." Then she disappeared.

If Reyna didn't know any better, she'd swear she'd seen a tear slide down her mother's cheek. It didn't matter, anyway. Not only was Reyna free of her mother's control, but also the anger she'd failed to direct at Chase had been successfully transferred to her mother. She felt light and relieved to have her freedom papers. She vowed right then that once she moved out, she'd never step foot in her mother's residence again.

Twenty-eight hours later, seated behind her desk at work, Reyna regretted cursing at her mother. At the time the disrespectful words rolled off her tongue, Reyna had forgotten she didn't have enough credit or employment history to lease an apartment on her own. The salary she'd received at her former church had been paid under the table, and the job description was simply catering to Pastor Jennings's needs. The current property management job was only two months old. An expletive slipped from her lips as she resigned herself to the fact that she'd have to ask her mother to cosign for the lease.

She folded her arms and slouched back in the faux leather wheeled chair. Mist seeped from her eyes as she took in her surroundings, her small workstation, and wondered, How did I get here?

She'd had dreams of being a family therapist. After experiencing the pain of a broken family, Reyna had wanted to help families solve problems and stay together. But she'd allowed that dream to die after Pastor Jennings insisted the Lord had spoken to her and wanted Reyna to work as her assistant at the church. At the time she'd readily agreed and dropped out of school just one year shy of completing her master's degree. Whenever Reyna had mentioned finishing school, her mother and Pastor Jennings would ambush her and coerce her into working for the ministry.

Reyna closed her eyes, leaned her head back, wondering when her common sense had vacated the building and left her dependent on others, like her mother and Tyson, to meet her basic needs.

Abruptly, Reyna sat forward, put her elbows on the desk, and voiced her thoughts. "Good old Tyson, he'll sign the lease for me. He just loves helping me out." Her lower lip curled. "Of course, I'll have to apologize for dissin' him the other night."

"What was that?"

The low monotone voice interrupted the conversation Reyna was having with herself and instantly set her on edge. Her boss had always had that effect on her. Paige was all about business all the time. Although the office hours were nine to five, Paige boasted that she arrived at seven every morning. For what, Reyna didn't know and didn't care to find out. When agents shared family photos and stories, Paige bragged about maintaining a prosperous real estate company during the housing slump, when most real estate companies were folding.

Reyna turned and faced her boss. Today, like every day, Paige was dressed in a black pantsuit, a white-collared blouse, and two-inch black sling-backs. Even without makeup and dressed starkly, the espresso-colored woman was beautiful. Reyna attributed Paige's singleness to her devotion to her job. In the short time Reyna had been with the company, more than a few admirers had appeared, but if the conversation didn't evolve around opening or closing an escrow, Paige would quickly dismiss them. Reyna would do just about anything to trade places with Paige.

Reyna pasted on a smile and gathered her thoughts. "Don't mind me. I was just thinking out loud."

A rare smile appeared on Paige's face. "It's okay to have thoughts of Tyson. He's a good man with a great work ethic, but don't let that interfere with your work." At rapid speed the smile disappeared, and the stoic demeanor emerged. "I need this month's lease renewals and inspections on my desk in ten minutes."

As Reyna watched Paige's hair bounce away, she remembered why she disliked her boss. Paige reminded her of Tyson. "Maybe I should fix them up," she mumbled, "right after I get him to sign on the dotted line."

Chapter 6

Tyson read the first paragraph of the brief for the wrongful death case for the third time. Like with the two previous attempts, his thoughts wandered off from the written words to the thorn in his flesh. Reyna. As hard as he tried, Tyson couldn't get her off his mind. Exercise didn't work; neither did meditation. All night and most of the morning, he had declared he no longer cared for her, but his heart had rejected the memo. He wanted what Kevin and Leon had, and he wanted it with Reyna.

Procrastination had never been a character trait of his, but Tyson willfully saved and closed the legal document for future review. He swiveled around from his maple-wood desk and stared out the window. Having an office on the sixteenth floor in downtown Oakland had its advantages, one being an overhead view of Lake Merritt. From his office window, Tyson also had an unobstructed view of the Oakland Estuary. The water, although murky, always had a cathartic effect on his spirit. On many occasions the freshwater and saltwater waves had settled his anxieties over a pending case. He closed his eyes, relaxed his shoulders, and mentally pictured the waves washing the stress away. Unfortunately for him, residue from Reyna's rejection was too deeply embedded in his spirit for the exercise to work.

At the slight knock on his door, Tyson rubbed his beard, then swiveled around and prepared to greet the knocker, who he assumed was his secretary. One of things he valued most about Lois was her ability to know when he wanted to be left alone. In their five-year employment relationship, Lois had yet to invade his professional and personal life.

"Yes, Lois?" he said in his customary monotone voice. As the door crept open, he expected to see Lois's salt-and-pepper hair and gold-rimmed eyeglasses. What appeared was a spiked hairdo, jean-clad legs, and spiked heels. Reyna.

Being caught off guard wasn't something he favored, and Reyna's jeans being at least one size too small added to Tyson's sudden discomfort. Instantly his body temperature rose, and he felt his temporal vein pulsate. His suddenly sweaty hands moved involuntarily, fingering the Montblanc pen set, then the telephone. As Reyna moved toward him, Tyson gave up and leaned back in his chair and stared at her.

Reyna was a beautiful woman, but the tight clothes she wore didn't leave much to his or anyone else's imagination. Her makeup was more conservative than the last time he saw her, and she displayed less skin, but the overall look stilled screamed "Will do anything for fifty dollars." Long gone were the days when they were members of Pastor Jennings's church and her wardrobe consisted of floor-length skirts and turtleneck tops.

Her full lips parted into the smile he adored, and an unexpected twinge caused his abdominal muscles to tighten as the thought that she'd given the lips he'd longed to kiss to another man brought him back to reality. The few remaining feelings he held for her were swiftly brushed away. Reyna had assaulted his ego, and he wouldn't pursue her again.

"What are you doing here?" He asked the question after redirecting his focus to the computer screen. He opened the Internet browser and checked two e-mails before realizing Reyna hadn't responded. He looked up to find a king-size package of Reese's Peanut Butter Cups—his favorite candy bar—surrounded by Reyna's decorated nails. He smirked but didn't accept the token gift. "You can keep that. You can't make up for the humiliation you caused me with a candy bar." He opened the next e-mail.

"What about two?"

"Unbelievable," he mumbled when Reyna presented another orange, yellow, and brown package.

Reyna pulled her arm back and plopped down in the leather chair reserved for visitors. "Come on, big guy. Stop playing hard to get."

"Give those to your new boyfriend." Tyson deleted the wrong e-mail as the bitter words spilled out.

Reyna crossed her legs at the ankle and shifted in the chair. "What boyfriend?"

Tyson pushed the computer mouse aside. "The one you used me to get at the Claremont." He looked her dead in the eyes. "I hope he's everything you need." For a second he thought he saw hurt cover Reyna's face. When she placed the Reese's on the desk and lowered her head, Tyson was certain things hadn't gone as well as he assumed with Mr. Dancin' Machine.

"There's absolutely nothing between us," she answered just above a whisper. "Turns out we're totally wrong for each other."

Tyson saw the tears Reyna attempted to hide by blinking rapidly, but his bruised ego prevented him from caring. With his elbows fixed on the desk, he asked, "And your point for being here is . . . ?" He let the question hang.

Suddenly Reyna's face split into a full smile, and Tyson's heart fluttered. Although he no longer liked her, he would always love her dimpled left cheek. The fragrance swirling around his nostrils wasn't bad, either.

"I've got some great news, and I wanted to share it with my best buddy."

Tyson leaned back and smirked. "And who might that be?"

Reyna threw her hands up. "Will you loosen up? Okay. I admit I embarrassed you at the Claremont. I could have worn something different, but you didn't have to call me cheap, either. And maybe I said some harsh words, but they were the truth. I mean, we're friends, but sometimes you act like I'm your woman, and we both know that's not the case." She pushed the candy toward him. "Why don't you eat this candy so we can go back to being buddies?"

Marlissa and Starla had been right. He had failed terribly in making his intentions known. Reyna was oblivious to his attraction. "Buddies?" he asked through a tight jaw.

"Look, you drive me crazy sometimes . . . okay, most of the time. But you've helped me to heal, and I value you as a friend. Actually, right now I *need* your friendship."

Tyson was determined to cut ties with Reyna, but her last statement piqued his interest. Reyna needed him. "What exactly do you need?"

Reyna relaxed and laced her fingers. "I've decided it's time for me to move out of my mother's house. I'll be thirty-one in a couple of months, and I've never lived on my own. Plus, my mother is still attached to Rosalie Jennings. I can't completely heal if my mother insists on being that demon's friend."

Tyson flinched. "That's a little harsh, don't you think? Pastor Jennings may be a little misguided, but I wouldn't label her a demon."

Reyna's eyes rolled. "Sugarcoat it any way you want, but she still has horns."

"I see you've taken responsibility for your actions," he responded with normal sarcasm.

"I am taking responsibility for myself by moving out. It's time I stood on my own two feet. With a little help, of course," she added when Tyson raised an eyebrow.

Tyson looked at his watch, then back at Reyna. "I don't have much time. Tell me exactly what you need me to do."

Reyna's eyes grew wide. "Promise you'll do it?"

"I promise to consider it, buddy," he said dryly, then tore open the Reese's Peanut Butter Cups. He bit into the chocolate-covered peanut butter without looking at it. He savored his one indulgence while watching Reyna's lips move. She mentioned something about needing credit for a car, or was it an apartment? He wasn't sure. The movement of Reyna's pouty lips had distracted him. He'd lost count of the times he'd wanted to taste those lips over the past four months, but he hadn't tasted them, and now he wouldn't.

"Well, what do you think?"

Tyson quickly swallowed, then cleared his throat. "Run that by me again. I want to make sure I understand you." Reyna appeared oblivious to Tyson's inattentiveness.

"So you want to use my signature to get an apartment?" he asked after she repeated the proposition.

"If you don't mind, buddy. It will only be for the first year," Reyna explained. "You and Kevin are the only people I know with good credit and a six-figure salary.

Kevin and I are cool now, but I don't think it's a good idea to ask the man I once stalked to cosign for me."

"I'm sure Kevin would help you, but I don't think Marlissa would appreciate that." Tyson took another bite, then slowly chewed as he mused over the request. Reyna needed to be on her own, but did he need to be the one to help her? Although she would be responsible for her living expenses, the arrangement would connect her to him in a way he didn't want, but that was all Reyna was offering. He had an offer of his own. "If I were your landlord, I wouldn't check your credit report. I'd give you a year lease and trust you to pay your rent on time."

Reyna's mouth dropped, then closed. She looked perplexed. "Tyson, what are you saying? Your house is big, but we can't live under the same roof."

Tyson balled up the candy wrapper and tossed it into the trash can. "You're right. We can't live under the same roof, but I have a vacant town house you can move into. It's already furnished."

Reyna's mocha-colored lips separated and closed three times before she found her voice. "Are y—you serious?" she stuttered. "I didn't know you owned a town house. You'll let me live in it?"

Tyson smirked and considered disclosing just how much he owned, then thought better of it. Everything material Reyna desired, he could provide with ease. If she weren't so obsessed with making up for lost time, she would see that what God had prepared for her was far better than anything she could ask for or think. For now, he would help her . . . might even pray for her, but that was all.

"You can move in anytime," he said as he scribbled the address and rental fee on a Post-it. "Of course, you'll need to have the utilities turned on. Since we're buddies, I won't require a security deposit," he added with a hint of sarcasm.

Reyna read the address. The paper slipped from her fingers, and before the yellow square touched the carpet, Reyna ran around the desk and wrapped her arms around Tyson's neck. "Thank you! Thank you!" She rained kisses over his forehead and bearded cheeks. "That's an exclusive development, a gated community." She released him and danced around the office, singing an updated version of McFadden & Whitehead's "Ain't No Stoppin' Us Now."

Beads of sweat lined Tyson's forehead and his breathing accelerated as he watched the celebration. Finally, he knew how Reyna's lips felt against his skin. All he had to do to reap the mediocre reward was meet her need.

He cleared his throat. "There is one condition."

"I'm on the move. Ain't no stopping . . ." Reyna stopped midway through a left turn of the electric slide. "What's that?"

"Come to church with me on Sunday." Both Reyna's neck and eyes rolled, but he ignored her antics. He stood and reached for his suit jacket. "I have to visit a client now, but I'll pick you up at ten o'clock Sunday morning." He fixed his gaze on her as he buttoned the tailored suit and waited for the excuses, but none came. Her face contorted, but Reyna didn't utter one word of protest.

"Fine," she finally agreed. "I appreciate this so much, I'm going to fix you up with Paige. You two are perfect for each other. Both of you are anal to the tenth degree." Then she danced out the door.

Tyson looked at the remaining package of candy on his desk and shook his head as if to clear it. What had just happened? He'd just offered his property to the woman he'd vowed not to pursue, and all it took was chocolate-covered peanut butter cups.

Chapter 7

"Ain't no stoppin' me now . . ." Reyna was still singing the seventies classic when she returned to her desk
at the real estate office. The crowded workstation appeared more spacious and the dark décor appeared
brighter now that her life was finally on the right track.
She was moving on up from a drab 350-square-foot
bedroom to a deluxe town house on the north side of
town. And it was furnished and had a pool, a gym, and
reserved parking. She'd shown and leased the development to several corporate clients seeking a place to ac-
commodate out-of-town executives, but never did she
think she'd be a tenant.

"Oh, Tyson, God used you to bless me today," she
said audibly, then frowned. "Where did that come
from? God had nothing to do with this. I got this on my
own." That was when she remembered Tyson's little
condition. He had a lot of nerve dangling a furnished
town house as bait to get her to even think about grac-
ing any worship service with her presence. As much
as she detested organized religion, she needed what
Tyson had offered. Which meant she had to play by his
rules. A couple of hours listening to religious rhetoric
couldn't hurt or change her resolve about God.

She twisted in the chair, and her abdominal muscles
quickly reminded her how much it had cost her to be
with Chase. She had received nothing in return, unless

she counted total humiliation. Her eyes slammed shut when tears threatened to spill. "I will not waste another tear on that loser." After the lump in her throat dissolved, she threw her head back and replaced the painful memory with thoughts of Tyson.

One day she'd tell him how she regretted not listening to him about her attire. Maybe. To pacify him, she'd attend church service—once—and as a bonus, she'd sit around the sanctified Sunday dinner table and listen to the Jenningses and the Scotts proclaim how good God was. "I guess the Bible is good for something. I asked, and then I received." She was laughing at her own joke when Paige entered her space.

"You're in a good mood."

Paige's stoic tone failed to place a damper on Reyna's jubilation. "I'm moving into the Broadway Terrace complex in North Oakland," she announced.

"Into Tyson's place." Paige voiced the question in the form of a statement.

"Yes," Reyna answered cautiously. "How did you know?"

Paige rested her hip against the wall with her arms folded. "He called me and canceled his rental listing agreement. He said he'd found a tenant, but I had no idea it was you. Interesting," she said and shook her head slightly. "At any rate, can you schedule the maintenance work for Cedar Heights for next week?"

"Sure." Paige turned to leave, but Reyna wanted to plant a seed. "Paige, you and Tyson have a lot in common. Have you considered going out with him? You'd have to unwind him first, but he's a good guy."

Paige retreated and offered Reyna some advice. "I know he's a good guy because I've already unwound him. I hope you learn to value his worth and don't take advantage of him. For the record, I know Tyson a lot better than you think, and I know for a fact he wouldn't appreciate you, of all people, playing matchmaker for him."

Reyna watched Paige's back pass over the threshold, not sure how to interpret her comment and too excited to care.

Three hours later, when she entered her mother's house and heard voices, the boxes she'd picked up from the storage company on the way home tumbled to the floor. Pastor Rosalie Jennings was there. Reyna hadn't seen her former pastor since Kevin and Marlissa renewed their vows five months ago. At the time Pastor Jennings had refused to acknowledge her presence.

Reyna gathered the boxes, and instead of heading upstairs, she marched into the living room. "Might as well tell them both to kiss my behind at the same time," she grumbled.

"I hate to interrupt this hypocritical bonding moment, but I have an announcement to make," Reyna yelled above their conversation. "I'm moving this weekend."

Jewel's head snapped around; then her shoulders slumped.

"I would move tonight, but the electricity and phone won't be turned on for forty-eight hours. I can't wait to leave the company of manipulators and thieves."

Pastor Jennings closed her Bible. "I beg your pardon, young lady."

"You heard me, lying prophet," Reyna sneered. "I can't wait to get out of here and live my own life."

"Reyna, that's not necessary," Jewel said. "If you're leaving, then leave, but don't insult my guest."

"You're always taking up for her. If I didn't know any better, I'd swear you're lesbians, but you're too *holy* for that."

Jewel gasped, and Pastor Jennings began speaking in tongues.

Reyna feigned innocence. "Did I say something too dirty for your holy ears?"

"Jesus, Jesus, Jesus." Pastor Jennings's words in an unknown tongue transformed into a chant.

"Be careful," Jewel warned, "how you disrespect those who have the rule over you."

Reyna stepped closer and towered over her mother. "That's where you're wrong, Mommy dearest. You can be her puppet for the rest of your life, but nobody rules over me." She shifted the boxes to the opposite arm, then stomped away.

Inside her bedroom, Reyna dropped the boxes on the floor and plopped down on the bed. Her eyes slowly roamed the cluttered room. What was once a place of refuge over time had turned into a dungeon. When she was a child, the plastered walls had shielded Reyna from her parents' arguments. During her high school years, her bedroom transformed into a place of fantasy as she envisioned falling in love with and marrying her Prince Charming. Later on, the room would become plotting headquarters for her futile pursuit of Kevin Jennings. She hated this room. She hated this house and the two women downstairs, who were probably still praying to some spirit and speaking jibber-jabber.

Reyna grunted. "I don't need them or their tired prayers. As long as God doesn't bother me, I won't bother Him."

Chapter 8

"Would they hurry up and sit down?" Reyna's irritation neared the boiling point when she shifted in her seat as the praise and worship ministry began the third song. God might be good to some people and His mercy might endure forever, but her tolerance for listening to praises to an invisible God had run out. She was there only to fulfill the condition of moving into Tyson's town house. Briefly she had considered reneging on the deal, then had reconsidered after inspecting the place.

The town house was perfect, with vaulted ceilings and granite countertops. Tyson's decorating budget must have been huge. From the butter-soft cream-colored leather furniture to the plush carpet, everything was top-notch. Both bedrooms were filled with Thomasville furniture, and the gourmet kitchen resembled something from the Food Network channel. The secure off-street parking wasn't bad, either. When she'd questioned Tyson about why he'd invested so much money in the rental unit, he'd explained that the town house was his primary residence before purchasing a home in the Oakland-Berkeley Hills.

"I promise to take good care of your property," was what she'd told him after the walk-through inspection two days ago. Now, seated next to him and listening to his monotone voice's pathetic attempt to keep up with the praise and worship singers, she wanted to rip the lease to shreds.

She'd grown up in the church, yet she'd never seen a group of people so uninhibited with their praise and devotion to God. Both Kevin and Tyson had told her Restoration Ministries had a membership of over one thousand, and Reyna believed them. As far as Reyna could tell, all the floor seats were taken and most of the balcony was full. The majority of the congregants were on their feet and were clapping their hands to the music. Others were seated with hands raised. In one form or another, it seemed everyone participated.

Reyna looked at the couples seated to her left, and a pang of jealousy jolted her stomach. Kevin stood with one hand raised, while his other hand rubbed Marlissa's back. Leon held Starla's hand while the pair did a two-step dance. Reyna desired what they had: a loving relationship. Just seven days ago, she thought she'd found that with a stranger going by the name of Chase. The good deacon was probably at church with his wife at that very moment. She hung her head in an effort to hide the lone tear that trickled down her cheek as thoughts of shame rushed to the forefront. Why couldn't she find someone to love her the way Marlissa and Starla had?

She felt a nudge on her right arm. "Would you like my handkerchief?"

Reyna reached out and accepted Tyson's offer without looking up and without thanking him. She quickly wiped the tear, then resumed glaring at the praise and worship team. Two songs and a praise dance break later, Reyna stood and clapped as the praise team left the stage.

During Pastor Drake's sermon, Reyna chose to play Tetris on her cell phone. She didn't listen to Pastor Drake, but on more than one occasion she looked up to find Tyson shaking his head at her.

"Finally, I can leave this place," Reyna grunted as soon as the benediction concluded.

"Could you at least pretend you have some respect for the house of God?" Tyson's face twisted with disgust. "You missed a good Word today, playing that game."

Reyna slipped the phone inside her purse. "At least I turned the sound off. You know the only reason I'm here is to satisfy the terms for letting me rent your place. I'm sure the Word was good to you, but I don't believe that crap anymore."

"Reyna!" Tyson's raised voice caught the attention of their friends and Mother Scott. "You grew up in the church. How can you be so callous?"

"You Holy Rollers made me this way!" Reyna yelled back.

"I know y'all are not arguing in church?" Mother Scott asked as the Jenningses and the Scotts looked on with stunned facial expressions.

Reyna's hostile attitude evaporated. She was still adjusting to Mother Scott's forward personality. "I'm sorry, Mother Scott, but he started it."

"Did not." Tyson pointed a finger at Reyna. "You're the one who played a game during service instead of listening to the Word."

Mother Scott's balled fist rested at her petite waist while she pointed her forefinger at the two. "I don't care who started it. Y'all are too old for this." Her hand gestured in the direction of Leon and Starla's kids. "My grandkids act more mature than you." She glared at Tyson. "She's unsaved. I expected her to act crazy. But you are saved and call yourself a lawyer. You wouldn't yell in the courtroom, so don't yell in God's house."

Tyson's head dropped. "Sorry, Mother."

Instead of apologizing for her behavior, Reyna rolled her eyes at Tyson, then turned and walked away. "I'll see you in the car," she said over her shoulder to Tyson.

Tyson entered Kevin's home without knocking and walked straight to the kitchen for the ceramic container that stored rice cakes instead of cookies. He'd nearly completed two whole cakes before he realized Kevin and Marlissa were staring at him. During nearly every visit in the past Tyson had voiced his dislike for Marlissa's healthy snacks and had begged her to bring back the Oreos. Now here he was, eating the rice cakes like sliced bread.

"What?" he asked, reaching for another caramel-flavored rice cake. "So what if I didn't knock? It's not like you didn't expect me."

Kevin retrieved a serving dish from the top shelf for Marlissa, then turned to his friend. "I see you and Reyna didn't resolve your issues on the ride over," Kevin smirked. "What did you do? Drop her off at the nearest bus stop?" Kevin laughed.

Tyson stopped chewing and discarded the remaining rice cake in the trash, but didn't answer. Kevin's laughter ceased.

"You wouldn't," Marlissa said.

Tyson pounded his fist against the granite countertop. "I didn't drop her off, but I should have. That stubborn goat is out in the car." Tyson winced at the sound of the doorbell.

Kevin stepped back. "Whoa, man. Reyna has really gotten under your skin. I've never heard you revert to name-calling. Maybe you should rethink this tenant-landlord thing." Tyson had shared his plan with Kevin two days ago.

"There's nothing to rethink," Reyna said upon entering the kitchen after Marlissa let her in. "I held up my end of the bargain. Now he's stuck with me."

Tyson whirled around to face the woman he cared about but at the moment found difficult to like. Reyna had publicly embarrassed him again, causing him to lose his placidity. He glowered at her from head to toe and then silently berated himself for admiring the yellow pantsuit she wore. Even though Reyna had a smug look on her face, her beauty excited him. She wore more makeup than he thought necessary, but it was what he saw beneath the surface that twisted his heartstrings into agony.

"How can you be so callous toward God?" Tyson asked through clenched teeth. "You once had a strong relationship with Him."

The doorbell sounded again, and Kevin left the kitchen.

Reyna planted a fist against her waist and stepped closer to Tyson. "What I had was a bunch of lies fed to me by people claiming to be His mouthpiece."

"It wasn't people, Reyna. It was one person," Tyson corrected. "And you need to forgive Pastor Jennings so you can move on with your life."

Reyna scowled. "You may forgive seven times seventy per day, but I'm not there yet."

"Well, at least you remember one scripture," Tyson shot back just has Leon and Starla joined them in the kitchen. Instead of greeting one another, the couples stood back and watched the interaction between Reyna and Tyson.

"I remember more than you think, but it would do you some good to remember the one about drawing people with love and kindness," Reyna sneered. "All you do is judge me for not wanting to serve *your* God anymore." She turned toward Kevin. "Sorry if this offends you, but your mother destroyed my life."

Tyson erupted before Kevin could respond. "You are not a child! You're a grown woman with a mind of your own. No one can make you do anything you don't want to do. You're just as much to blame for your bad decisions as Pastor Jennings. You were a willing participant."

Reyna's fist pounded the granite countertop. "Shut up! You're self-righteous, just like Pastor Jennings!"

Tyson's cheeks burned, and he lost control. The words tumbled out before he could stop them. "Come off it, Reyna! Were you a victim, and was Pastor Jennings the reason you spent the night at the Claremont with a man you barely knew?"

Tyson heard the collective gasp of his friends behind him, but the pain etched on Reyna's face held him captive. In seconds the arrogance and bravado evaporated, and tears welled up in her eyes. Tyson hadn't meant to expose her, but her careless act had hurt him to the core. Her boorish behavior only added salt to the open wound.

"Who I spend my nights with is none of your business!" Reyna blessed Tyson with a string of expletives, then stomped toward the front door.

"How could you put Reyna's business on Front Street like that?" Marlissa said, letting Tyson have a piece of her mind at the same time the front door slammed.

"I didn't mean to, but that woman drives me past crazy," Tyson replied, defending himself.

Starla joined in. "You were so wrong for that. I never thought I'd see *you* stoop so low." She planted her balled fists against her waist, which caused her swollen abdomen to stick out even farther. "Now, you go outside and apologize!"

"Now!" Marlissa added, while pointing at the door.

Kevin and Leon didn't offer any support.

Sure he was wrong, but apologizing to Reyna for bringing out the worst in him was getting old. He detested public scenes, yet in less than one hour, he'd allowed Reyna to pull him out of character twice. As much as he wanted to cast the blame on her, deep inside Tyson accepted full responsibility for his lack of self-control. Not to mention his efforts to steer Reyna back to the household of faith had just been derailed. Exasperated, Tyson threw his hands up, then went to find Reyna.

He assumed she'd be sitting in the car, but she wasn't. He was about to panic when out of his peripheral vision he spotted yellow fabric floating down the slope. Kevin lived atop a hill.

"Reyna!" he yelled and caught the attention of Kevin's neighbor. "Sorry," Tyson offered when the older gentleman dropped the water hose, then proceeded to trot after Reyna. "Reyna, wait!" he huffed as he picked up momentum. When he purchased the tailored suit and dress shoes, chasing Reyna down a hill was not what he had in mind. The spiked heels that minutes earlier had adorned Reyna's feet were now swinging wildly in her hands.

Reyna turned and paused long enough to tell Tyson to take a permanent trip to the dark side, then continued trekking down the hill.

When Tyson caught up with her and grabbed her from behind, Reyna whirled around and swung her heels at him. "I can't stand you!" she screamed.

With ease, he held her hands stationary and steadied his breath. "Would you calm down and listen to me?"

"Why? You just told all my business." Reyna yanked her arms free and glared at him. "How did you know what happened at the Claremont? I didn't tell you that."

"I saw your car in the parking lot on Saturday, when I went to retrieve my coat," Tyson answered, still hoping his deductive reasoning would prove incorrect. Tyson observed the anger seep from her, only to be replaced by shame. Her shoulders slumped, and she turned away. "So I was right?"

"Yes," she answered just above a whisper. "You were right about more than you think." The stilettos slipped from her hands and clanged against the cement the second her shoulders started to heave.

Tyson grabbed her shoulders and turned her to face him. "Baby, I'm sorry. I didn't mean to make you cry." Seeing Reyna shed tears because of his behavior made his insides quiver. The last thing he wanted to do was cause her pain in the literal sense. He reached inside his jacket pocket for a handkerchief and wiped her face. "Please forgive me. I didn't mean to hurt you." He searched for words. "You're my friend and I care about you, but sometimes you drive me crazy and I don't know how to handle that," he admitted.

Reyna snatched the handkerchief. "Would you shut up and let me talk? This is hard enough, but since you put it out there, you might as well know the whole truth. I only got mad because somebody found out about my stupid mistake."

"Go on." Tyson nodded, wondering if he would ever understand this woman.

Reyna didn't hold his gaze as she confessed, "You were right about everything. I spent the weekend with that guy from the dance floor. He liked me, but not enough to tell me about his wife and kids until after I'd gotten drunk and given him my virginity."

Tyson flinched but didn't respond verbally.

"From my clothes, he thought I was a hooker, and paid me for my services before he left." Reyna covered her face and shed silent tears. "I feel so stupid. I actually thought he cared."

Lost for words, Tyson molded her against his chest and held her. When Reyna didn't resist, his heart acknowledged the truth. He was really in love with Reyna. What else could explain why he felt the urge to shield her from an opportunist like the guy from the dance floor, although she'd purposely set out to use the man to hurt him.

"Reyna, you're not stupid. You've just been making bad decisions lately," Tyson said, attempting to comfort her.

Reyna raised her head and met his gaze. "You don't consider what I did pathetic?" she questioned.

Tyson held her gaze and for the first time shared his heart. "Sweetheart, you're wounded and looking for love. The problem is you're looking too hard and in the wrong places. You're a beautiful and intelligent woman, and you deserve the best. You need to slow down and open your eyes. What you need just may be in front of you. I'm here for you, and I'll help you in any way I can."

Reyna's face twisted as if she was pondering his words. Tyson's heart pounded against his chest cavity in anticipation of her response to what he considered a declaration of his feelings.

"You're right. I do deserve the best, and I'm going to find it on my own," she finally answered.

Frustration threatened to overtake Tyson's emotions once again. He released her and stepped back. "Were you listening?" He didn't allow her time to answer. "Slow down. Stop being angry, and allow God to direct you."

"Tyson, you're a good friend and a smart man. And as much as I hate to admit it, you're right about me being wrong to blame Pastor Jennings without shouldering some of the blame for the wreck I've made of my life. Maybe one day I'll consider God again, but today is not that day." She closed the distance between them and cradled his cheek with her thumb and forefinger. "Please try to understand that right now I have to do me. I want to experience life. I missed that being Pastor Jennings's shadow. I want to know what fun is. I want to go—"

Tyson wasn't sure if he meant to or not, but before Reyna could finish the sentence, he pressed his lips against hers. When Reyna didn't protest, he held her and deepened the kiss. Thoughts of good and evil battled in Tyson's mind. He shouldn't be kissing Reyna like this in public, for all the neighbors to see. He shouldn't be kissing her at all, but it felt good.

"Whew!" Reyna said, fanning herself after breaking the kiss. "Not only are you a good friend, but you're also a good kisser. If you weren't so anal and wouldn't get the wrong idea, I'd let you kiss me again." She bent over and retrieved her shoes. "You're going to rock Paige's world." When she returned to the upright position, Tyson was walking back up the hill.

Chapter 9

Reyna activated the Bose sound system and moved to the rhythm as she prepared a breakfast of bacon and eggs with wheat toast. Having a place of her own was liberating. Jewel would keel over and die if she could see Reyna now as she stood at the stove in her underwear, gyrating to the R & B hit and singing the lyrics about dancing the night away. She switched off the stove and transferred the bacon and scrambled eggs to a plate the precise moment the toaster dinged. After pouring a glass of orange juice, Reyna sat at the counter and devoured her breakfast. As she licked jelly from the corner of her lips, thoughts of Tyson tainted its sweetness.

The previous day's events on the hill had rocked her world more than she cared to admit. In his anger Tyson had embarrassed her, but then with tenderness he'd comforted her without condemnation. His kiss had not only seared her lips, but had also warmed her soul. Reyna had been so discombobulated that before dinner back at Kevin's house she'd offered to say grace. If the gesture had pleased Tyson, he didn't show it and didn't mention it on the ride home. In fact, he didn't say much to her at all after the incident on the hill.

Tyson was a good person, but why Reyna felt compelled to expose her vulnerability to him was a mystery to her. It had always been that way with him. When her world began spiraling out of control, Tyson was right there, trying to break her fall, but she wouldn't take heed of his advice. He was the one who had bailed her out of jail and helped her nurse the wounds. She'd mastered the art of cursing him out, yet Tyson respected her. Whenever she needed help, Tyson was right there, such as when he offered his home to her. She had noticed his patience was starting to wear thin with her attitude about church, but she wasn't ready to change. One day she'd face reality and acknowledge that Tyson desired much more than friendship from her, but today wasn't the day. Not as long as he worshiped the God she detested.

The clock above the stove chimed, indicating she had forty-five minutes to iron and get dressed. Today she wanted to arrive at the real estate office early. She was on a mission to fix Tyson up with Paige as a way to direct Tyson's affections away from her. In compliance with the office dress-code policy, Reyna selected a black pencil skirt that stopped just above the knee and a tapered jacket with a white-collared shirt. After applying makeup and styling her hair, Reyna slipped her nylon-covered feet into four-inch pumps and headed for the office.

Before backing out of the driveway, Reyna turned on the satellite radio station and blasted the latest number one R & B hit. Traffic was unusually light for a Monday morning, and she made it work with ten minutes to spare. Just as she suspected, Paige was already seated in her office, with her eyes glued to the computer screen. As usual, Paige's model-like physique was covered in a dark-colored business suit.

After the previous warning, Reyna wasn't sure how to approach the subject of Tyson. "Good morning,

Paige," she cheerfully greeted from the doorway, then looked down at her watch. "How long have you been here?"

"About two hours," Paige answered, without turning her attention away from the computer.

Reyna inched into the office and looked around. Paige was one of the best; the multiple wall plaques proved it. Paige was beautiful, self-sufficient, and successful. A tinge of jealousy and regret sparked in Reyna as she wondered what her life would be like had she finished her master's degree and started her own practice. Would she be as successful as Paige? She quickly decided that she would be phenomenal. She directed her thoughts back to the task at hand.

"How was your weekend?"

"Church was wonderful," Paige answered as her fingers glided across the keyboard.

Reyna rolled her eyes but stopped short of smirking. "What about the rest of the weekend? Surely you didn't spend the whole weekend at church, did you?" The more Reyna thought about it, the more it seemed possible for Paige to spend the whole weekend at a shut-in prayer session.

Paige continued typing. "No. I also visited an art gallery."

"Really?" Reyna saw the opening she'd been waiting for and took the liberty of sitting in one of the guest chairs. "I didn't know you like art."

"I collect pieces as a hobby." Paige smiled, just slightly, but continued typing. "Not to brag, but I have an extensive collection. Are you a collector also?"

"Well, no." Reyna leaned back and crossed her legs. "But Tyson is. You should see his place. He has art everywhere. Maybe the two of you could compare pieces or visit galleries together."

Paige's fingers ceased their movement, and for the first time, she looked up at her employee.

Reyna sat in anticipation until Paige scowled at her, then stood, with her fists planted on the desk. "Reyna, I told you to leave that alone. Tyson and I are adults with a long history. If we want a relationship, we know how to establish one without any interference from you."

Reyna's jaw fell.

"Furthermore, you don't know Tyson as well as you think. If you did, you wouldn't waste your time trying to fix him up." Paige sat back down. "I suggest you go to your workstation and focus on the job you're paid to do and leave my personal business alone." With that, Paige redirected her attention back to the computer screen.

Humiliated, Reyna stood and swiftly left while she still had a job, but she wondered just how much history Tyson and Paige shared.

By lunchtime, as she waited in line at the Chinese buffet, the early morning events were long forgotten. After hours of inspection reports and credit checks, the only thing on Reyna's mind was chicken chow mein and garlic chicken wings. To get her daily serving of vegetables, she added a spoonful of broccoli to the already loaded plate and approached the cash register.

"Someone has worked up a big appetite."

Reyna paused momentarily to see to whom the bass voice belonged, and almost lost her desire to eat. The six-foot-plus-tall man standing behind her was gorgeous. Normally, she wasn't attracted to Caucasian men, but this dark-haired, bearded man was built like a bodybuilder and had deep sea–blue eyes. He was dressed in a tailored suit, complete with silver cuff links. His skin wasn't pale, but olive, like he'd just stepped from a tanning salon.

"Excuse m—me?" she stuttered.

The man's smile revealed a straight set of teeth. "I didn't mean to distract you, but it's not every day I find a woman who can eat more than me."

Reyna's eyes traveled down to the stranger's plate, and she blushed. Her plate held double the amount of food in comparison. "I guess I am pretty hungry." She sobered. "Do I know you?"

He extended his free hand. "Now you do. My name is Peyton."

Reyna took note; he had presented his left hand. The ring finger was bare. After resting her tray on the counter in front of the cash register, Reyna shook his hand. "I'm Reyna."

"Nice to make your acquaintance, Reyna," he responded while squeezing her hand.

"You hold up line. You ready to pay for your food, miss?" the Chinese cashier interrupted in broken English.

Embarrassed, Reyna snatched her hand back and reached inside her purse.

"We're together," Peyton said and handed the cashier a twenty-dollar bill.

"I can't let you do that," Reyna protested. "You don't know me like that."

"That's exactly why I'm treating you to lunch. I want to know you like that."

Reyna didn't know how to respond to his aggressive behavior or to the wink that followed. What she did know was that she wanted to know more about this fine white man with the blue eyes. While Peyton collected his change, she secured a table near the door, just in case he turned out to be crazy. Before she sat down, she checked her clothes. She wasn't dressed like a hooker today, so Peyton's interest in her had to be genuine.

"Thank you for sharing this meal with me," Peyton said once he had fitted his long frame in the chair.

"You're welcome," Reyna said while twirling a noodle around her fork. "I am curious, though. Why do you want to know me?"

Peyton poked a broccoli spear, then looked up. "Do you want the truth or some corny line?"

"The truth," Reyna answered before biting into a chicken wing. "The truth is always best."

"Okay, but don't say I didn't warn you," he said after swallowing. "I saw you walk in, and I liked what I saw. You look like a woman who could stimulate my mind."

Reyna smirked. "That last part was corny. But thanks for the compliment." She looked down at his left hand again. Reyna was determined not to make the same mistake twice. "Are you married?"

"No," he answered without hesitation.

"Gay? Bisexual? In a relationship of any kind?" Reyna rattled off the questions, then held her breath for the answers.

Peyton chuckled. "No. No. No. And no, I don't have any children running around. What about you?"

Reyna finally exhaled. Peyton had potential. "No to all of the above."

"Now that that's out of the way, tell me about yourself." Peyton appeared visibly relaxed as he listened to Reyna talk about working in real estate.

"What about you?" she asked.

"I'm an investment banker in the city." That was how local residents referred to San Francisco. He went on to share some experiences related to his position at one of the top firms in San Francisco.

As she ate, Reyna observed his mannerisms and listened to his speech. Peyton appeared confident in his ability at work but said nothing about family and God. That scored well with Reyna.

"Do you live near here?" Peyton asked as Reyna finished the last chicken wing.

She washed down the garlic delight with a drink of water before answering, "I'm about ten minutes away, in Broadway Terrace." A smile creased his face, and Reyna felt proud to say she lived among the Bay Area elite, even if she was renting from a friend. "What about you? Do you stay in the city?"

"Most of the time." He paused and leaned in so close, Reyna felt his breath against her skin. "But for the right person I'd be willing to commute."

Reyna pushed back from the table. Peyton was handsome and employed, but she still didn't know him. "I have to get back to work," she announced as she stood.

Peyton stood and gently grabbed her arm. "Please, may I have your number before you go? I'd love to see you again."

Reyna looked down at the light manicured hand touching her and was amazed she felt the heat of his touch through the fabric of her jacket. For a brief moment she entertained the truth: dating someone outside of her race fascinated her.

"Sorry, Peyton, but I don't think that's a good idea. Lunch was good, but it didn't earn my phone number. After all, I don't even know your last name." She reclaimed her arm and made a dash for the exit.

"Covington. My full name is Peyton Ryan Covington."

Reyna stopped dead in her tracks. By stating his full name, this stranger had given her more than the man she'd naively shared her body with. She ignored the intuitive warning and retraced her steps.

Chapter 10

"Do you want to talk about it, or what?" Kevin asked after Tyson threw his racket on the wood-paneled floor after missing the ball for the third time.

Tyson usually excelled in racquetball, but today his game was way off. His whole day had been off-kilter. He'd overslept and almost missed a preliminary hearing. In the rush to make it to the courtroom on time, he'd parked in a handicapped space and received a four-hundred-dollar parking violation ticket. Now he was losing to Kevin in their weekly game of racquetball.

He paced the length of the court, wiping his forehead with a towel.

"Well?" Kevin said and sat on the floor and adjusted his prosthesis.

Tyson ceased pacing and leaned against the wall near his friend. "I hate to think how you'd whip me if you had two full legs." Kevin's right leg had been severed below the knee in a car accident when he was a teenager.

"My remarkable athletic skills are the least of your problems," Kevin smirked. "My prowess on the court can't touch the whipping Reyna has put on you. And just think, she doesn't even know it."

Tyson's denial came out as incomprehensible grunting.

Kevin stood upright and asked, "Have you reconciled your feelings for her yet?"

Tyson threw his hands down. "Man, I know I'm in love with her." The admission left a bitter taste in his mouth. He frowned at Kevin's laughter. "It's not funny." He threw the towel at his friend.

"You're right. It's not funny." Kevin bent over, holding his stomach. "This is downright hilarious. The stoic anal retentive attorney Tyson Stokes has fallen in love with Reyna Mills. What are the odds of that? You guys are like oil and water."

"Whatever, man." Tyson picked up his racket and started for the exit.

Kevin caught him by the shoulder. "Hold up, man. Just having some fun at your expense." Tyson stopped walking. "I'm just saying, for someone who detests drama, you've selected a drama queen."

Tyson slumped back against the wall. "Trust me, it wasn't on purpose. Man, I don't know what I'm going to do." He slid down the wall and rested on the floor with his knees bent, his head in his hands.

Kevin quickly sobered and sat next to him. "Man, this is really tearing you up. I've never seen you look so defeated and confused." Kevin broke the silence that followed. "Do you plan on telling her?"

Tyson raised his head and forced out the remaining air from his lungs. "I did." Kevin's incredulous facial expression pushed him to explain further. "Okay, maybe not directly, but I told her I cared about her." He paused. "Oh yeah, and I kissed her."

Kevin's whistle echoed through the court. "How did she respond?"

"She said I was a great kisser, and then renewed her ridiculous quest to fix me up with Paige."

Kevin's face twisted. "Paige? Why Paige?" Kevin paused. "Reyna doesn't know about you guys?"

Tyson shook his head from side to side.

"Are you going to tell her?"

Tyson thought the idea absurd. "Heck, no! I'm not telling that woman that if Paige and I weren't such self-centered and selfish adults back in the day, we'd be the parents of a twelve-year-old kid. You know Reyna will use that as an excuse for her crazy behavior. I can hear her now. 'You had the chance to sow your oats. Why can't I?'" His head shook, almost involuntarily. "No way, man. She's already accused me of judging her. Besides, that's not something I'm proud of."

Tyson wasn't proud. In fact, the decision he made almost thirteen years ago was his biggest life regret. When he met Paige in college, they were the perfect match. Both were driven by ambition, and neither wanted the emotional attachment that came with relationships. Their exclusive "friends with benefits" arrangement worked for a year, until a night of drinking led to an unplanned pregnancy. Neither wanted or needed a baby. Both admitted that although they shared their bodies, their hearts were far apart, and they mutually agreed to an abortion. Tyson paid for the procedure and supported Paige through the process. They had remained friends over the years, but the "benefits" part of the relationship ended with the pregnancy. The experience left them both scared and, eventually, led them to the altar and into a relationship with the Lord.

"Are you still haunted by it?" Kevin asked. Tyson had shared with him the nightmares he used to have.

"No, but I still regret it." Tyson cleared his throat in effort to steady his voice. "I wonder what could have been." He looked his friend in the eyes. "And to be honest, I'm jealous of you and Leon. I'm starting to think maybe Paige and I don't deserve a family, because of our selfish decision. Look at us. We're both workaholics and can't relate emotionally to anyone."

Kevin grabbed his shoulder. "Man, don't do this to yourself. God forgave you and Paige a long time ago. You're workaholics because you choose to be. You can't express your feelings, because you've suppressed them for so long, you can't identify what they are."

Tyson's head dropped.

"And you need to learn what unconditional love is," Kevin said after shaking him until he lifted his head. "Not that legalistic stuff you experienced growing up."

"How do I learn anything else?" Tyson asked, hunching his shoulders. "I'm thirty-six years old, and I have yet to receive that from a human. I have to give my father a list of my winning cases in order to get one compliment out of him. And Mother, she's always been too busy enjoying the prestige of being the wife of a judge to care about me."

"Man, you know I love you. So does Marlissa. We accept you no matter how anal you are." Kevin pushed him with his shoulder. "Come on, dude. You're going to be my child's godfather, remember?"

Tyson maneuvered himself upright. "That's right. And don't forget to name him after me."

"Hmm. Anal Jennings." Kevin said the words slowly, then stood up. "It has a nice ring to it."

Tyson retrieved his towel and racket and once again started for the exit. "Just for the record, I love you too. I don't think I could care for you more if you were my biological brother. And Marlissa? Well, she's become the bossy little sister I never wanted, but I love her like crazy. And Leon and Starla have grown on me like mold on bread."

"That wasn't so bad, now was it?" Kevin asked once he stopped laughing. "Sharing your feelings is good for the soul."

"Yeah, well, if you tell a soul about my emotional meltdown, I'll sue you for defamation of character."

Kevin slapped him on the back. "And lose the only friend you have? I doubt that."

Tyson chuckled at his idle threat. Kevin's unconditional friendship had carried him through the hardest times in his life. When he confided in him about the Paige situation, Kevin didn't judge him. When he passed the bar exam on the first try, it was Kevin who celebrated his achievement before his parents did. And it was Kevin who'd accompanied him to the altar the day he dedicated his life to the Lord.

Tyson treasured their bond, but he'd trade in his law practice to have a happily ever after with Reyna.

Chapter 11

Strutting before the full-length mirror in her bedroom, Reyna admired her reflection. "Girl, you look good!" she exclaimed. The black lace–strapped dress was perfect. It showed just enough cleavage, without revealing too much, and flared just below the knee. She'd learned her lesson the hard way; it was possible to look sexy without impersonating a lady of the evening. If she spent the night with Peyton, he wouldn't feel obligated to leave money on the nightstand.

She and Peyton had spoken on the phone every day since their chance meeting five days ago. During those conversations, she learned Peyton had relocated to the Bay Area from Oregon less than a year ago. He had a business degree and ambitions to one day open his own brokerage company. The closest thing Peyton had to family in the Bay Area was an old college buddy. And although he claimed to have a close relationship with his parents, Peyton always changed the subject when questioned about them. That didn't bother Reyna; she didn't want to discuss Jewel or her runaway father, either.

It was Friday, and Peyton had promised to make it a night she'd never forget after she revealed she'd never been on a real date before. At first Peyton didn't believe her, but then she shared how she'd grown up in the church under strict supervision.

At 6:00 P.M. sharp, the telephone rang. It was Peyton at the security gate, seeking access to the exclusive subdivision. After buzzing him in, Reyna rushed to the vanity and sprayed Mariah Carey's fragrance on her neck and pulse points. After the Chase disaster, she'd thrown out Halle Berry's fragrance. The doorbell chimed just as she slipped on the black stilettos. "This is my night," Reyna declared, then raced to the front door.

"Hello. I . . ." she said after opening the door.

The red long-stemmed roses resting in the crook of Peyton's arm took her breath away. The cologne he was wearing didn't help, either. The black Versace suit must have been tailor-made to fit his chiseled torso so perfectly. His even skin appeared darker than when they first met. Either Peyton had a tanning salon membership or he spent countless hours lying in the sun. His beard had been trimmed, making his thin lips appear bigger and more attractive.

Using his free hand, Peyton took her hand and raised it to his lips. "Hello, my beautiful Reyna."

She was no match for his cologne combined with his soft touch. Reyna exhaled and almost fell when she attempted to lean against a wall that wasn't there. Peyton caught her just in time.

"Are you all right?" he asked once he'd steadied her.

Reyna downplayed her embarrassment. "It must be these shoes. I lost my balance." There was no way she'd let this man know he'd blown her mind in less than sixty seconds. She stepped to the side. "Please come in. It'll just take me a minute to grab my wrap."

"Where would you like for me to put these?" he called after her.

Reyna stopped mid-stride. "He must think I'm a moron," she mumbled to herself before turning around and offering him a smile. "Thank you. I'll put those in water first."

"Why don't you let me do that?" he offered. "Just show me where you keep the vases."

He followed Reyna into the kitchen. "Let me get that for you," he said when Reyna reached into the top cabinet.

Her skin burned while his body pressed slightly against hers as he retrieved the crystal vase. Now she wished for long hair again so she couldn't feel his warm breath against her neck. *Genesis, Exodus, Leviticus* . . . She mentally recited the books of the Bible to calm her nerves. "Where the heck did that come from?" she scolded.

"What did you say?" Peyton asked.

Reyna cleared her throat and stepped away. "Nothing. Be back in two minutes."

Inside her bedroom, Reyna decided Mariah Carey's fragrance yielded better results. Never in a million years did she think she'd be attracted to a white guy, but so far Peyton was the total package. He was attractive, attentive, and came with his own resources.

When Reyna returned from the third-level bedroom, the vase filled with roses rested beautifully on the granite countertop, but Peyton was nowhere to be found. Reyna retraced her steps into the living room. Still no Peyton.

"Peyton," she called out.

"Down here." The distant response came from the bottom level.

"What the heck is he doing roaming around my house? Even Mother taught me better than that," she muttered on the way downstairs. "What are you doing down here?" she asked when she reached the landing.

Peyton either didn't detect her attitude or simply ignored it. "Just checking out the place and admiring your impeccable taste. The real estate market must be turning around."

Reyna almost asked what he was talking about, until she realized Peyton thought the town house and the furnishings inside belonged to her and that maybe she was a broker. With those perfect teeth smiling at her, Reyna didn't find it necessary to correct him. Peyton didn't need to know the space had once served as Tyson's home office. The oak cabinets lining the walls had once contained law books. He'd left the matching desk and leather chair. Mounted on the wall was a forty-six-inch flat screen. The cabinet below housed a Bose sound system and a DVD player. Regal crown molding outlined the earth-tone walls, and the beige carpet would almost envelop your toes when walked on barefoot.

"I do my best," she lied. "We should be going," she said, reaching for the light switch.

"How long have you owned the place?" he asked, assisting her up the stairs.

She didn't know how to answer that. Besides her car, the only things she owned were the clothes on her back. Before she could think of an answer that wouldn't disclose that she'd just mailed the last payment on her five-year-old Camry two days ago, they reached the landing. She stepped aside and allowed him to open the front door.

"Thank you," she said and stepped onto the walkway after locking the door. "I haven't lived here long," she answered and then changed the subject. "Someone's having a special evening," she stated in reference to the black limousine blocking her driveway.

Peyton placed his palm on the small of her back and nudged her forward. "I couldn't agree more. This will be an evening you'll never forget."

Reyna was midway down the walkway when the chauffeur got out, walked around the vehicle, and held the door open. She ceased walking. "Wow," she mouthed without sound. She'd never been in a limousine before, not even for the prom or a funeral.

"Don't look so surprised." He leaned so close, his breath warmed the hairs on her neck. "You're worth it, beautiful."

Reyna blushed but secretly agreed she was worth it. And she was beautiful. He urged her forward and helped her into the vehicle.

Once inside, Peyton filled two glasses of champagne before the limo left the subdivision.

Remembering the last time alcohol touched her lips, Reyna hesitated before accepting the golden bubbly liquid. Unlike before, the sip she took barely moistened her tongue. She casually held the crystal and admired the vehicle's interior. Every detail, from the butter-soft leather seat to the lighted floor and bar, was exquisite, the highlight being the mini flat-screen TV.

Any anxiety she had was relieved once the smooth jazz sounds floated through the speakers and relaxed her to the point where she closed her eyes and hummed the notes along with the alto saxophone.

"You like that, huh?"

She heard Peyton's words at the same time she felt his hand rest on her thigh. With more calmness than she felt, Reyna returned the glass to the bar and in the process removed Peyton's hand. Flowers and a limo ride didn't translate into free roaming.

"I didn't realize how beautiful jazz can be until recently," she responded honestly, without going into details about her strict religious upbringing. "Now I can't get through the day without the soothing sounds." When she turned and faced him, the lights from the bar illuminated Peyton's blue eyes, causing her to temporarily lose her train of thought. "What music helps you select the right investments for your clients?" she asked once she recovered.

Instead of answering the question asked, Peyton said, "Let's not ruin the evening with work talk. I don't want to think about anything but you." He leaned back and rested his arm against the leather. "You are so beautiful, and I want you to enjoy the evening."

Her mouth was dry, but she swallowed, anyway. This white boy was saying and doing all the right things.

"You still haven't told me where we're going," she said.

He took a few sips of champagne before responding, "Don't worry. Stick with me, and I'll take you for a ride you won't forget."

Reyna wanted to respond but couldn't think of a flirtatious comeback. She decided to sit back and enjoy the moment. Thirty minutes later, she stepped from the limo, awestruck. Peyton had taken her to a historical restaurant that stood on Ocean Beach in San Francisco. The city known for fog was uncharacteristically clear. The dark blue sky and the deep blue water ran together and met in a kiss. Slow waves with white-foam caps slammed against the rocks at the base of the structure. She inhaled, and the salt water tickled her nose.

"This is beautiful," she said once they were seated. The glass window provided an unobstructed view of the Pacific Ocean. "Thank you for bringing me here," she said, at the same time calculating how much money was in her checking account, just in case Peyton acted a fool, and she had to pay for her own meal.

"Order whatever you like," he said after the waiter explained the specials for the evening and took their drink orders.

Reyna scanned the menu. She couldn't decide between the prime rib and the Dungeness crab cakes. Peyton settled the dilemma by ordering two of each.

"Now who's hungry?" she asked when the waiter left.

He rested an elbow on the table and closed the gap between them. Reyna leaned back against the window. Peyton was handsome, but his eloquence reminded her of the Claremont. Under no circumstances would tonight be a repeat performance.

"This is not your first time here, is it?" he asked.

She took a sip of water with lemon. "Actually it is," Reyna admitted.

"Really?" Peyton appeared surprised. "Where do you normally take your high-end clients?"

Before Reyna could explain she wasn't a broker, the food arrived. Before tasting the food, she paused. Peyton picked up his fork and began eating. Tyson would have blessed the food, she thought, then scolded herself for thinking about Tyson. She was on a date with a handsome man who obviously had resources and respected her. She was not going to ruin the evening by thinking about a man she didn't want or need. She picked up the fork and dug into a crab cake.

During the meal, Peyton dominated the conversation with questions about the real estate market. Reyna evaded most questions and manufactured answers from conversations she'd overheard at the office.

"What happened to not ruining the evening with work?" she finally asked, putting an end to his questions.

He shrugged his shoulders. "You're right. I'm sorry. It's just hard to turn off at times. Excuse me. I'll be right back." Peyton left the table and returned ten minutes later, wearing a radiant smile.

After dessert of hot lava cake and vanilla ice cream, they enjoyed a walk along the pier before heading back to the waiting limo. The door had barely closed when Reyna felt Peyton's breath against her cheek and hand on her thigh.

"Mind if I kiss you?"

His breath was hot, but a shiver ran down her spine, and not from passion. Before she completed the nod giving her consent, Peyton crushed his mouth against hers. Right when she started to pull away, his tongue pushed her lips apart and freely explored every crevice of her mouth. "Ouch," she wanted to scream but didn't. When he finished, her hand covered her now aching lips.

Peyton must have thought she enjoyed it, because he said, "There's more where that came from," with a satisfied grin.

"You can keep it right where it is," was what she wanted to say but didn't. Instead, she turned and stared out the window for the remainder of the ride. Peyton took the opportunity to get acquainted with her body parts.

She wanted to stop him from touching her, but found the attention, although rough, refreshing.

"We're here," she announced when the limo turned into the subdivision. She pushed him away and replaced the lace straps on her shoulders.

Peyton ran his index finger down her arm. "Aren't you going to invite me in? I have the perfect way to end a perfect evening."

She found his smile sexy, and the attention he lavished on her appeared genuine. But after the last mistake, she needed more.

"Why would you want to spend the night with me?" she asked and waited for him to confirm what she assumed: Peyton wanted a return on the money he'd spent that evening.

He kissed the tip of her nose. "I enjoy being with you, Reyna. I know it hasn't been long, but I'm starting to care about you . . . a lot. I want to be with you."

His answer sent shock waves through her. No one had told her anything similar to that before, except Tyson, but he didn't count. She stared at Peyton long and hard, debating if she was making the wrong decision. On the surface, Peyton was everything she wanted, but what did she really know about him? He could be serious, and her indecisiveness could ruin something special. Or he could be a dog like Chase. She decided there was only one way to find out.

Chapter 12

Tyson switched on the hands-free Bluetooth device, then touched the icon on the touch-screen phone. The beads of sweat accumulating on his forehead and wet palms had nothing to do with the interior temperature of his home. A central heating and air-conditioning unit kept his home at a comfortable sixty-eight degrees. He hated making this weekly phone call. He gulped down nearly half the bottle of water, trying to lubricate his parched throat. He'd tried numerous cases before some of the most difficult and uncompromising judges, but only one judge caused him to second-guess sound decisions and doubt his ability. Repetitive vows of affirmation and declaring deliverance hadn't left him secure with the judge. On the third ring, the judge answered the phone.

"Good morning, Attorney Stokes," the stoic voice greeted.

Just once Tyson wished the judge would drop the legal image and be Fredrick Stokes—his father. "Good morning, Father. How are you and Mother?"

"The trial is taking much longer than I anticipated. I can't believe the antics of these young lawyers. Their ambition gives leeway to sensationalism." Judge Stokes was currently presiding over a case involving a local businessman accused of murdering his wife and then hiding the body. "I can look at that man and tell he's guilty as sin, and the evidence supports it. His money has bought him enough legal muscle to make him look like the victim. The media is having a field day."

Tyson nodded in agreement, as if his father could see him. Listening to his father's complaints about the injustices in the criminal legal system, Tyson affirmed his decision to practice civil law. He'd announced the decision over dinner with his parents after passing the bar. Judge Stokes's disappointment was evident when he stood and walked out of the restaurant, leaving his wife and son behind. His father didn't speak to him for an entire month. According to Tyson's mother, Judge Stokes had been boasting to his colleagues that his son would one day follow him on the criminal bench. Tyson could still sit on the bench one day but presently didn't have the desire.

Tyson opened the refrigerator and removed a take-out carton from the previous night's dinner and placed it inside the microwave. "Father, you've been on the bench over twenty years. You know the press thrives on cases like this."

"I'd bet the house the jury is not as slow as they look." Judges Stokes chuckled at his own dry humor. "Once they convict the imbecile, I bet he'll try to cut a deal by offering to disclose where he hid the body."

When the microwave beeped, Judge Stokes was still on his soapbox. Tyson twirled the chicken chow mein around the fork and savored the taste.

"Anything else interesting?" Tyson interjected after the last forkful. He'd grown tired of his father's work talk. Would they ever share simple father-son conversation? Normal topics, like the score of a basketball game or the NFL draft, were never discussed. New books came up on occasion, but the subjects pertained to the law.

"What else is there?" the judge asked.

Tyson opened his mouth to point out the obvious and then decided against it. For the Honorable Fredrick Stokes, there wasn't anything else. His life had revolved around the law since childhood. His father had helped organize the local Association of African American Lawyers in the early sixties. The law was in his blood.

Tyson changed the subject. "Brian Culbertson is coming to town. I have tickets. Would you like to attend with me?"

If the question caught the judge off guard, he didn't show it. Without missing a beat, he answered, "Maybe next time. Your mother has my free time booked solid with those charity events she loves so much."

Tyson took measured swallows from the water bottle. He should be immune to his father's rejection, but it still hurt. He didn't give up. "What about dinner?"

The offer piqued the judge's interest. "You have a case you'd like to discuss with me? I'm a little rusty on the civil side, but I'm sure I could help you."

"No, Father," Tyson answered, defeated. "I thought we could just hang out." During the long silence that followed, he prayed his father would finally hear the longing of his only son. Tyson needed more than bland weekly telephone conversations. He would give anything to gain some insight on his latest dilemma: Reyna.

"I'll get back to you on that," Judge Stokes finally answered, his voice less brisk. "Hold on. Let me get your mother." There was a pause. "Bev," he called.

Tyson tossed the empty plastic bottle into the recycle bin. The Honorable Fredrick Stokes was a leopard who refused to change his spots.

"Hello, son," Beverly Stokes sang into the phone.

"Hello, Mother," Tyson replied dryly.

"Are you available on the twenty-first?" Beverly was never one for idle chitchat. Every conversation had a purpose, usually raising funds for an organization. "I'm chairing a benefit for the Autistic Children Fund. The president of the group, Mylan, is a delightful young lady. No children, single, and around your age."

From the giddiness in his mother's voice, Tyson suspected she had already committed him to attending. "I'll have to check my calendar," he answered, in anticipation of his mother's rebuttal. She didn't disappoint him.

"It's six o'clock in the evening on a Saturday. I'm sure there's nothing on your schedule. Unless"—she paused—"you're dating someone and working on some grandchildren before the judge and I are too old to enjoy them."

Ever since his father's bench appointment twenty years ago, his mother had addressed his father by his judicial title. Before then Tyson couldn't recall his parents using endearing terms for each other. It was either Fred or Bev. *No wonder I'm so emotionally constipated*, he thought, but said, "No, Mother, I'm not dating anyone."

"Good." His mother sounded relieved. "Bring your checkbook, and I'll let Mylan know you can't wait to meet her."

Tyson nodded rhythmically while his mother raved about how great and beautiful Mylan was, and then said good-bye.

Tyson disconnected the call and lamented that neither of his parents were interested in his life outside of the law and his checkbook. Being a glutton for punishment, Tyson phoned Reyna.

Chapter 13

Reyna hadn't noticed there were exactly twelve tan panels covering the master bedroom ceiling until today. She'd been too busy in the mornings rushing to the shower to leisurely lie in bed and take note. This morning was different. It was Saturday, her day off, and a snoring mass of tanned flesh held her stationary.

After little contemplating, Reyna had invited Peyton inside last night. She had offered him a seat on the couch, but he'd helped himself to her bed without much resistance. A few kisses here and a stroke there, and Reyna had succumbed to his demands. "At least I know his last name," she'd mumbled when it was all over.

While the experience had left her with many emotions, satisfaction wasn't one of them. Peyton had showered her with glorious words and promises but had failed to deliver on any of them. In many aspects the experience was similar to her first encounter—painful. The only difference was Peyton cared about her. She'd basically yielded and allowed Peyton to have his way with her. She'd never admit it to Jewel, but Reyna now understood why her mother rationed out physical activity to her father.

Reyna stretched and brushed Peyton's black waves from her chin, then attempted to squeeze out from underneath him. With her every motion, his grip tightened. Frustrated, Reyna gave up and wondered how she'd ended up in bed with a white man and in what direction their relationship was headed. Peyton hadn't expressed love but had repeatedly told her how beautiful she was. Reyna certainly wasn't in love. After all, she'd known the man only a week. Yet she trusted him enough to spend the night with him.

She frowned as drool from Peyton's mouth moistened her skin. "Ugh! Get up," she shrilled and vigorously shook him.

Peyton braced his weight on his elbows and raised his head, shaking it as to clear it. Reyna watched as thick eyelashes gave way to those piercing blue eyes.

"Sorry. Was I too heavy for you?" he asked, at the same time using the back of his hand to wipe his mouth.

Not the picture of sophistication from the night before, Reyna observed. In fact, the second he'd stepped back into the town house, the word *class* vacated the premises. He acted more like a starved animal than a refined investment banker. He'd practically ripped off her clothes with more energy than the Energizer Bunny.

"You're not too heavy, but I need to use the bathroom," she answered with her head turned away from him. Peyton took morning breath to a new dimension.

He rolled over onto his back and stretched, but before Reyna could gather the sheet around her, Peyton jumped from the bed and trotted into the bathroom.

"Selfish—" The ringing telephone cut off the choice adjectives she had for Peyton. She rolled her eyes at the closed bathroom door before answering the phone. "Hello."

"Good morning, Reyna."

Shock waves flowed through her at the sound of Tyson's voice. It took her a moment to gather her bearings.

"Reyna?" he said when she didn't respond.

"I'm here," she said, recovering. "What do you want?"

He cleared his throat. "I just wanted to see how you're adjusting to the town house. Is everything in working order?"

How lame, she thought but said, "Everything is fine. If it wasn't, you'd be the first to know, Mr. Landlord." After an extended pause, she added, "Is there any more of my business you'd like to know?"

"No. Sorry to bother you. Good-bye." The line went dead.

She felt a pang of guilt for being rude but didn't have time to dwell on it. Peyton exited the bathroom, wearing her robe.

"Hey, what's for breakfast?" he asked. "I'm starved."

"Excuse me?" Reyna was stuck on the fact that he had the audacity to wear her clothing. They weren't that close, were they?

Peyton stepped over his clothing, which was heaped on the floor, and plopped down on the bed. "I know you have some food in the house. Go find me something to eat."

"Why don't you get back into that limousine of yours and find your own food?" The words poured out before Reyna's feet hit the floor.

"You're kidding, right? The limo is long gone. I only rented it for last night."

Her head snapped up.

He reached over and pulled Reyna toward him. "Come on now. After all, I gave you last night. Don't I deserve some pancakes and eggs or something?"

"I don't feel like cooking," she stated, digesting the fact that he'd rented the limo and that it was now gone. Then she realized he'd planned all along to spend the night. That explained the pack of condoms in his pocket. Fighting a feeling of déjà vu, Reyna tightened the sheet around her. "How are you getting home?"

"I was hoping you could give me a ride," he stated while scratching his forearm.

Reyna stepped back and planted a fist against her waist. "You live in the city, and I'm not fighting week-end bridge traffic to take you home. You better take a cab or catch BART." Her neck rolled with every word. "You should have thought about that before you dismissed your driver."

This time when Peyton reached for her, he pulled her to him and used his legs to hold her stationary. "Come on, sweetheart. Don't be mad at me for wanting to give you the best."

"So it's my fault you don't have a ride home?" she snapped.

"It's not your fault." His fingertips stroked her cheek. "You're a special woman, and I care about you. I wanted our first date to special. You deserve that and more."

Peyton's deep sea–blue eyes transformed into a soft sky-blue shade and mesmerized Reyna. His gentle tone relieved her misguided agitation. She was irritated at Tyson for calling and disturbing her imagined peace. All night she'd been trying to convince her conscience that Peyton was the man for her, but hearing Tyson's voice had squashed her efforts. His voice across the phone wires had touched her in a place Peyton's physical presence hadn't. But she didn't want Tyson.

"I want to give you everything." His arms opened and he gestured at the expansive master bedroom suite. "You have so much already, but I'm willing to work hard for you."

Reyna's tense muscles relaxed, and imaginary music sounded in her ears. Peyton planned to stay around.

"Okay," she said, surrendering with a smile. "I'll feed you, but you can find your own ride home." She gave him a quick peck, then skipped into the bathroom.

"I'm sure you have clients scheduled for today, but what do you have planned for tomorrow?" she heard him ask behind the closed door. "I was thinking, maybe you could show me around Oakland."

She covered her mouth to keep from shouting. Peyton wanted to spend time with her. Without thinking, she let the words fly from her lips. "After church, I don't have anything planned." Did I just stay that? she thought. She cleared her throat. "What I meant to say was, since I no longer attend church, I'm free."

He opened the door and stepped inside. "Good. Let's spend the day together."

"Close the door!" she yelled. Liberation for her had finally come, but some things would always remain private. Sitting on the commode was one of those things.

"Why? I've seen everything already," he smirked, then walked over to the sunken tub.

"Get out!"

He ignored her and turned on the water. Then he searched the cabinet and pulled out scented bubble bath and bath salts.

Reyna watched, speechless, as the tub filled with water.

"Soak in this for a while," he said, pointing at the tub. "It'll help with the soreness. Forget about breakfast. We can pick up something on the way. I don't want to make you late for any million-dollar deals," he added on the way out.

Reyna's mouth hung open, but she couldn't form any words. His thoughtfulness warmed her, yet guilt caused her to shiver. Peyton's intentions were honest, but hers were built on false pretenses. Sooner or later she would disclose the truth about her job.

An hour later, when Peyton frowned first, then got into her five-year-old Camry, Reyna decided the sooner the better.

Chapter 14

"Reyna?"

The shrill voice put an abrupt end to Reyna's attempt to sneak into the office undetected. She'd planned to slip into her workstation and act as if she'd been busy working for the past hour. In actualilty, Reyna was an hour late, thanks to Peyton. Sunday's sightseeing excursion had turned into dinner and dessert at the town house, with her being the main entrée. She wouldn't have minded so much if Peyton hadn't decided to spend the night and then overslept. That required her to drive him into San Francisco in Monday morning commute traffic, since he'd ridden BART into Oakland the day before. She had tried unsuccessfully to persuade him to take mass transit back, but he'd insisted he wouldn't have enough time to go home and change and make it to work in time. Peyton was still under the impression she was a real estate broker and set her own hours. Now, as she prepared to face Paige's wrath, she wished she'd told him the truth. She wasn't a real estate broker, but a secretary/assistant with a no-nonsense boss.

"Reyna," Paige called again. "You're late."

"As if I didn't know that," she mumbled and then slumped into the chair and placed her head on the desk.

"Are you all right?" Paige's tone softened as she stepped into Reyna's workstation.

Reyna launched into performance mode. "I'll be fine," she groaned. "I have a bad case of cramps." She moaned and gripped her abdomen.

Paige's hand rested on her shoulder. "Would you like me to get you some tea? I'm sure we have some in the break room."

Reyna lifted her head but kept her eyes closed. "If you don't mind. That might help." She pronounced the words as if every syllable was a labored effort.

"I'll be right back."

Reyna opened her eyes and watched Paige's departing back. She smirked and whispered, "That was easy," once Paige was no longer within earshot. Although lying was a recently acquired trait, Reyna had discovered she was very good at it. She had dodged a bullet this time but would be more careful in the future. She turned on the computer, and while waiting for it to boot, she sorted the papers in her in-box.

A few minutes later, Paige returned, carrying a steaming mug.

Reyna let the papers fall onto her desk. "Thank you so much," she offered weakly and reached for the mug. She placed the mug under her nose and inhaled the steam from the minty hot liquid.

Paige continued standing in front of the desk with her arms folded, but with a look of concern.

Reyna guessed Paige wanted to make sure she drank the mint tea. She blew into the mug and took a small sip. "Um," she moaned as the warm liquid slid down her throat. "This is helping all ready," she lied and prepared to take another sip.

"Good," Paige said and planted her palms on Reyna's desk. "Before Mother Nature pays you another visit, stop by your neighborhood Walgreens and pick up some Midol, Tylenol, or whatever your medication of choice is. Get up an hour earlier and take the medicine. Then get to work on time. The telephone was invented in eighteen seventy-six. Learn to use it next time." She started for the door, then stopped. "One more thing. If you think my friendship with Tyson is your ticket to special treatment, you're sadly mistaken." Then she left.

Reyna swallowed prematurely, causing the tea to burn her throat. Once the fire in her throat was extinguished, she cursed Paige's authority. She spent the rest of the day blaming Peyton for her predicament. If he'd only driven his own car and gone home at the end of the evening, like most dates did . . .

On the surface, Peyton was the total package, but there were things about him that nagged at her. His preoccupation with her supposed deep pockets being one. When they reached the Bay Bridge this morning, he didn't even offer to pay the toll. He didn't offer money for gas on their excursion, either, but he did bring back her change along with a receipt. He had spent the night at her place twice but hadn't invited her to his apartment.

By the end of the workday, Reyna had justified any misgivings about the new man in her life. Peyton was her man. After making a fool of herself by chasing a man who didn't want her, Reyna finally had a man who adored her. Peyton constantly expressed his adoration verbally and touched her affectionately. She would work with him on time management but would fight to the death to keep him in her life.

After a quick shopping trip after work, Reyna ran into the town house and dropped the grocery bags on the kitchen table. Peyton had also managed to eat what little food she had the day before. By the time she reached the ringing telephone, she was breathless.

"Hey, you," she panted into the phone, hoping it was Peyton. "Hello," she stated more firmly when the caller didn't respond.

"Reyna, this is your mother."

She pulled the phone from her ear and jumped up and down while silently screaming, "Why did I answer the phone?"

"Are you still there?"

Reyna settled down and spoke through clenched teeth. "What do you want, Jewel?"

"Young lady, just because you've moved from my home doesn't give you a blank check to disrespect me. I'm still your mother. . . ." The words trailed off, giving way to heavy breathing. "I just wanted to check and see how you're getting along," Jewel said in resignation.

"I'm good," Reyna said dryly.

"Well . . ." Jewel hesitated. "Do you need anything? I know you're grown, but you've never been on your own before. . . ."

"No, Mother," she snapped. The time had passed long ago for the tired, concerned mother act. "I don't want or need anything from you." Reyna heard huffing and puffing and envisioned her mother with that red head scarf, speaking in tongues.

"Please call if you need anything."

Reyna wasn't moved by the resignation in her mother's voice. "Bye," she sang, then replaced the cordless phone on its base. Without a second thought, she put the groceries away and made a quick meal of spaghetti, a tossed salad, and garlic bread. She ate the satisfying meal seated at the kitchen counter, next to the cordless phone. Peyton had said he'd call after meeting with a client, and she didn't want to miss his call.

By the time she'd filled her lunch containers with leftovers and cleaned the kitchen, Peyton still hadn't called. She pressed the talk button on the phone to make sure the device was working. After calling the phone company's twenty-four-hour problem line and having them run a test on her line, Reyna dialed the cell number Peyton had given her. When the call went to voice mail, she disconnected without leaving a message.

Her alarm sounded at 6:00 A.M. the next morning, but her phone remained silent.

Chapter 15

Tyson leaned back in his chair and rested his size-eleven Brooks Brothers shoes on his expansive desk. He'd never done that before, but an early morning workout, lunch consisting of Reese's Peanut Butter Cups and a banana, and two deposition hearings in five hours had left him mentally and physically drained. His thumbs and forefingers massaged his temples and forehead in a circular motion in an effort to ease a throbbing headache. After a few minutes, Tyson gave up and retrieved a bottle of aspirin from his desk drawer. He concentrated so hard on removing the foil seal from the pill bottle, he didn't see or hear his visitor arrive. His secretary had left shortly after he returned from the courthouse.

"Tyson, are you all right?"

His head snapped upward, and the pill bottle—still sealed—fell onto his desk. He met his father's concerned stare with one of his own. His father rarely addressed him by his name and visited his office even less. Was the judge sick?

"Father?" Tyson's brow furrowed as he questioned his father's sudden appearance.

"What brings you here? Is Mother all right?"

Judge Stokes stepped completely into the office and dismissed his concern with a casual wave of the hand. "Other than being mad at you for no-showing at the fund-raiser last week, your mother is fine. Are you sick?"

Tyson lazily shrugged his shoulders, as if standing Beverly Stokes up was a common and acceptable practice. He had wanted to attend the event but hadn't been up to the matchmaking his mother had orchestrated. It didn't matter how captivating this Mylan person was; he wasn't interested. His heart belonged to his new tenant. He did, however, send a substantial contribution.

Tyson retrieved the pill bottle and replaced the plastic red cap. "No, just a little tension headache." He placed the bottle back in the drawer, deciding that having difficulty opening the bottle was a sign he didn't need the drug. He'd endure the pain; he didn't like taking pills, anyway. "What brings you by?"

Judge Stokes uncharacteristically stuck his hands in his front pants pockets, then looked nervously around the office. "Well," he began, then paused. "I'm free this evening. I called from the car, and your secretary said you were finished for the day." He cleared his throat and sat down. "A few weeks ago you mentioned having dinner. Well, son, I haven't eaten. I thought, well, maybe . . ." Judge Stokes's words ran together. "If you're hungry, we could eat together."

The strain on the judge's face didn't go unnoticed, and if his head wasn't throbbing, Tyson would have been elated his father wanted to spend time with him. The best he could offer was a weak smile.

"Thanks." Tyson paused and knitted his eyebrows. "Wait a minute. Father, are you sick?"

Judge Stokes looked perplexed. "No. Why?"

"Because you haven't addressed me as son since . . ." Tyson thought for moment. "I don't recall hearing that since I passed the bar. That day I went from being Tyson, your son, to Attorney Stokes." Remorse gripped him when his father's shoulders dropped. He had never seen the judge's face clothed in regret and didn't know how to respond, so he remained quiet.

"If we hurry, we might beat the dinner crowd at Skates," Judge Stokes stated, ending the awkward moment. "We can take my car, and I'll bring you back to pick up yours later."

Tyson glanced at the desk clock, then pushed back from his desk and stood. "Sounds good. Nothing beats fresh seafood and prime rib," he said, seconding his father's choice. He felt the judge's stare follow him as he gathered his jacket and briefcase. As they walked through the reception area, Tyson felt the urge to say something, but he didn't know what. The precise moment the office door lock clicked, he realized the ride to the restaurant and dinner would be the most uninterrupted time he had had with his father in years. The realization saddened him, but at the same time it gave him hope that he would gain a better understanding of the Honorable Fredrick Stokes.

During the drive to the Berkeley Marina, Tyson wasn't sure if his headache had subsided or if he was focusing too hard on the driver to notice the pain. Unbeknownst to him, the judge had purchased a new sports model Jaguar, and now he chatted nonstop about the luxury vehicle. Although Tyson didn't heed them, he recalled numerous speeches made by the man seated inches from him about the importance of buying American-made cars. Every three years Judge Stokes purchased new vehicles for himself and his wife, but they were usually top-of-the-line Cadillacs or Lincolns. "It keeps Americans working," he'd said.

Now all of a sudden he's the spokesperson for a foreign car? Tyson couldn't believe it.

"I know what you're thinking," his father said when Tyson's head shook from side to side. "What happened to my stance on American-made goods?"

"Let me guess. You converted during the test drive?" Tyson joked but stopped short of laughing. The merriment pouring from his father took his breath away. He leaned back in the leather seat and tried to recall the last time he heard his father laugh so freely, and couldn't.

"Something like that," Judge Stokes confirmed. "I grew so tired of Judge Oliver bragging about his new ride that I went to check it out for myself." He turned his gaze from the road and glanced at his son. "Up until recently, Ford Motor Company owned Jaguar, so technically the car has American in its blood."

Tyson's mouth gaped. Who was this man? "I can't believe you said that with a straight face."

"The Lincoln gave me a good ride, but this baby," he said, stroking the wood grain, "she's *smooth*."

Tyson threw his hands up. "Okay, who are you, and what have you done with my father?" He turned and looked in the backseat. "Is there a camera somewhere? Am I being punked?"

Judge Stokes pulled into a parking stall and shut the engine off. "Son, don't look so surprised. It may take a while, but with prayer and patience, people can change."

Tyson pondered his father's words while exiting the vehicle. Perhaps his father was in the process of changing. He hoped so; otherwise, he'd credit the sudden changes in his father to a midlife crisis.

The moderate seventy-degree weather yielded a postcard-perfect evening at the marina. The sky was clear, and the foam-capped waves rolling in from the bay were violent as they crashed against the rocks and pillars that surrounded the restaurant. Tyson paused long enough to sniff the saltwater scent of the marina and discovered the throbbing in his head had disappeared. Relieved, he walked briskly through the parking lot alongside his father.

"You're looking better," Judge Stokes said after they had been seated in a secluded corner and had ordered drinks. "I would ask you about the case, but I don't want to talk about law tonight."

"You d—don't?" Tyson stuttered, then recovered. "The law is your life. As you've said, what else is there?"

Judge Stokes broke eye contact and looked out the window. "I know I said that," he acknowledged with more than a hint of sadness. "But there is so much more to life." Before Tyson could ask what he meant, the waiter delivered their drinks.

As the sweet-tart taste of strawberry lemonade slid down his throat, Tyson took note of his father's attire. Whereas most judges wore casual clothing beneath their judicial robes, Judge Stokes dressed daily in tailored suits. A trait Tyson copied. Today Judge Stokes was dressed in khakis and a collared shirt, but no tie. *If this midlife crisis includes trading in Mother for a twenty-year-old, he'll have to deal with me,* he thought before taking another sip.

"So, Father, you seem to have undergone a slew of changes since we last talked. What gives?" he asked after the waiter returned for their dinner orders, then left.

"Judge Oliver is always bragging about something," his father began after fumbling with the bread and the butter knife that had been placed on the table. "He held a party to show off the new addition to his home. I started not to go, but you know your mother is a socialite." Judge Stokes finally buttered a piece of bread but didn't take a bite. "His son, the one who graduated from Harvard, was there."

Tyson started to ask how Judge Oliver's new home addition was relevant to the topic at hand, but held his tongue. Although his father complained about Judge Oliver's lack of modesty, he was still considered a close friend, and his father valued his opinion. The new Jaguar was proof of that.

"Would you believe he and his son started wrestling in the backyard in front of everybody?" his father continued after a sip of iced tea. "At first I couldn't believe it. That man is almost sixty, and there he was, tumbling around on the lawn in front of all those people and appearing happy about it. In the twenty years we've worked together on the bench, I'd never seen that side of him. He's six-five and about two hundred fifty pounds. His son is just as big. It was hilarious. I watched and laughed along with the other guests. I laughed so hard, I cried."

Tyson observed his father's expression change from amusement to melancholy. Another indication of how much the judge had changed. His father never revealed his emotions, aside from anger.

Judge Stokes took several deep breaths, then after another sip of iced tea, looked his son in the eye. "The tears I shed weren't tears of joy. I cried because out there in front of all those people I realized I've never shared any moments like that with you."

Tyson reached for his glass but retreated as the weight of his father's words penetrated, leaving him speechless.

"To be honest, I've always been jealous of Oliver's relationship with his sons."

Tyson's mouth gaped at the revelation, but his father didn't appear to notice.

"He's always boasting about their accomplishments. I can handle that because I can brag about your accomplishments. But I couldn't compete—not that I would want to—with what I witnessed that day. Oliver actually enjoyed embarrassing himself with his son. He loves his son and wasn't afraid to let everyone there know that his family came first. I never learned how to do that. . . ." His voice trailed off.

Both father and son changed sitting positions during the silence that followed Judge Stokes's confession. Tyson leaned back and rubbed his beard. His father sat back and looked out over the bay through the window. They remained that way until the waiter delivered two steaming bowls of clam chowder.

Still at a loss for words, Tyson bowed his head and listened to his father say grace. After adding cracked pepper to the soup, Tyson savored a small spoonful. His father didn't move.

"Aren't you going to eat?" Tyson asked, still unsure how to respond to his father.

"Of course," his father said, shaking his head as if to clear it, then, like his son, adding pepper to his soup.

Tyson ate the soup too fast and burned his tongue, but he didn't care. Something was happening to his father, and he sensed it was for the better. The silence continued throughout the appetizer course. Just when Tyson summoned the courage to speak, his father opened up.

"Your grandfather was a good man and an excellent lawyer. I can't count how many family members of former clients rave about how he helped them. He's been gone ten years now, but he will be forever remembered for his legal mind." Judge Stokes paused and regained eye contact. "I remember my father working all the time on civil rights cases and traveling around the country. I read about his successes in the newspaper and watched him on television. I heard him debate topics with the best. He wasn't an affectionate person, but tough and tenacious. From him I learned the importance of hard work. I learned to measure success by accomplishments. He taught me to provide for a family by working long hours. Mama and I never wanted for anything material.

"You're also reaping the benefits of his hard work with the money and property he left you. For that, I'm grateful, but I needed more and didn't know how to express it. I craved his time and friendship but was afraid he'd be disappointed or consider me soft. Besides, he was a very busy man. So I sucked it up and focused on making him proud. That's why I initially studied law. I wanted his approval. As time went on, I learned to love the law. He was proud too. Our best conversations were centered on the law. I still desired more but settled for what he gave me."

Tyson swallowed hard to force down the sob threatening to escape. His prayers were being answered, yet he didn't feel like celebrating. His heart broke for his father, because he'd walked in those same shoes.

"Watching Oliver enjoy his son shook me to the core. I couldn't deceive myself any longer. I made a horrible mistake. I vowed I'd be more to my son than my father was to me, but I'm ashamed to say I've repeated the cycle. I never learned how to relax and just be. I don't have memories of you and me playing around or hanging out. There weren't any fishing trips or one-on-one basketball games, because I too busy working. When I wasn't working, I pushed you to work hard. Outside of graduations, I missed those father-son bonding moments. To be honest, I really don't know you as a person." He reached out and patted his son's shoulder.

"You're grown and probably don't need me, but, son, I would like to work on getting to know you. I'd like for us to be friends."

Tyson didn't realize silent tears had escaped his tear ducts until he felt the fluid drip from his beard and onto his folded hands. He used the cloth napkin to wipe his hands without taking his eyes from his father, who appeared to have grown ten inches taller since they'd entered the restaurant.

"I wanted to accept the invitation to that concert, but I was afraid to say so. Your mother fussed at me all night for being a coward. I'd been telling her how you and I should spend more time together, and when the door opened, I slammed it shut."

Tyson cleared his throat. "The concert's isn't for another month. The ticket is yours if you want it." A warm sensation permeated his being at the sheer happiness on his father's face.

"Thank, you, son." Judge Stokes squeezed his son's shoulder. "I don't believe I've ever told you this, but I've always loved you and I'm very proud of you."

The declaration proved too much for Tyson. Why did his father have to feed him the words his soul craved in a crowded restaurant? He bowed his head into the cloth napkin and wept. After soaking the cloth, it occurred to him that his father needed the same thing. He stood and walked to his father's side. Judge Stokes was barely out of his seat when Tyson hugged him. "I love you, Dad." His father shook in his arms as he said a prayer of thanksgiving.

"Perfect timing," Judge Stokes said when the waiter arrived with their entrées just as they sat back down. Both were oblivious to the stares of fellow patrons.

"I can't tell if this is the best prime rib in the world or if I'm so happy that everything tastes good," Tyson said after taking a bite.

"I know what you mean, son. It feels like a huge weight has been lifted. I know we have a long way to go, but it's a good start."

"Yes, it is," Tyson agreed.

They talked more about the past and made plans to improve the present, then shared a dessert the judge wasn't supposed to have due to an elevated blood-sugar level. For the first time Tyson heard his father tell jokes and discovered his laugh was similar to his own.

As they headed toward the door, another laugh stopped Tyson dead in his tracks.

"What's wrong, son? Did you forget something?" his father asked when Tyson turned and started in the opposite direction.

"No. Nothing at all," Tyson answered, shaking his head at the sight of Reyna seated in a booth, cuddled up to a white man and giggling too much to notice him. Tyson retraced his steps and exited the restaurant, determined not to let Reyna ruin his evening.

Chapter 16

The blaring sound caused Reyna to literally jump out of bed. This was her final chance; she'd hit the snooze button twice already. She shut off the alarm and rushed to the bathroom. After Paige's rebuke a few weeks ago, she'd vowed never to be late for work again. She needed this job, no matter how mundane it was, until something better came along. More often than she cared to admit, Reyna fantasized about returning to school and finishing her master's degree. The idea of one day opening a practice excited her, but the reality that millions of Americans with multiple degrees were unemployed due to the economy discouraged her from pursuing the possibility. She decided to focus on the here and now. Peyton.

Reyna forgave his disappearing act from a few weeks ago when he arrived at the town house three days later with roses and offered to take her to dinner at Skates. Up until that moment, she hadn't heard from him, and depression had started to set in. When she saw him standing on her porch with the red, fragrant beauties, all was forgiven. She didn't question his excuse about working late with special clients. He still wanted to be with her, and that mattered above his absenteeism. The regret and depression had lifted, and she'd been with him every day since, mostly in the evenings. Since his car was in the shop, she'd pick him up from the

BART station and he'd spend the night, then drive her to work the next morning.

A steady stream of hot water gushed from the showerhead and massaged her sore and achy body. Muscles she didn't normally use and certainly couldn't name had been used during Peyton's latest sexual escapade. Since their union, she'd been flipped, dipped, and contorted, and they'd gone through a max pack of condoms, but never had she been satisfied. Most of the time her mind wandered off to other things during what Peyton swore was a mind-blowing experience.

"I'm tired of this," she mumbled as she lathered the sponge with drops of mango shower gel. She wasn't sure what she should be getting from the deal, but was convinced there was more to sex than sore muscles and a stiff back.

Marriage is honorable in all and the bed is undefiled.

"No!" she declared when the Bible verse broke through her thoughts. "I don't want to hear that mess now. This is my life, and I'll live it the way I want." She turned up the water pressure and rinsed twice before exiting the shower stall.

Intense anger traveled through her and seared her heart. "Just because I'm living my life the way I want, and not the way some ancient book says I should, doesn't mean a thing," she said, rambling, and yanked a towel from the rack. "I determine what makes me happy, not God." The rambling continued while Reyna dried herself off and rubbed lotion into her skin, but she stopped short of adding an expletive. Still shy about her body, she snuggled into a robe before exiting the bathroom.

"Get up, sleepyhead," she said, shaking Peyton on her way to the walk-in closet. "We have to be out of here in fifteen minutes." By the time Peyton sat up, Reyna had dressed in a magenta pantsuit.

"It's too early to be up." His voice lacked its normal sophistication. "You're the boss. Go in late once in a while."

She walked from the closet and leaned against the bed for support and stepped into her pumps. This morning Reyna didn't have the time or the energy to come up with a lie to keep the facade going. "Look, Peyton, I'm not the boss. I don't make, as you say, *big bucks*. I'm not a broker. I'm an administrative secretary at best, and I need this job." She ignored the shock on his face. "And what about you? Don't you have a job to get to? Every bank I know opens before noon. You sleep more than any investment banker I know."

She hadn't meant to say the last part but had grown tired of Peyton's blasé attitude about his work and his overzealous interest in hers. Peyton's position didn't require him to work set hours Monday through Friday. From what he had revealed, Reyna figured Peyton enjoyed a flex schedule, which she secretly envied. By her calculations, Peyton worked no more than four hours a day. After dropping her off at work, he'd drive into the city, work a few hours, and then he would be waiting for her in her car in the real estate office parking lot at five o'clock.

"So you're not a broker?" He pronounced the words as if reading them from a delayed teleprompter.

"You heard me. Now, get up and get ready." She picked his pants up from the floor and threw them at him. "When will they be done with your car?" The extra mileage he placed on her car every day had her concerned she'd need an oil change long before the recommended three months.

"In a few days," he said in response to her question, then asked again, "You're not a big-shot broker?"

"You heard me the first time." Reyna wanted to stick to the subject of his invisible car. "A few days? You said that last week." Peyton's car had been in the shop for two weeks, without Reyna having a clear understanding of what was wrong with the foreign vehicle she'd heard about but never seen.

He stepped into his pants, another thing Reyna didn't like. Peyton rarely bathed.

He didn't address her question. "If you're just a secretary, how can you afford this place?"

The "just a secretary" remark struck a nerve. "Don't worry about my finances," she snapped and rolled her neck. "You need to worry about why it's taking so long to fix your car." She removed her silk scarf on the way back into the bathroom to apply makeup.

"You didn't answer my question," he stated from the bathroom doorway. "How can you afford this place and everything that's in it on a secretary's salary? Are you seeing someone else? Is he paying the mortgage?"

Reyna dropped the liquid eyeliner onto the vanity, then spun around. Peyton's voice had dropped an octave, and his once olive skin blazed like brimstone. Tender eyes had been replaced by piercing daggers.

"Why w—would you ask me something like that?" she stammered.

His bare chest heaved and his nostrils flared, but his gaze never left hers, and that frightened her. "Answer me."

She shivered at his flat tone. "How can I be seeing someone else when I spend all my time with you?" She couldn't tell him about Tyson. Not that there was anything to tell. He'd been generous toward her by charging her below market rent, and yes, he was attracted to her. He was the closest thing she had to a friend, but Peyton didn't need to know that.

Peyton stepped into her space, pinning her against the vanity. "I'm going to ask you one more time. Are you seeing someone else?"

The morning breath stench wafted to her nose and nearly made her gag. She would have turned away, but his hand gripped her chin. For the first time since meeting him, Reyna thought Peyton could harm her. "I'm not seeing anyone but you. I don't have a mortgage, and I pay my own rent," she answered with more bravado than she felt.

He stepped back. "Good. Make sure you keep it that way. If I find out you're cheating on me, it won't be good for you." After pausing, as if to let his words sink in, Peyton smiled.

The grin he offered wasn't one of joy, but of satisfaction, she thought. She remained glued in place while he gathered his shirt and the tan pouch he carried everywhere.

"Hurry up," he ordered. "I need to drop you off so I can take care of my business."

Reyna stood there for so long, she didn't have time to finish applying makeup. Peyton had just threatened her, and he had done so with such calm, Reyna wondered if he had previous experience. He hadn't shared any details about previous relationships. "The past doesn't matter," was his answer to any question about his past. Looking at her unmade face in the mirror, Reyna second-guessed her decision to accept that answer.

"Come on," he called, leaving the bedroom. "You need your entry-level job."

The words stung, but she didn't have the time or the strength to retaliate. She turned out the bathroom light and grabbed her purse, then sprinted for the front door. Her trot came to an abrupt halt as she passed through the dining room. The mahogany table was bare. Tyson's bronze candlesticks were gone.

Chapter 17

Irritated beyond measure, Reyna grabbed her purse and stomped off the bus and walked the three blocks to her subdivision. Reyna hadn't used public transportation in years, but thanks to another one of Peyton's disappearing acts, she'd been reacquainted with bus schedules and timed transfers.

For two days he had failed to pick her up from work on time and hadn't bother to call. Last night he'd shown up at the town house after eight o'clock, claiming he'd been too busy with an important client to call. Reyna wanted to ask how important the client was if Peyton hadn't bothered to shower and shave, but before she could pose the question, he collapsed on her bed and began snoring.

This morning she'd awakened to the smell of bacon, eggs, and pancakes. From the towels crumpled on the bathroom floor, Reyna assumed he'd finally showered. After a quick shower, Reyna wrapped herself in a robe and padded into the kitchen.

All it took was one glimpse and Peyton's transgressions were forgiven. Not only had he showered, but his face was clean shaven. The black turtleneck accentuated his pectorals, triceps, biceps, and all the muscles in between. Navy blue dress slacks hugged his trim waist and brought attention to his muscular thighs. His thick, dark, curly hair hung loosely around his shoulders. This was the Peyton she liked. Not the one who'd threatened her and left her stranded.

After flipping an egg, he turned and smiled, and his blue eyes washed over her. "Sorry about last night. I promise it won't happen again."

His good looks and sincerity took the sting from the choice words she had for him. "Make sure it doesn't," she said firmly, then added, "What time will your car be ready today?" Handsome or not, it was time for him to find his own transportation.

"About that," he said while transferring the fried egg to the plate. "I've decided to sell my car. Too many problems."

Reyna's hand stopped midair as she reached for a glass in the cabinet. "What?"

"Oh, well, the cost of the repairs is more than the car is worth. So I told the mechanic to keep it and use whatever he can sell it for as payment."

"Okay," she said as she grabbed the glass in the cabinet. "When are you going to buy a new car, and what are you going to do for transportation in the meantime?" From behind, Peyton wrapped his arms around her waist. She sniffed his cologne but pretended the woodsy scent didn't have an effect on her.

"I'm in no hurry to go into debt," he responded after kissing her neck.

"You live in the city." She paused. This was another reminder that although he'd spent countless nights at her place, she'd yet to see where he lived. "BART is good, but you need a car. You make good money, so you can afford it," she said, although she had no proof of it. Peyton carried large amounts of cash, but from what she'd seen, his wardrobe was limited to three suits and a few slacks and countless T-shirts and turtlenecks. She hadn't seen the fancy jewelry since their first date.

He squeezed her. "I can use your car, like I do now. Since you're stuck inside at a little desk all day, you don't need it."

The glass fell from her hand and crashed to the floor. She spun around. "What do you mean, I don't need my car?" She thought of all the sacrifices she'd made to make every car payment and became livid. "You can't tell me what I need. I'm a grown woman. I know what I need. I need my car!"

Peyton retreated with both hands raised. "Hey, slow down. If you don't want to help your man out for a while, fine. But I thought we were a couple. I thought we were in this together."

"In what together?" she asked with her head cocked. "I seem to be the only one sharing in this relationship."

"What do you mean?"

She rolled her eyes at his look of naïveté. "I share my house, my car, my food, and my body. The only things I get in return are your dirty clothes all over the house. I don't know where you live or if you really have a job." Exasperated from voicing what she'd been thinking since they began dating, she stomped to the utility closet for the broom to sweep the shards of glass up. When she returned, Peyton relieved her of the broom and cleaned the mess up in silence, except for the sniffles.

She mumbled an expletive, regretting her tirade. Her hand rubbed the back of her neck, and she was reminded of her need to visit the hair salon soon. She longed for the old days of long hair. Maintaining a short spike cut was hard for someone who didn't like to comb hair. She'd figure it out, but first she had to find a way to handle the weeping, fine white man in her kitchen.

After returning the broom to the utility closet, Peyton stood in front of her. "I'm sorry you feel I've taken advantage of you," he said between sniffles. "I care about you so much, and I thought you felt the same. My mistake. I didn't know you were so unhappy." He wiped his cheek with the back of his hand. "I'll get my things and leave. Enjoy your breakfast."

Her eyes followed his slumped shoulders out of the kitchen; then she turned her attention to the plate of food. Peyton had cooked her a hearty breakfast and nothing for himself. "What am I supposed to do now?" she grumbled, then slowly retraced her steps to her bedroom.

"What are you doing?" she said just as Peyton zipped up his travel bag.

"I told you, I'm leaving. It's over."

Watching Peyton prepare to walk out of her life unleashed fear and old memories. Another man she cared about was leaving her. First her father, now Peyton. Sudden anxiety consumed her, sending tremors racing through her. Sweaty palms rubbed involuntarily against her robe. A lump formed in her throat, and before she could prevent them, the words "Please don't go" gushed out.

"You don't want me, Reyna, and you don't trust me," he said, reaching for his jacket, which was draped across the chaise.

"I do trust you." Her voice quivered. "It's just sometimes I s—say the wrong things," she stammered. "I told you, I've never had a real relationship before, but I really care about you." She bowed her head to hide the tears. She didn't want him to go but didn't want him to see her cry, either. He might consider her weak.

His thumb and forefinger, warm against her chin, lifted her head. "Do you really love me?"

She nodded, hoping she wasn't lying. For the most part Reyna enjoyed his company and the attention he lavished on her when he was around, but she wasn't sure if what she felt equated to love. Needing him to stay around, she told him what he wanted to hear. "Yes, I love you."

"Prove it, then," he said, then sat on the bed with his arms folded.

Paige is going to kill me, she thought as she untied and removed her robe.

Now, as she unlocked the door to the town house, she wished she'd kicked him out and kept her car key. It wouldn't have mattered; Peyton had taken the liberty of having a duplicate made.

After neatly placing her stilettos on a shelf in the walk-in closet, Reyna sat on the couch in the living room, browsing through the supermarket's weekly sales ad. Anything to keep her mind off of Peyton and what he was doing with her car. She compiled her weekly shopping list, then affixed it to the refrigerator with a magnet and decided to call Peyton again. Like countless times before, his voice mail answered. "Where are you?" she whispered, then pressed the end-call button.

As she paced around the house, anger gave way to worry and then to confusion. She hadn't been downstairs in Tyson's old office in weeks, but the second she stepped inside, she sensed something wasn't right. The forty-six-inch flat-screen television was missing. Even the wall mount was gone.

"Oh, my God." Her hands flew to her mouth. "I've been robbed. First the candlesticks, now this. I wonder what else is missing." The answer to her question revealed itself quickly. The twenty-four-karat gold pen set and the gold-trimmed globe were both absent from their spots on the desk. A twelve-inch figurine was also missing, along with the Bose sound system. "I better call the police."

She started for the stairs, then stopped. What if Peyton was here when this happened? she thought. He could have walked in on the burglar and . . . She didn't finish the thought for fear of what could be. She raced around the town house, checking windows for broken glass. The door that led to the garage appeared to be intact, and so did everything else. Nothing had been vandalized, just stolen. She lifted the cordless phone from its base and punched 9-1-1. She'd just given the dispatcher her information when Peyton finally walked through the front door.

"Thank God, you're all right!" she exclaimed, then shushed him until she finished with the dispatcher.

"What are you so fired up about? I thought you'd be angry about the time."

"I've been robbed!"

Peyton rushed over to her and enveloped her in his arms. "I'm so sorry, sweetheart. Did it happen while you were waiting for me?"

"No," she answered, seeking comfort in those deep blue eyes. "Someone broke in here and ripped off the downstairs office." She wasn't sure, but she thought she recognized relief in that sea of blue.

"Did you see anything?"

She shook her head. "No. It happened before I got home. I was so mad at you for making me take the bus, but if I hadn't, I might have been here when it happened." She kissed his cheek. "I'm sorry."

He squeezed her. "I'm just happy you're all right."

"I have to go online and fill out a report for the police."

"All right. I'll go downstairs and check things out. Then I'll make sure the door locks are secure."

Relief washed over her as she watched Peyton trek downstairs, but it was only temporary. Her living space had been violated, ending her sense of security. She didn't know exactly when the intruder had entered her home or how many times. What bothered her most was the violation appeared to have occurred with little effort. No doors or windows had been broken, and she'd set the alarm system every morning when she left. The perpetrator was a professional, she figured.

She returned to the kitchen after completing the electronic police report and found Peyton had set the table. In her anxiety over the break-in, she hadn't noticed the Chinese takeout he'd brought.

"I wanted to surprise you with a romantic evening, but after what's happened, that's not going to happen. At least we can enjoy dinner." He pulled out a chair. "Have a seat. I just need to pour the wine."

Reyna did as instructed and savored the moment for what it was—a temporary distraction from her present dilemma. Sure she was safe now with Peyton there, but what about later?

"I doubt the police will recover anything. At least your renters' insurance will give you a payout to replace everything," he stated between bites of Mongolian beef.

Reyna stopped chewing. She didn't have renters' insurance. She advised rental clients at the office of the necessity of carrying renters' insurance, but she'd figured she didn't need it, since the furnishings in the town house belonged to Tyson. *Tyson.* She repeated his name in her head. How was she going to tell him about the burglary? Tyson, a man of substance, probably wouldn't miss the stolen items. He certainly didn't need them. If he did, surely he would have taken them when he moved into his new home. Even still, she regretted he'd suffered a loss.

They hadn't spoken since his phone call a few weeks ago, when she reminded him that her interest in him didn't extend beyond their tenant/landlord relationship. He hadn't called since but had sent her a certified letter with an address to mail the monthly payments to. He'd finally gotten the message that they would never be anything more than friends. There was no way she'd open that door again. *I'm not going to tell him,* she decided and took a sip of wine. *I'll just save money until I can replace everything.*

"I don't have renters' insurance."

Peyton's fork fell to his plate. "What? Why not?"

"I don't need it," she said with a nonchalant shrug.

"That's the stupidest thing I've ever heard. You have over a quarter million dollars in furnishings in this place, and you don't think you need some type of insurance? Unbelievable," he said, shaking his head.

The disdainful look on his olive face made her wonder if Peyton really considered her stupid. "It's not mine," she whispered, then stuffed the remaining piece of egg roll into her mouth.

"What's not yours? Common sense?"

Too embarrassed to admit she didn't own anything except her car, she let the insult slide. "All of it. I mean, none of this is mine. It belongs to the landlord." She sighed. "I rented the place fully furnished," she added when his brow wrinkled.

He leaned back in his chair and scrutinized her for what seemed like forever. She twisted in the chair under those piercing blue eyes. Her breathing accelerated, and her hands picked lint from her shirt that wasn't there as anxiety took over. What was Peyton going to do now that he knew the truth? Would he end the relationship?

"Well," he finally said after gulping some wine. "At least you're not out anything. I'm sure the landlord has insurance with all the customized amenities in here."

Reyna's breathing returned to normal and then accelerated again at his next statement.

"Reyna, you deceived me. You presented yourself as a smart and intelligent woman of substance. You're none of that. I like you but don't know if I can overlook your failure to trust me due to your own deceitfulness."

"I wasn't being deceitful," she countered. "You assumed I was a broker and that I owned the place. You never asked me."

He pushed back from the table and stood. "So it's my fault you're a liar?"

"No." A lump formed in her throat; she swallowed hard. "You're right. I should have told you the truth, but you haven't exactly been an open book with me, either," she declared. "I still don't know where you live. For all I know, with your disappearing acts, you could have a wife and kids somewhere."

His fists pounded the table. "Look, if you still don't trust me, I'm out of here." He knocked over the chair on his way to the front door.

"Wait!" Reyna ran after him. Peyton couldn't leave her alone tonight. What if the burglar came back? Even with insults, Peyton's presence gave her a sense of security.

She grabbed his arm just as he twisted the doorknob. "Please, Peyton, don't go." He huffed but didn't turn around to face her. "I'm sorry I didn't tell you the truth in the beginning. I didn't know how," she admitted. "I was afraid you wouldn't like me anymore." He still didn't budge. "Come on," she added while stroking his triceps. "You said you cared about me. Doesn't that earn me another chance?" His muscles flexed beneath her touch just before he finally turned to face her.

"What about trust, Reyna? We can't have a relationship without trust. You keep questioning me, like I'm hiding something."

"I do trust you," she answered but hoped he wouldn't ask her to prove it again.

"Prove it. Let's move in together."

Reyna covered her open mouth with one hand and, with the other, massaged the rapid pounding in her chest. "Are you asking me to move to the city with you?" she blurted out.

"No. Since your place is larger than mine, and I'm sure the rent is more economical, I'll move in here with you. That is, if you can trust me enough to live under the same roof with me."

She didn't miss the sarcasm, just didn't address it. Thoughts of how she would explain a live-in boyfriend to Tyson and her mother filled her head. Then she wondered why she cared what her landlord and her mother thought of her. As long as she kept the rent current, why should Tyson care who she took up residence with? To date, she had yet to invite her mother to her home. That wouldn't change.

"That's a great idea. We can split everything fifty-fifty. With you around, I'll feel safer. Besides, you've practically been living here, anyway," she said, hoping that was enough to make him stay.

He released the knob. "All right, if you're sure this is what you want," he said, exasperated.

The anticipation of finally getting what she desired most caused flutters to roll through her stomach. Her fantasy could become reality, depending on her words. Peyton wasn't perfect by far, but then, neither was she. There were many things she didn't know about him, but with them living together, she would find out all she needed to know soon enough.

"Yes, I'm sure," she answered with a smile.

Chapter 18

Tyson's BMW came to a screeching halt after rounding a sharp corner in the hospital's parking garage. He steered his ultimate driving machine between two SUVs, hopped out, and dashed toward the garage stairwell. Kevin had called him forty-five minutes ago with the news that Marlissa's water had broken and that they were on their way to the hospital. Tyson, not wanting to chance missing the birth of his godson, had his secretary reschedule his morning appointments. Before leaving the office, he'd traded in his tailored suit for a pair of casual slacks and a pullover.

After securing a visitors' pass and before taking the elevator to the labor and delivery unit, Tyson stopped at the hospital's gift shop and purchased a floral arrangement for Marlissa and a huge stuffed teddy bear for the new arrival. He stepped from the fifth-floor elevator with gifts in tow, and instead of asking for Marlissa Jennings's room number, Tyson followed the noise, which resembled what one might encounter at a revival tent meeting. Mother Scott's and First Lady Drake's praying and singing vibrated down the hall.

He doubted the soft knock he gave on the door was heard over the makeshift praise and worship service happening on the other side. When the second knock didn't yield a response, Tyson eased the door open and stepped inside.

Marlissa's corner room was complete with a full-sized couch, a chair with an ottoman, a flat-screen television, a dresser bureau, and a full-sized crib. Soft pastel animals and shapes covered the walls. No doubt Marlissa had the best birthing room in the facility, thanks to Kevin being on staff as a highly respected ophthalmologic surgeon. Tyson guessed Kevin's status also served as the reason why the hospital staff tolerated the scene before him. First Lady Drake was stationed at the end of the bed, on bended knees, praying in her heavenly language. Mother Scott stood at the head of the bed, singing "Come on in the Room" and beating a tambourine. Both women were dressed in white. Marlissa lay panting while Kevin massaged her back. On the bedside table rested a large canister of what the prayer warriors referred to as anointing oil.

Tyson would have shaken himself to make sure he wasn't dreaming, had he not witnessed the same scenario two weeks ago, when Leon and Starla's daughter was born. Starla's labor lasted only two hours, but by the time little Miracle entered the world, two nurses had received Christ as their personal savior. At the time, Kevin had cautioned the prayer warriors against repeating the shenanigans at his place of business. As usual, the plea fell on deaf ears. The prayer team of Scott and Drake operated by its own set of rules.

"How's it going?" Tyson asked his friend with a tap on the shoulder.

Kevin appeared startled when he turned and found his friend standing behind him with flowers and a teddy bear that was big enough to occupy a chair of its own. His weary eyes relaxed a bit. "Hey, man. Glad you could make it."

Tyson leaned forward. "They're not bothering you too much, are they?" he asked, with a nod toward the prayer warriors.

"What do you think? The supervisor has been in here twice all ready," Kevin said through clenched teeth. "I've never been more embarrassed in my life. Would you believe they rubbed oil on the nurse's hands before they allowed her to hook Marlissa up to the fetal monitor?"

"Did you expect anything less?" Tyson said between chuckles. "Marlissa is their adopted baby. My guess is you haven't seen the worst yet." He sobered at the sound of Marlissa's moan. "How is she holding up?"

"She's doing great." Kevin turned back toward his wife. "Hey, babe, look who just walked in."

When Marlissa ceased panting long enough to look over her shoulder and acknowledge his presence, Tyson thought his knees would buckle. The same thing had happened with Starla. For as anal and as stoic as he was, seeing a woman in pain reduced him to mush. He had to lean against the chair for balance, and it made a sound and interrupted the prayer warriors' flow. First Lady Drake stopped speaking her heavenly language, and then Mother Scott stopped singing.

"Do you mind?" Mother Scott asked, with a fist planted at her waist. "We're trying to have a baby here."

Tyson started to apologize but considered that useless when it came to the radical mothers. He had learned early on to just let them rant.

"What do you mean 'we'?" Marlissa panted out.

"Now look what you've done." First Lady Drake swatted him with her prayer cloth. "You've made Marlissa lose focus. We're bringing a future prayer warrior into world. The atmosphere needs to be as spiritual as possible. If you can't get with the program, you're going to have to wait outside."

"And what's with that big bear?" Mother Scott barked. "By the time the baby is big enough for that, he'll be old enough to read the Bible. I guess they didn't teach you common sense at that lawyer school."

Tyson thought if Mother Scott considered the bear impractical, she'd be flabbergasted by the gifts he had in his garage for his godson, which included an electric train set.

"You're right, Mother. I should wait in the waiting room." He set the flowers on the bureau. "Hang in there," he said to Marlissa, then turned to exit the room. By the time his fingertips touched the doorknob, First Lady Drake's talk with the Lord had resumed, and so had Mother's Scott's off-key singing and tambourine beating. "I should have assigned them to Reyna," he mumbled as he headed down the corridor, then wondered if he still cared about her.

He hadn't interacted with his wayward tenant in three months, outside of the monthly rental checks he picked up from his post office box. He knew she was still employed from conversations with Paige, but that was all he knew. He'd shared his predicament with his father. "Move on. If you can't be with the woman you love, then find a woman who loves you. She'll treat you right and make a happy home," was what his father had told him. After the last rejection, that was exactly what he'd done. Tyson had moved on and had stopped praying for a relationship with Reyna. He hadn't meant to start dating; it had just happened that way, thanks to the tenacious Beverly Stokes.

Bonding with his father meant spending more time at his parents' home. Every Saturday, instead of a bland phone call, Tyson enjoyed brunch on the deck of his parents' home overlooking the San Pablo Bay. True to form, every Saturday, his mother had sung Mylan's praises, until finally orchestrating a "chance" meeting.

After a visual inspection, Tyson's first thought was to thank his mother for poking her nose into his personal life. Mylan's beauty was the perfect mix of her African American and Korean heritage. She complimented him on all points, from a keen intellect to a love of art. Most importantly, Mylan was a devoted Christ follower. Her only negative characteristics were the long hours she worked at the nonprofit organization she'd founded and an obsession with her smartphone. Ironically, Tyson categorized himself as a workaholic, yet he disliked the trait in Mylan. If and when he decided to make them an official couple, the constant texting and Facebook and Twitter updates would have to end. They had been out on a few dates and had engaged in numerous phone conversations. He relished the companionship and her physical beauty but had yet to develop feelings for Mylan equal to what he'd once felt for Reyna.

A rare emotion caused him to pace the waiting room. An excitement he hadn't felt in years bubbled in his belly. A few feet away his godson was being born. A life that he would have total responsibility for should Kevin and Marlissa become incapacitated. The thought that this could be the closest he'd come to actual fatherhood dulled the moment. Images of what could have been with the life he and Paige had created resurfaced. He'd long ago admitted the abortion was a mistake, but the remorse remained.

Pastor Rosalie Jennings and Reyna's mother, Jewel, entered the waiting room before Tyson could sulk over the worst decision he'd ever made.

"Where's Kevin?" Pastor Rosalie Jennings had a habit of asking him questions she already knew the answers to.

Tyson wasn't in the mood for his former pastor's games. "Where else would he be but in the delivery room with his wife?"

"How is Kevin holding up? Is the baby all right?" Pastor Jennings quizzed.

The fact that Pastor Rosalie Jennings didn't express concern for Marlissa didn't come as a surprise, but Tyson's blunt answer did. "Why don't you go and see for yourself how your son *and* your daughter-in-law are doing?"

Tyson's jaw dropped when Pastor Rosalie Jennings's shoulders slumped and she retreated to a seat, looking like a lost child. In all the years he'd known her, he'd never seen her look so defeated. Even when Kevin moved his membership from her church, she had had more spunk. Although she was to blame, the estranged relationship between her and Kevin had taken its toll on her.

"No," she responded, looking around the waiting room, confused. "I'll just wait in here."

Uncertain if the hopelessness act was genuine or manipulative, Tyson readily agreed. "Suit yourself," he said, then went back to pacing, only this time he added a prayer for peace. If Pastor Rosalie Jennings caused Marlissa an ounce of distress, the prayer warriors would lay hands on her.

"It's time to push!" Mother Scott rushed into the waiting room, shaking the tambourine. "Come on, Ty . . ." Her words fell short when Pastor Rosalie Jennings stood up next to Tyson. She cleared her throat. "Hello, Rosalie."

Pastor Rosalie Jennings returned the greeting in the same dry tone it had been offered.

Mother Scott turned back to Tyson. "Are you coming or not?"

He wanted to witness the actual birth but doubted he could handle it. The brightness in Pastor Rosalie

Jennings's eyes helped him make up his mind. "Pastor Jennings, why don't you go?"

Pastor Rosalie Jennings sucked her breath in and placed her right hand over her heart. "Oh my, do you think I should? I mean, it is my grandchild. If anyone has a right to be in there, it's me." She gripped Tyson's arm. "But do you really think I should go?"

Some things never change, Tyson thought. The Holy Spirit prevented him from voicing his opinion of Pastor Rosalie Jennings's shenanigans.

"Look, we ain't got time for all this drama, Rosalie." Mother Scott pried her hand from Tyson's arm. "You know you want to be in the delivery room—that's why you're here. We all know you don't like Marlissa. *We* ain't too fond of you, either, but we'll tolerate you for Kevin's sake. It ain't his fault he drew the shortest stick and got you for a mama." She pulled the pastor toward the door. "Come on. We're bringing in a prayer warrior. Maybe with all that anointing in there, you'll finally get delivered of your issues. Hurry up so you can get washed up."

Thunderous laughter poured from Tyson as soon as his former pastor cleared the door. "I love that pushy old woman," he said between chuckles.

"Uh-huh!" Jewel cleared her throat.

He quickly sobered. With Pastor Jennings's dramatic performance taking center stage, he'd forgotten Jewel was there.

"Sorry, Ms. Mills. No disrespect intended."

Jewel's lips twisted, then relaxed. "I know, and that was funny, but don't tell Rosalie I said that."

Tyson observed Jewel carefully. A smile rested on her cinnamon face, but worry lines framed her ebony eyes. He hadn't seen her since Reyna moved into his town house. She appeared to have lost about twenty pounds. Tyson wondered if she had an illness.

"How have you been, Ms. Mills?" he asked, hoping to gain some insight into why she looked so tired.

"I'm good. How is Reyna? Have you seen her? Is she still working? Does she have enough food?" The questions gushed out like a geyser. "She won't return my calls, and I'm worried about her." She began pacing back and forth. "That girl thinks she knows what she's doing, but she doesn't. She hates me, thinks I'm the reason her father abandoned her. She has no idea the sacrifices I've made for her." She stopped pacing and plopped into a chair. Tears rolled down her cheeks and gathered beneath her chin.

Her agony sapped his strength. He sat beside her and rode out the emotional wave. Out of habit he reached for a handkerchief, intending to offer it to her, and then he remembered he wasn't wearing a suit.

"I haven't been the best mother. I haven't always given her the attention she needs, but I do love my daughter. I'm scared of her resentment of me. She's going to end up in something she can't get out of, just like I did. There are so many things I need to tell her."

He groaned as he listened to Jewel's sobs. He didn't have a clue how to comfort her. She acted like Reyna had died and not just moved out on her own. He didn't know much about the Millses' family history, but Jewel's words and disposition indicated the pain ran deep.

He patted her hand. "Ms. Mills, stop worrying so much about Reyna. She's much stronger than you think. From what I've heard, she's performing well at the real estate office, and she pays the rent on time. She's doing well on her own," he said, conveniently leaving out that he'd seen her at Skates, where she was practically sitting in some man's lap.

Tyson hoped his words reassured her; he wanted the conversation to end. His godson's pending birth deserved his full attention. Besides, Reyna had made it crystal clear she didn't want him in her business.

"I hope you're right, but I don't feel good about it," Jewel said between sniffles. "She won't even give me her address." She looked up at Tyson with glossy eyes. "If I had her address, I'd feel better."

Unbelievable, he thought. Tyson now understood how Jewel and Pastor Rosalie Jennings had managed a thirty-year friendship. They could teach a course in manipulation.

"Ms. Mills," he stated firmly so she wouldn't take his words lightly, "I will not give you Reyna's address. Neither will I deliver a message to her. I will not drive you over there. I will not be placed in the middle of your and Reyna's feud."

Tyson restrained a chuckle when Jewel's mouth opened but no words followed. Her bewildered expression communicated that she hadn't expected a direct answer. Finally, she closed her mouth and relaxed back in the chair.

Tyson leaned back and rested his right foot on his left knee. He intertwined his fingers, but before he could prop them above his head, Mother Scott's tambourine, combined with a chorus of "Praise the Lord Everybody," echoed down the hallway.

Tyson welcomed the joy that enveloped him, and embraced the moment. Uncharacteristically, he stood and gave public thanks to God, then trotted off to meet his godson.

Chapter 19

Reyna slammed her desk drawer closed, then pro-ceeded to shut down her computer. Business at the real estate office was usually slow the last Friday of the month. Today was no exception. The calm before the storm, she called it. Monday morning her desk would be cluttered with clients' rental payments and her voice mail would be full of messages from clients with excuses for why their rent would be late. She'd heard it all, from "I lost my job" to "My job messed up my check." Her favorite excuse was "The dog ate my last check."

The phone rang, but she let the call go to voice mail, figuring it was the parade of excuses getting off to an early start. She concentrated on her number one pri-ority: getting home early to fix a surprise dinner for Peyton to commemorate one month of living together.

Cohabitating with Peyton left much to be desired, but being determined to make it work, Reyna accentu-ated the positive. His presence had given her the secu-rity she needed after the break-in. He contributed to the food and utility bills, and she hoped he'd cover the upcoming rent payment so she could put some money away to replace the items stolen during the burglary. He still didn't have his own transportation. He did, however, have what appeared to be a phobia to water. Peyton bathed on average twice a week, but only after Reyna stated his natural scent offended her.

Only after Peyton moved in with only two suitcases did she realize he didn't own any possessions. "The furnishings at your place are much nicer than mine," he'd said when she asked about the furniture he'd left in his old apartment. She had never seen the furniture, or the apartment, for that matter, but doubted anything would be nicer than Tyson's custom pieces. She accepted his explanation without question.

Although Reyna didn't have much say in the matter of transportation, since Peyton didn't have a car, the two quickly fell into a daily routine. Peyton would take her to work and then would drive into the city to meet clients. On most days, he'd return in time to pick Reyna up at work. She now owned a monthly bus pass for the days Peyton's meetings went over, which was often. Their physical activity had decreased slightly, thanks mainly to Peyton's special evening clients. Reyna didn't miss it at all. Ironically, having Peyton for a companion didn't quench her desire for companionship. Something was missing, and tonight she hoped to discover what it was.

"You must have big plans for this weekend," Paige said from the entranceway just as Reyna reached for her blazer. "I assume this is so since you're taking the afternoon off."

Explaining that her weekend didn't promise anything special wasn't something Reyna wanted to do with her boss. The rough edges had been smoothed over since Reyna had remained punctual, but they weren't friends. "Thanks. We're driving up to Mendocino for the weekend," she lied. Her car probably couldn't make the three-hour drive with all the miles Peyton had clocked on it. Nowadays the three-thousand-mile/three-month oil change rolled around in half the normal time.

"It's beautiful up there. Enjoy." Paige turned and left.

Reyna stared at her retreating back. *That could be me,* she thought as envy and bitterness surged through her. Reyna wanted the authority and power Paige represented. "One day I'll have it all," she whispered, then glanced at her watch. She had four minutes to make it to the bus stop if she wanted to stay on schedule for the romantic dinner celebration.

Ninety-minutes later, Reyna stumbled into the subdivision, trying to balance her purse, grocery bags, and a bottle of wine while walking in four-inch heels. She nearly lost her balance when she turned the corner leading to her unit and saw her car parked in the driveway. It was two o'clock in the afternoon. Peyton should be at work.

She steadied herself and walked purposefully to the front door. With each forward step, she wanted to run ten steps in the opposite direction, but she had to confront Peyton. By the time she sat the bags and the wine bottle down on the porch, she'd convinced herself that Peyton had come home early to plan a surprise of his own.

"Hello, Reyna," the neighbor adjacent to her called from his rosebushes before she inserted the key into the lock. "It's a beautiful day, isn't it?"

She imitated happiness, which she didn't feel. "It's a great day," she answered with a smile. She turned back toward the door.

"Did Peyton get that big flat-screen TV fixed yet?"

The keys fell to the ground. She wasn't aware Peyton and her neighbor were on a first-name basis.

"I recommended my brother's shop. He does great work, but he said Peyton never showed up."

She eyed the neighbor suspiciously. "What are you talking about?"

The neighbor stood upright and adjusted his hat to shield his face from the sun. "I saw him loading the TV into your trunk a while back. He told me the picture appeared distorted. I told him about my brother's shop. My brother would have fixed it for a little of nothing." He shrugged his shoulders. "But like I said, Peyton never showed up."

"Are you sure you have the right person? This is a big subdivision, and it's easy to get people mixed up," Reyna observed, hoping the man was mistaken.

His eyebrows narrowed, like he'd been insulted. "You're right. It is a big subdivision, but only one blue-eyed white guy with a ponytail lives next door to me." His face softened. "If you need anything, let me know. Have a good day."

Reyna bent over to retrieve the keys and then gripped her stomach to combat the sudden wave of nausea. The neighbor's revelations couldn't be right. She refused to believe Peyton had removed the TV without her permission and then had allowed her to think it had been stolen. Peyton was her man, and she trusted him. *The old man is mistaken,* she decided and proceeded to unlock the door. Three steps inside the foyer Reyna learned that vision and memory didn't always dim with age.

Peyton wasn't at work, and he wasn't planning a celebration for them, either. However, the neat white lines on the coffee table provided a surprise she doubted she'd ever forget.

"What are you doing?" she asked in a voice so low, Reyna wondered if she'd only thought the words.

Peyton's deep blue eyes, shielded by a glossy haze, peered up at her for only a second. "What does it look like I'm doing?"

In stunned silence she watched him use what resembled a glass straw to transport the white substance into his nose with precision. This wasn't his first time. Now she knew what was in that tan pouch he carried everywhere.

"Get out!" she sneered. "Pack your bags and get . . . out of my house."

Hoarse laughter poured from Peyton for so long, Reyna thought he'd choke. That would save her the trouble of killing him for bringing drugs into her home.

"I mean it, you lying thief." She pointed toward the door. "Get out of my house. I'm not playing," she added when he continued laughing.

"Shut up and sit your broke behind down, before I knock you down. You're messing up my high. This isn't your house, remember? The only thing you own is that raggedy car parked outside, which, by the way, needs a tune-up. You don't even own your body. I own that. But lately, even that hasn't been good. I'm only with your sorry butt because I'm between jobs right now. "

"I thought you worked in the bank?"

His laughter boomed louder. "Are you really that stupid? What banker only works three hours a day? I haven't worked as a banker since I moved here from Oregon."

She was afraid to ask but needed to know what he'd been doing with her car every day. "What do you do all day?"

"Mind my business, which is what you need to do."

"Why did you steal from me?"

The booming laughter changed to chuckles, but his eyes remained glossy and his cheeks flaming red. "Do you really want to know?"

She nodded and wrapped her arms around her waist, bracing for the answer.

"You got it all wrong. I didn't steal anything from you. You"—he pointed at her—"don't own anything. You're just a wannabe and you're not too smart and you're too easy. The owner of this place won't miss the few items I took. I did him a favor. I gave Mr. Big Shot a tax write-off."

Reyna stared at him, wondering how he could laugh while saying those horrible words. Cocaine must work like a truth serum for him. She had learned more about him in the past five minutes than she'd learned the entire time they'd been together. She'd been playing house with a stranger. Every aspect of the life she'd manufactured crumbled, and so did her heart. Peyton didn't care about her. In the process of doin' herself, she'd got done.

"Leave now!" When he didn't move, Reyna grabbed the cordless phone. "I'm calling the police."

"You're not calling anybody!" He wasn't laughing anymore.

The phone tumbled from her hand as she fell to the floor, reeling from Peyton's backhand slap across the face and from being called a female dog for the first time. She tried to brace herself against the ottoman, but Peyton yanked her head back and grabbed her by the throat.

"Do you hear me?" he snarled in her ear. "I'm not going anywhere, and you're not calling anyone. We're in this together. Got it?"

"Yes," she whimpered, fearing he'd choke her. The ferocious look in his eyes suggested he could do just that.

He pulled her to her feet by the throat and began grinding against her and kissing her face. Reyna attempted to pull away, and he tightened his hold. "Are you trying to get away from me? I told you, you belong to me. Not that you're worth anything."

Reyna didn't have an answer that wouldn't result in more contact with the back of his hand or his fist. She was stuck at the mercy of a drug-controlled mad-man. Peyton could kill her, and no one would know. She hadn't told her mother where she lived, and Tyson wouldn't think to check on her until the five-day grace period for the rent had expired. Even Paige wouldn't miss her until Monday morning. Wanting to do her own thing, Reyna had alienate everyone in her life. She bit her lower lip and let the tears flow. *God, please don't let my life end like this,* she prayed inwardly to a God she no longer believed in.

Peyton released her throat, and she forced oxygen into her lungs. Maybe he was on his way down, coming back to his senses. Her hope vanished when he ripped open her blouse and groped her roughly.

"Stop!"

"Shut up!" Peyton pushed her to the floor and hiked up her skirt. "I'm going to remind you who the boss is around here."

She crossed her legs tightly and shielded her face from another blow.

"Open your legs!"

Dazed from a blow to the head, Reyna yielded to his demands. She closed her eyes and mentally tried to remove herself from the abuse about to occur. At the sound of his belt buckle hitting the glass table, she imagined she was at Disneyland, spinning in the teacups, laughing. Then the knocking—more like bang-ing—started.

"Reyna! Reyna!"

Her name was being called by a voice she didn't readily recognize. The banging intensified, but only after Peyton ordered, "Don't move. I'll be right back," did she realize the banging was real and not a fantasy. Someone was at the front door.

Cautiously, her eyes followed Peyton's shirtless body to the foyer. She didn't know the identity of the uninvited visitor, but she planned to use the intrusion to her advantage. With what strength she had left, she removed her shoes and straightened her skirt, then stood and walked over to the fireplace and removed a poker. Adrenaline surged through her veins as she gripped the deadly object. She had never played baseball and didn't know the mechanics of a good swing, but she figured one hard blow to the head would deliver her from Peyton's evil. Or better yet, the weapon would intimidate him and he'd leave of his own accord. She heard the front door close and lifted the poker to striking position. Tremors shook her body, but she held the poker steady.

"That was your nosy neighbor," Peyton said, walking past her into the kitchen. "You left these grocery bags outside on the porch."

She stared at the bags as he placed them on the center island. In a rush to confront Peyton, she'd totally forgotten about them. The dinner and celebration, it all seemed like an obscure dream now. In hindsight, her life with Peyton had been a nightmare.

She lowered the poker but kept enough distance between herself and Peyton just in case she needed to strike if he was transformed once again. Moments earlier he had tried to rape her; now he whistled as he put away groceries.

After putting the last item away, he turned to face her. "You forgot the eggs and a few other things I need." He walked past her and retrieved his shirt from the floor. She remained motionless while he buttoned his shirt and removed her car key from the hook. He reached the door and then turned back like he'd forgotten something.

"I'm going out for a while, See you later," he said after collecting his paraphernalia in that tan pouch.

The force of his tongue pressing against her mouth combined with his stale breath sent rolling waves of nausea through her. Before she could gag, he was gone.

The tremors that shook her commingled with the nausea and sent her running to the guest bathroom to empty the contents of her stomach. Self-reliant and independent, Reyna now knew the taste of fear and degradation. With each heave, a bitter taste rested on her taste buds. Gargling and rinsing removed the tangible residue but did nothing to ease the insecurity and anxiety.

With shaky fingers, she fumbled with the remaining buttons on her blouse and removed the remnants of it, then discarded them in the trash. Using the vanity to support her weight, she turned on the faucet and reached for a washcloth but stopped short of wetting it. The image captured by the mirror temporarily paralyzed her. Even her tears ceased to fall. The disheveled hair and the swollen jaw and lip were a far cry from beauty marks. At that moment, Reyna felt uglier than the image staring back at her. Until today, *stupid* wasn't an adjective she'd use to describe herself, but the reflection said otherwise.

"How did I let this happen to me? How did I end up living with an unemployed, stealing drug addict?" She didn't have answers to the questions her conscience asked. "I should've known better," she said aloud.

Reyna cleaned her face, thinking maybe it was her fault for trusting a man she knew little or nothing about—again. Once he said he cared about her, the trust she had for Peyton surpassed all doubts. Her greatest desire was for someone to love her, but all men did was use her and take advantage of her inexperience. Every man except Tyson, but she didn't want him.

Too stubborn to admit she needed his comfort right now, Reyna ignored the temptation to call Tyson and admit he'd been right about her looking for love in all the wrong places. In fact, Tyson had advised her against looking for love, period. "*W*hoso findeth a wife findeth a good thing," he'd say early in their friendship. "Focus on learning who you are, and let the man pursue you." She might have heeded his advice had he not included a scripture. She'd been controlled long enough by the sixty-six books. It was time to do things her way. Pride prevented her from admitting her way wasn't working.

Heavy steps carried her back into the living room. She surveyed the room, as if seeing it for the first time. The cozy, welcoming feeling had departed, and in its place was gloom. A chill ran down her arm, reminding her she wasn't wearing a shirt. She ignored the coolness and straightened the room. While replacing the poker on the stand, she noticed several figurines were missing from the mantel. Peyton had stolen more of Tyson's belongings. "What else is missing?" she wondered out loud, then went to check the guest bedroom. She hadn't checked the room since dusting it over a month ago.

"Oh, Tyson, I'm so sorry," she groaned when she turned the light on. The once cozy mauve and cream decorated room had been stripped of a wall-mounted flat-screen TV and most of the artwork. She had to tell him, now, but how? She turned out the light, closed the door, and headed back to the living room for the cordless phone.

The shaking returned as her fingers keyed in his home phone number. How was she going to tell the one man who'd been nothing but good to her that she'd moved a substance abuser into his home, someone who had robbed him blind right under her nose?

She was about to disconnect the call when he answered on the sixth ring. "Hello."

She hadn't realized how much she had missed talking to him until she heard his tenor voice. She swallowed, and the soreness sent flashbacks of the afternoon's events rushing back.

"Hello," he repeated.

"Tyson, it's me. Reyna," she said after clearing her throat.

"I know," he responded, sounding a little agitated. "I have caller ID. What's up? Is something broken?"

If it were only that simple, she thought. "Nothing's broken, but I need to talk to you about something."

She heard shuffling, like he was moving the phone from one ear to the other.

"Can it wait? I'm about to head out for the evening."

Her heart constricted, and she wasn't sure why. Then it occurred to her this was the first time Tyson didn't make himself available to her.

"It can wait. Sorry I caught you at a bad time," she said with both resignation and relief.

"Call my secretary and make an appointment at the office next week."

"Sure. Maybe we could do lunch?" she offered, thinking a public place would be best to have the conversation.

"I have to go. See you next week."

Reyna stared at the phone in disbelief. Tyson had hung up on her without saying good-bye. He hadn't addressed the lunch invitation, either. The abrupt dismissal could mean only one thing: Tyson had gotten over his infatuation with her. Any other day she would have been happy, but right now Reyna needed someone to feed her self-esteem after Peyton had shredded it.

The more his venomous words and actions replayed in her mind, the angrier she became. He considered her stupid and worthless, yet he was unemployed and basically homeless. The insults to her sexual ability might have some validity, considering she didn't have much experience, but he didn't have to be so cruel in expressing his displeasure.

She had replaced the phone on the base and was starting for her room to take a shower when Peyton's last words pounded her already throbbing head. Fear gripped her at the realization that Peyton wasn't out of her life yet. He'd said he'd be back. That didn't concern her; she wanted him to return her car and get his belongings. What worried her was whether he'd be under the influence or not when he showed up. She turned back and grabbed the poker, just in case the monster decided to rear its nasty head.

"Reyna! Reyna!"

Reyna jumped from the bed and swung the poker wildly. She chopped the air three times before realizing Peyton wasn't in the room with her but was on the other side of the bedroom door, banging on it and begging her to let him come inside.

"Sweetheart, please open the door. We have to talk."

Fully awake, Reyna placed the poker on the bed and tightened the belt on her robe. The numbers on the nightstand clock read 11:38 P.M. Peyton had been gone for over eight hours. "Go away, Peyton. Leave my keys on the table, and get out of my house," she hollered, hoping he'd comply.

"Can I at least get my clothes?"

"Your clothes are in those garbage bags by the front door." She'd packed his belongings before dozing off. "Now, get your . . . and get out!"

She heard footsteps retreat, then return to the door. "Please, Reyna. I'm sorry. Please talk to me."

A sense of satisfaction surged through her at Peyton's pleading. "Hours earlier you called me worthless. Now look who's begging who!"

"Reyna, please. I didn't mean what I said. To be honest, I don't even remember what I said or did. That stuff had me messed up."

"You hit me! You tried to rape me!"

First she heard the sobs and then what she assumed was the thud of Peyton's body as he hit the door.

"Sweetheart, I'm so sorry. That wasn't me. It was the coke. I care about you too much to ever hurt you."

"Is it you or the coke that's been stealing me blind?"

He twisted the doorknob. "Please open the door. I'll explain everything. Then if you want me to go, I will. I just want you to be happy, even if it's without me."

Reyna paced around the room. The tender Peyton had returned and had weakened her resolve. What if he really didn't mean all those nasty things he'd said? Drugs and alcohol had a way of altering ones personality. She reasoned, if the words spoken earlier were true, he wouldn't be begging for forgiveness now. He wouldn't care. The least she could do was hear him out, then put him out.

"You've got five minutes, and then you're out of here."

"Okay. Whatever you want," he said in resignation.

She reached for the poker. "Just in case," she mumbled and then opened the door.

Chapter 20

Tyson's chest swelled with pride as he looked down into his godson's face. The tiny white Armani suit fitted him perfectly. After a long lecture from Marlissa, Tyson conceded he'd gone overboard with the silk christening gown, but his godson deserved the best. Although he bore his father's name, two-month-old Kevin Hezekiah Jennings, Jr., had inherited Marlissa's complexion and pointed nose. A slight twinge of jealousy rushed through him, and he wished the roles were reversed—that it was Kevin standing at the altar in the role of godfather at the christening of his son. As quickly as that thought came, it passed, and he silently repented for coveting his best friend's family. He glanced to the side section of the church, where Mylan sat between Starla and Mother Scott, and allowed his thoughts to drift to what a child with Mylan would look like.

After three months of dating, Tyson still hadn't had the status talk, but he was growing content with the idea of a committed relationship with the woman both his parents loved. Every conversation with his mother began with, "When was the last time you talked to Mylan?" and Judge Stokes didn't end a conversation without stating, "That Mylan is a fine young woman. She'd make a good wife and mother someday."

Tyson didn't doubt she would. He had visited her at the center and was amazed at the patience and attention she lavished on the autistic children. Her smartphone took a backseat to her babies, as she called them. Tyson had also noticed that recently she'd begun turning off the phone during their dates. Mylan had also initiated affection by reaching for his hand or stroking his arm and shoulders whenever possible. The gestures should have prepared him for the kiss she gave him on their last date, but it had stunned him. Not that the soft brush wasn't pleasant; it just didn't move him like he thought it should have. He liked her, but the beauty and gentleness permeating Mylan had yet to touch his heart, which was a minor detail, since he refused to allow his emotions to control him any longer. He'd learned well from his experience with Reyna that the heart could be deceitful.

Reyna. He hadn't heard from her since that strange call two months ago. Whatever she had to say must not have been important, since she hadn't followed through with making an appointment. Her rent was current, although last month he had to charge her a late fee. She included the additional fee without him having to call and speak to her. Another indication their time had passed.

Little Kevin kicked his leg against Tyson's left arm at the same time Marlissa pinched his right one. His mind had drifted so far, Tyson had missed his cue to affirm his commitment to help rear the child up to reverence the Lord.

"I will," he responded after Pastor Drake repeated the question. Tyson bowed his head but kept his eyes focused on the chubby face smiling back at him as Pastor Drake stretched his hands and prayed a blessing over the group. Tyson returned to his seat with the baby snuggled against his chest, regretting more than ever the decision he and Paige had made over a decade ago.

***

"Give me that baby," Mother Scott ordered the moment she stepped into the Jenningses' home for the celebratory dinner after the christening. "I need to impart some anointing to this prayer warrior."

Tyson complied without protest. "If you had your way, the first words out of the baby's mouth would be 'Thank you, Jesus.'"

"Get your facts straight, lawyer," Mother Scott corrected. "His first words would be 'the blood of Jesus.'"

Mylan, who sat next to him on the sofa, laughed.

"What are you laughing at?" Mother Scott said.

Unfamiliar with Mother Scott's bluntness, Mylan sucked in her breath and looked at Tyson for help.

Tyson patted her hand. "Don't worry. She's harmless."

"You don't have to worry about me unless you got some demons you need casted out." Mother Scott laid the baby facedown on her lap and patted his back. "I don't think that's the case with you."

Mylan relaxed, but the reprieve was short lived.

"I discerned your spirit during service. You're saved. You praised God like you really love Him. You're pretty, and you and Tyson look good together, but you do know Tyson is not the one for you."

"Mother," Tyson warned.

"How many times do I have to tell you?" First Lady Drake walked in. "Stay out of folks' business. You don't have to tell everything."

"I'm just saying. The Lord showed me who Tyson's wife is, and she ain't it." She looked at Tyson. "We all know who she is, but I'm not going to bust you out by stating her name. Especially since she's not here to defend herself."

First Lady Drake took the baby without protest from Mother Scott. "We're not quite through casting all those demons out of her yet. She's got some old tough ones, but they're coming out. I guarantee that."

Mylan's head bounced from the mothers to Tyson. "What are they talking about? Are you seeing someone else?"

"What do you mean, someone else?" Mother Scott interrupted before Tyson could come up with an answer that didn't sound flaky. "He's not really seeing you. He's just killing time while my baby, Reyna, gets herself together." Her hands flew to her mouth. "Oops. Did I just say her name?"

"That's enough!" Tyson roared.

Both Mother Scott and First Lady Drake waved Tyson off and continued playing with the baby.

Tyson stood and beckoned Mylan to do the same. "Come on. Let's get something to eat. I'll explain later in private. To answer your question, no, I'm not seeing anyone else. Outside of my mother"—he gestured toward the prayer warriors—"and these nosy mothers, you're the only woman in my life."

She nodded. "Okay."

Tyson didn't miss the uncertainty clouding her adorable face. Hopefully, by the end of the day, he'd come up with an explanation to reassure Mylan of his interest. More importantly, he needed time to figure out why his heart had fluttered at the mention of Reyna being his wife.

"You look troubled. Man, what's up?" Kevin asked when he joined Tyson on the deck after dinner.

Tyson was troubled, but the day belonged to his godson. "I am troubled that you ate the last of the banana pudding your mother made. I thought I was your boy."

Kevin licked the spoon clean. "You are my boy. That's why I had Marlissa put a bowl aside for you before Leon devoured it."

"Thanks." Tyson turned his back to his friend and stuffed his hands into the front pockets of the designer jeans he'd changed into after the ceremony. The views of the bay and the city from Kevin's deck were breathtaking. The view from Tyson's bedroom balcony equaled their glory. Unfortunately for Tyson, the peace he normally enjoyed eluded him today. He still didn't know how to broach the subject of Reyna with Mylan.

Kevin stood beside him and offered him a bottle of water. "So how are things progressing with Mylan? She's a beautiful woman."

"That she is," Tyson agreed.

"Is it serious?"

Tyson took a swig. "Not yet, and it might not ever be thanks to our nosy friends."

"They mean well," Kevin said when he recovered from laughing after Tyson told him about the prayer warriors' shenanigans.

Tyson turned and looked through the sliding glass door into the great room. "Maybe I should go and get her before they start round two."

Kevin dismissed his concern while twisting the cap off of his water bottle. "Mylan is perfectly safe. The dynamic prayer duo is too busy commanding devils out of my mother to pay your girl any attention."

"Do they ever turn it off?"

"I doubt it. Mother Scott probably speaks in tongues in her sleep. So is she your girl?" Kevin said, probing.

Tyson sat down on a lounge chair and leaned back.

"Well?"

"I want her to be," Tyson answered honestly. "She's gorgeous, smart, and considerate. She loves the Lord, and my parents love her."

"But—"

"There are no buts. I'm just taking it slow. What?" he asked when Kevin continued staring at him.

"It's me you're talking to, remember? What's the problem?"

Tyson looked back toward the great room, then leveled with his best friend. "Here's the deal. I like the package. My father said it's more important to marry someone who loves me than to wait for the love bug to strike me. A good woman like Mylan will help build a good home. Love can come later."

"Is that what he did? Marry your mother without love?"

The question stung. The idea that his father didn't love his mother when they married had never occurred to him. What was worse was that he couldn't say unequivocally that love had ever arrived for his parents. They shared a bond, but in Tyson's opinion, they lacked intimacy.

"Is that what you want? An arrangement?"

"That's not what I'm saying. Mylan's a good catch, and I—"

"Look, man," Kevin interrupted. "I'm thrilled you're building a relationship with your father. You've loosened up a great deal. Look at you. I haven't seen you in jeans since college. Granted, it's an eight-hundred-dollar pair, but jeans nonetheless."

"I have my standards," Tyson joked.

"Yes, you do, and the judge isn't an expert on relationships. That's why you haven't committed to Mylan. Your heart's not in it." Kevin let the words marinate before continuing. "On the surface you and Mylan look good together, but I don't see anything equal to the passion you have for Reyna."

"Had!" Tyson jumped up. "I *had* passion for Reyna, but that's over. I've moved on. Pursuing her was a big mistake. That's why I'm taking my time with Mylan. I don't trust my heart. Everyone doesn't have what you and Marlissa and Leon and Starla have. As much as you loved each other, you had to go through hell to keep that love. Love doesn't guarantee happiness." Tyson paced the length of the deck. "Maybe my father is right. Marriage doesn't have to equal love, at least not in the beginning. Love can come later."

Kevin downed the rest of the water, then tossed the bottle in the recycle bin. "If you really believe that, then commit to Mylan and move the woman you love out of your property."

Chapter 21

Reyna rushed into her workstation at the real estate office and dumped her bag on the floor. She had two minutes to swap her Nikes for a pair of heels and get to the conference room for the weekly staff meeting. She hated these meetings, but Paige thought them necessary to keep the agents on target and motivated. Reyna's role was primarily that of a note taker, but through the process she learned about the business, and she hoped to one day own her own home.

Home. That was a place she hadn't been in a while. Although she ate and slept at the town house, it no longer felt like home—not with an unemployed substance abuser living there.

After she caught him snorting Tyson's furniture up his nose and then suffered his subsequent verbal and physical attack three months ago, Peyton apologized profusely and begged for forgiveness. He swore the cocaine had spoken those vicious words and not his heart. He had even vowed to enroll in to a rehabilitation program and get a legitimate job. "It won't happen again. I promise. I love you." He'd made the declaration on his knees, with tears and snot running down his face. His sincerity and his profession of love had convinced Reyna to give him another chance, but she slept with the poker underneath her bed, just in case.

Peyton had lived up to his promises. He even bathed regularly. He catered to Reyna's every need. He did the housekeeping and cooked and presented Reyna with the results of his Internet job search when she returned home from work. He compiled a list of rehab programs, and not once did he ask to use her car. He discussed every decision with her, no matter how small, and showered her with affection. The new and improved Peyton was the man of Reyna's dreams. After seven days, she learned dreams could transform into nightmares.

Thinking all Peyton needed to overcome his habit was her support, Reyna ignored the subtle signs that she was being manipulated again. When fifty dollars disappeared from her purse, Peyton convinced her she'd miscalculated on their last trip to the grocery store. Two days later, she planned to run errands during her lunch break but couldn't find her car. It wasn't where she'd parked it that morning. Reyna called the police to report it stolen, only to have Peyton drive up while the officer was taking her report. Peyton swore he'd told Reyna he planned to use the vehicle for a job interview. She knew he was lying. As much as they needed the money, she would have remembered an employment opportunity. She gave him the benefit of the doubt until she came home and found her debit card on the coffee table, next to his mirror and glass straw. She called the bank and nearly fainted when she discovered that not only had he stolen her card, but he'd snorted the rent money up his nose.

Hours of yelling and screaming climaxed with more tears and confessions of love from Peyton, and Reyna once again rescinding her demand for him to move out. Instead of asking Paige for an advance, she went to the local payday loan broker and borrowed enough to cover the rent plus the late fee. She still owed *Fast Cash* money. Then she rented a post office box and opened new bank accounts. She kept the new debit card locked in her drawer at work. It was inconvenient, but necessary. Peyton had already hocked everything of value in the town house. Their sex life had dwindled to nothing, but she didn't miss it, and apparently neither did Peyton, because he didn't approach her. To dilute the painful reality of her dismal life, Reyna indulged in a nightly dose of vodka and orange juice.

This morning she ran behind schedule because Peyton accused her of hiding money from him because she didn't trust him. As usual, during the weekly argument Reyna lied and said that she wasn't hiding any money and that she trusted him, but not the drug that controlled him. She thought she'd soothed him, until he cursed her out and then punched a hole in the bathroom wall. Just what she needed: something else to replace. At this rate she'd be in debt to Tyson the remainder of her natural life.

She made it to the conference room with ten seconds to spare. Paige acknowledged her presence by telling her to pass out the agenda.

"Sure," Reyna said through gritted teeth. Even though Paige was her boss, she hated whenever the woman told her what to do.

Paige opened the meeting with prayer. The downside of working for a Christian employer, other than being jealous of her, was the weekly "Come to Jesus" prayer. Although Reyna no longer believed the hype, she bowed her head, but instead of praying, she hummed the beat to her favorite song.

An hour later Reyna's to-do list overflowed with requests not only from Paige, but from other agents as well.

"Reyna, I need to speak to you privately for a moment," Paige stated at the close of the meeting. "The rest of you may leave."

What did I do now? she wondered as the agents filed out of the room. Reyna hoped she wasn't being fired when Paige stood and closed the door after the last agent.

"Reyna, you're doing a good job."

Reyna exhaled.

"I've noticed a remarkable change in your work habits since you joined us six months ago. I'll admit I hired you only as a favor to Tyson, and your meddling almost got you fired. However, you've changed. Tyson was right about you. You have the potential to do great things. I hope you consider returning to school. According to Tyson, you're close to obtaining your master's."

The last thing Reyna had expected was a compliment from Paige. Pride prevented her from saying thank you. She swallowed the lump in her throat, wondering what else Tyson had said about her. "I might go back someday, but right now I have to support myself."

Paige nodded as if she understood completely, and Reyna knew what was coming next. "Well, pray about it. God can turn things around if we trust Him. Until then, you've earned your six-month salary increase. The other agents and I have agreed to pay you an additional stipend to perform code calls and set listing appointments. This will free us to devote more time to our existing customers and gain new ones."

Reyna jumped up. "Really?" She'd forgotten all about the six-month increase provision in her employment contract. The code-calling stipend was an added bonus.

For the first time, Paige's laughter filled the room. Reyna's gut contracted; even the woman's laugh was eloquent.

"It's not much, but it'll help." Paige turned to leave but stopped short of the door. "God has so much more for you than what you're settling for. Find a way to finish school. I'll help in any way I can."

Reyna heard the words but didn't have time to take heed. Paige had just given her the means to pay off the payday advance loan. The company called her so much, she had to download a Chinese-speaking voice mail message to throw them off.

Reyna floated through the rest of the day. The increase in pay would eventually solve her money problem. The extra money would give her the chance to catch up on some bills and finally get a tune-up on her car. On the way home, she debated whether to share the good news with Peyton, then decided against it. He'd find a way to snort the money up before she earned it.

She stopped short of opening the town house door when she arrived home that evening, opting to sit on the bench swing on the porch for a few minutes to gather the strength to deal with Peyton. Every day when she came home, he badgered her for money, and when she swore she didn't have any, he'd curse at her, then leave, only to return in the middle of the night.

She looked around the subdivision and noticed something was missing—her car. Which meant Peyton wasn't home. She entered the town house with renewed energy, only to have it sapped from her the next minute and replaced with anger.

An unfamiliar skinny blond woman lay on the couch. The stranger offered an empty smile before her glossy eyes rolled to the back of her head.

Reyna violently shook the woman. "Who the . . . are you? Why are you in my house?"

"Will you shut up?" Peyton said, emerging from the bedroom, wearing jeans and no shirt, with the glass straw in his hand. "Stupid broad, you're always messing up somebody's high. What are you doing here this early, anyway? Shouldn't you be at work?"

Reyna huffed and jumped in his face. "Cokehead, it's six o'clock in the evening." She pointed back at the semiconscious woman. "Who is she? What is she doing here?"

Peyton's head shook and his eyes blinked like he was confused. "I guess I lost track of the time. We're usually done before you get home."

"I said . . ." Reyna paused when his words resonated. "Are you telling me, you and this cokehead tramp have been snorting up in my house every day?"

"Don't talk about Laci like that. She's a good person who enjoys the same recreation I do." He turned to walk away and then turned back, like he'd just remembered something important. "If it's really six o'clock, she's late picking up her kids from the child-care center." He went over and shook her. "Come on, Laci, wake up."

Reyna's visual field flooded with red dots, and rage consumed her the longer she watched Peyton attempt to awaken the woman. Disdain dripped from her lips. "I can't believe you're cheating on me with that. You're leaving me for that?" Before she could strike his back, he turned around.

"I'm not stupid like you are. Laci and I are only friends."

"I don't believe you!"

"I don't care. As pathetic as you are, I'm not leaving you. I'd be as stupid as you are to walk away from my bread and butter. All I have to do is show you a little attention and you'll believe anything I tell you."

The corners of her eyes burned with tears. Peyton's truth serum was working again, and like before, the truth hurt.

"You promised you were going to stop using." If her heart wasn't broken, Reyna would have laughed at the ludicrous promise. What drug addict doesn't promise to stop using?

"I lied. I told you that only so I could stay here."

Reyna flinched.

"I don't ever plan to stop. I'm in love with the rock. So stop hassling me about it, because I'm not going to stop. I'm not moving out, either." He snapped his fingers like he had a thought. "I bet if you tried some, you wouldn't be so uptight."

"I believed you. I thought you were different."

"Why? Because I'm white? See, that just proves how slow you are. Darling, a man is a man no matter what color he is."

Both of their heads turned in the direction of the squeaky sound. Laci was pointing up at the ceiling and laughing.

"Good. She's awake. I'll call the cab to pick us up." Peyton pulled out the cell phone Reyna had paid for, and dialed a number. "You should think about what I said. A rock-climbing trip will relax you, and then maybe the three of us can have some fun." He winked. "You know what I mean?"

Reyna knew exactly what he meant, but was too stunned by the invitation to speak. She wanted to slap his face, but her hands felt like lead. As she listened to him arrange for a taxi, Paige's parting words recycled through her brain. She deserved better than Peyton. He had to leave. She wanted him gone, far away from her, but first she had one more question.

"Peyton, where is my car?"

He glanced at Laci, and they both burst into laughter. Mirth poured from Peyton with such force, he leaned against the table for support.

"Darling, your car is probably in three states by now."

Reyna fell back against the wall for support. "What?"

"How do you think we financed our adventure?" he asked, pulling his shirt out from underneath Laci. "We sold your car for parts to one of Laci's friends. At least now you don't have to worry about getting a tune-up."

Reyna felt her body sliding down the wall but didn't stop its descent. "You chopped my car?"

"Got over three grand for it." The words rolled off his tongue as if his actions were rational.

Peyton lifted Laci from the couch and steadied her as she stood upright. "The taxi will be here in a minute. We have to get Laci's kids before the child-care center calls CPS again." Laci followed him mechanically. "Don't forget to call the insurance company and report the car stolen so we can get a new car soon. Laci's husband is away on business, so I probably won't be home tonight," he called over his shoulder. Then the door closed.

Reyna's bottom hit the floor with a thud.

Chapter 22

Reyna jolted upright at the sound of the alarm clock. Blindly, she aimed for the nightstand to silence the noise. When her hand hit the wall, she remembered she wasn't in bed, but on the floor. She'd rolled over and fallen out of bed sometime during the night. Too drunk to gather her bearings, she'd slept on the carpeted floor.

She opened her eyes, but the throbbing in her head allowed her to stretch only briefly. No body aches, thanks to the extra padding beneath the once plush carpet. How or why Peyton had cut patches out of it was a mystery to be solved at another time. Right now the ocean waves rolling around inside her stomach demanded her immediate attention. After brewing a cup of tea, Reyna showered and prepared for the long trek to work—on the bus.

The option of driving to work in the vehicle she owned had been stripped from her. Thanks to Peyton, that luxury would elude her indefinitely, since she'd let the insurance lapse on the car after she paid it off. Taking care of Peyton had drained her resources, and she just hadn't been able to keep up with everything.

Taking care of Peyton. How did that happen? Reyna had asked that question before every swig of vodka and orange juice last night. Three-fourths of the way through the bottle, she still hadn't had an answer to that question but had decided Peyton was right about one thing: she was stupid. That was the only theory she could come up with to explain why she had shunned a good man who could provide for her and had embraced one who sought only to take from her.

Peyton had succeeded in his quest. The only tangible thing Reyna had left was some money in her secret bank account. The measly amount would last only a week, if that. The salary increase she'd hope would solve her money problems would now have to be used to purchase some form of reliable transportation. Her self-esteem had gone out the door with Peyton and his new woman. She literally had nothing left.

For the first time, Reyna walked into her workstation and appreciated the small space. At least she had a job, and eventually she'd recover from the mess Peyton had made of her life.

"Good morning, Reyna . . ." Paige stopped in the entrance to greet her but didn't finish. "You look sick. Are you okay? Cramps again?"

Reyna swallowed the bitter words she had for her Holy Roller boss. No doubt Reyna's appearance had fueled Paige's reaction. For the first time in months Reyna wasn't wearing makeup. The "always in place" spiked hair was gelled back. According to Reyna's own evaluation, she looked a mess, but she didn't care.

"No. I'm okay. I had a rough night, but I'll be fine."

"Can I bring you some tea?"

On any other day, Reyna would have enjoyed Ms. High-and-Mighty serving her, but today worthlessness had sucked her so deep into despair that taking advantage of Paige lost its appeal.

"No, thank you. Once I drown myself in work, I'll be fine." Reyna booted her computer, hoping Paige would recognize the dismissal tactic. She didn't.

"Reyna, may I pray with you?"

Paige asked the simple question with such sincerity, Reyna would have yielded had the throbbing in her head not returned.

"Look, Paige, I hope this doesn't affect my employment here, because I really need this job, but I don't believe in God. And I don't care much for prayer. I assumed Tyson shared that with you." She paused for Paige to confirm this.

"No, he didn't. He did tell me you were the most remarkable woman he'd ever met."

Reyna's mouth hung open. How could Tyson know all the senseless things she'd done and say that about her? Technically, he knew very little, but that was enough to tarnish her record.

"It doesn't matter what you believe," Paige continued. "You don't have to say a word. I'll pray on your behalf. I don't mean to push, but I sense you could use some divine guidance."

"No offense intended," Reyna lied, "but I don't need your prayer. I know what I'm doing."

For the first time Reyna witnessed sadness resting on Paige's stoic face, and she didn't care.

"No offense taken," Paige uttered so low, Reyna barely heard her. "Enjoy the rest of the day."

"How am I supposed to enjoy my day with Tyson on the brain?" she mumbled after Paige had cleared the entrance. For a brief moment Reyna permitted the truth to flood her pores and seep out. Thoughts of Tyson hadn't surfaced minutes earlier, when Paige mentioned him. Every time Peyton disrespected her, thoughts of Tyson's concern and gentleness comforted her. He was her one true friend. He said he would always be there for her, and she really needed him right now. She needed to do what she should have done months ago, when she discovered Peyton had stolen his belongings.

An hour later she made up her mind to drop by his law office during her lunch break, but first she needed to stop by the store for a bag of Reese's Peanut Butter Cups.

"Excuse me," Reyna panted after she bumped into Tyson's secretary. The two had collided when Reyna rushed into the reception area as the secretary was leaving.

"Ms. Mills? I haven't seen you in a while. What are you doing here?"

"I was hoping to catch Mr. Stokes before he left for lunch, if he's not in court. I would have called, but I wanted to surprise him," she explained.

"Oh, he will be surprised," his secretary responded after she recovered from the collision. "He's in his office, as usual, working through lunch. It was good seeing you again, but I have to go. I'm meeting my husband for lunch."

Reyna couldn't be sure, but she thought she heard the woman chuckle as she went out the door. She repositioned the shoulder strap of her purse and picked up the bag of candy that had fallen upon impact. To her surprise, little flutters filled her stomach with each step she took toward Tyson's office. She attributed the anxiety to fear of how he'd respond once he knew she had watched passively as a drug addict destroyed his property. She knocked on Tyson's door, then opened it and timidly stepped inside.

"Lois, I thought you went to lunch," he said without looking up from the computer. "Did you forget something?"

Her mouth ran dry, and her heart rate instantly accelerated at the sight of him. Instead of a tailored suit and collared shirt, he wore a polo shirt and what appeared to be khakis. Had his upper body always been that chiseled? It had been so long since she'd seen him, and for a brief second Reyna entertained the idea that she might have made a mistake by pushing him away.

"It's me," she said, walking to his desk and trying to keep from running to him.

Tyson's head jolted around. In seconds his facial expression changed from shock to pleasure to confusion. He looked down at his desk calendar. "Do I have an appointment with you today?"

It was not the response she'd hoped for, but certainly the one she deserved.

"No. I needed to talk to you." When he didn't respond, she held up the orange, brown, and yellow plastic bag. "I brought your favorites." When he didn't reach for the candy, she followed his eyes to the crystal bowl on the corner of his desk. It overflowed with the chocolate peanut butter candy. "For when you run out," she said, then laid the bag on the desk.

"What can I do for you, Reyna? Is everything in working order at the town house?" he asked before she could sit down.

Reyna changed her mind and decided to stand, just in case she needed to run. "You look good," she said honestly, stalling for time.

"Thank you. So what's up?"

"Well . . . um . . ." She stammered not from fear, but from the fact that for the first time Tyson didn't comment on her beauty. Then she remembered her appearance and didn't blame the man. "First, let me say—"

"Surprise."

Tyson jumped up and Reyna whirled around at the sensuous sound coming from the doorway.

"Lois told me you planned to work through lunch. So I brought you something to eat," Mylan said, holding up the picnic basket. She looked at Reyna. "I'm sorry. I didn't know you were with a client."

"Sweetheart, you're fine."

Reyna's head snapped around. *Sweetheart?* Her jaw dropped as she watched Tyson walk around the desk and take the large basket from the woman, who could easily win the Miss Universe Pageant. Her flawless makeup-free skin had a natural glow, and her long, thick hair reminded Reyna of what her gelled-down spikes used to look like. Feeling inadequate, she wrapped her arms around her body. Her breath caught when Tyson leaned over and kissed the woman on the lips.

"She's not a client. This is my tenant, Ms. Mills." He turned to Reyna. "This is Mylan."

Reyna's mouth moved to speak, but she got distracted by the toned arms wrapped around Tyson's waist.

"Hello, Ms. Mills."

Reyna acknowledged the greeting with a nod.

"Give Lois a call later and schedule an appointment, and then we can discuss the town house," Tyson said. "I think I have some time free on Friday."

It wasn't until Tyson called her name twice that she realized he'd just dismissed her for the beauty queen. She didn't miss the smirk on Mylan's face, either.

"Sure. Enjoy your meal," Reyna said in resignation.

Before exiting, she paused and looked back at the happy couple preparing to eat, and her heart sank even further. She was no longer the object of Tyson's affection. He had moved on to someone much prettier and smarter. An empty, hollow feeling engulfed her as she left the building. She had lost something valuable but refused to identify the true emotion. Thanks to the bottle of vodka tucked inside her bag, which she'd picked up at a corner store along with the candy, she wouldn't have to anytime soon.

Reyna spent the afternoon scheduling inspections and posting rental listings. After clearing her to-do list, she rearranged the file cabinet and dusted. Anything to keep thoughts of Tyson and his newfound love at bay. Tyson was a good man, and she should be happy for him, but a gloomy sadness consumed her. Except for the few tears that managed to escape, the strategy worked. At quitting time, she locked her desk, changed into her Nikes, and prepared to make a dash for the bus stop. Unfortunately, her mother and Pastor Jennings were waiting in the reception area.

Reyna smirked. "Let me guess. The happy couple is coming out of the closet and buying a house together."

"Satan, the Lord rebuke you!" Pastor Jennings exclaimed, waving an index finger in Reyna's face.

Reyna rolled her eyes. "Whatever. What are you doing here?" She directed the question to her mother.

Jewel went to hug her daughter but retreated when Reyna scowled at her. "I've been worried about you, and I miss you."

"And you couldn't say that with a card?" Reyna started for the door. "I don't have time for this. I have a bus to catch."

Jewel gripped her arm. "Reyna, please. It's been six months since you left my house, and you still won't tell me where you live. You won't even return my calls. Please have dinner with me. I really need to talk to you."

Reyna looked down at her arm. The bony hand gripping her didn't belong to the woman she'd grown to hate. She stepped backward and studied Jewel. Her mother had lost at least thirty pounds. The weight loss gave her face a sunken look, especially since she didn't wear makeup. Jewel had also abandoned her monthly Miss Clairol treatments; she now had more salt than pepper covering her head. Although she didn't care, Reyna couldn't help wondering if her mother had contracted an illness.

"What do you want to talk about? I don't have anything to say to you," Reyna replied. "Or you," she added, scowling at Pastor Jennings.

"Reyna, please hear us out."

Oddly enough, hearing her mother beg for her attention didn't give Reyna the satisfaction she'd imagined it would. The idea that her mother might be stricken with a terminal illness piqued her interest. Jewel's life insurance policy would provide her with a way out of the financial mess Peyton had created. She looked up at the wall clock; the interaction had already caused her to miss her bus. The next one wasn't scheduled to arrive for fifteen minutes. Since she'd skipped lunch to meet Tyson, she was hungry.

Reyna snatched her arm free. "Fine. I'll hear what you have to say this once, but then I don't want to see you or talk to you again." She glared at Pastor Jennings and added, "That includes you."

"Okay," Jewel agreed, but Reyna didn't miss the tear sliding down her cheek. She just didn't care.

"So where are we going? I have a taste for prime rib and lobster." If the two women who had ruined her life wanted to spring for dinner to ease their conscience, the least she could do was help them by going to an expensive restaurant. "Horatio's sounds nice." She waited for a protest but didn't get one.

"Whatever you want," Jewel agreed.

Reyna huffed and brushed past the women. "Let's go. I don't have all night."

"Do you want to ride with us, or would you like us to follow you?"

At Pastor Jennings's question, Reyna stopped mid-stride. Eating a free meal in a public restaurant with her nemesis was one thing, but being enclosed in a compact car for the forty-five-minute drive was another. Reyna didn't doubt for a second, she would be bombarded with personal questions and would have to endure that wretched gospel music the hypocrites played constantly.

"On second thought, let's have pizza at Zachary's," she suggested. The popular Chicago-style pizza parlor was located within walking distance from the town house. "I'll meet you there in an hour." That would give her enough time to catch the next bus and change into casual clothing and walk the short distance to the restaurant. It would also give her time to indulge in some of the happy juice tucked away inside her bag.

"We'll be there," Jewel answered. "Please show up."

"Don't get your panties in a wad. I said I'll be there."

Chapter 23

Reyna practically floated down the street and into the pizza eatery. A pint of vodka plus orange juice had rendered her joyous enough to sing to the birds along the street and bob her head to music no one heard but her. Over the past few months she'd developed a tolerance to alcohol that rendered her functional. She'd meant to take only a sip to calm the anxiety the last twenty-four hours had piled on her. First, Peyton and his drugged-out piece on the side had chopped her car. Then Tyson had dumped her for a new and prettier model. He hadn't actually dumped her, but that was the story she fed her psyche to avoid facing the truth. Now her mother wanted to have a heart-to-heart chat, but the problem was that Jewel didn't have a heart and Reyna's heart had hardened too much to care. At least she'd get a few meals for the inconvenience; she planned to order enough chicken and spinach-stuffed pizza to last the two days until payday.

Reyna slid into the booth in the back left corner. "All right, Jewel, Rosalie, what's up?"

"Thank you for coming," Jewel began, then sniffed. "Have you been drinking?"

"Have you been lying?" Reyna countered. "I said I'd hear what you had to say, but that doesn't include telling you my business. The last time I checked, I was a grown woman."

"Do you have to be so disrespectful? I know we taught you about respecting your elders and honoring your parents."

Pastor Jennings's rebuke fell on deaf ears. "You also taught me how to manipulate and use people."

"I will not—"

"Rosalie, please let me handle this," Jewel said, cutting in.

Reyna didn't miss the glare Pastor Jennings shot her mother. This marked the first time she'd witnessed Jewel stand up to her.

"Reyna, I ordered that chicken and spinach pizza you like and a diet Pepsi. I ordered a large so you'd have enough to take home for later."

Too ornery to say thank you, Reyna opened her mouth to say something derogatory but couldn't think of anything. Not only had Jewel remembered what she liked, but she'd robbed her of the pleasure of draining her wallet.

"Reyna, earlier you said you had to catch the bus. I don't mean to pry, but where is your car?"

"Mother Jewel, you are prying, but since you're paying for the meal, I'll answer. I don't have a car anymore. It was stolen and stripped." Reyna gave enough of an answer to keep Jewel from asking more questions, or so she thought.

"Have you contacted the insurance company?"

"Now you're asking too many questions that are none of your business."

The waitress delivering the drink order silenced a rebuttal from Jewel.

Reyna sipped the diet Pepsi and wished it were something stronger. "What's so important you had to hunt me down at my place of employment? Oh, by the way, don't do that again." She didn't miss the nervous glances her mother and Pastor Jennings exchanged. Her mother's hands shook so much, lemonade dripped from her glass when she attempted to drink. She had a bombshell, all right. Even semi-drunk Reyna could see that.

"Reyna, I need to tell you something I should have told you long ago," Jewel began after cleaning up the spilled liquid.

"You'll have to wait a few minutes longer to clear your conscience. I gotta pee." She covered her mouth and giggled. "Oops. I mean I need to use the ladies' room." The only negative about drinking for Reyna was alcohol sent her bladder into overdrive.

Reyna left the table and sideswiped a waiter carrying a hot pizza. The man's quick reflexes and steady hands saved the pizza from kissing the floor.

"Sorry," she giggled, then stumbled toward the restroom.

When she returned, Jewel and Pastor Jennings were waiting to bless the food. "I don't do that no more," she said, then loaded her plate with a pie slice. She'd eaten half the slice before noticing her mother and Pastor Jennings weren't eating. She wiped off the cheese dripping from her mouth. "What? Y'all don't like stuffed pizza anymore?"

"We've been fasting all day. I have some soup back at the house for us," Jewel explained.

Reyna rested the knife and fork against her plate and folded her arms. "All right, spill it. What's the big news flash?"

Jewel played with the folded napkin and sipped lemonade.

"Come on, Jewel," Pastor Jennings said, encouraging her. "You can do this."

"Do what?" Reyna wanted to know.

"Please promise to hear me out," Jewel begged.

Reyna didn't like it, but the dread in Jewel's tone pulled at her heartstrings, which caused her to sober some. "I'll try."

Jewel's eyes closed, and her mouth moved. Either she was praying, speaking in tongues, or both.

"Come on, I don't have all night," Reyna said, pressing. She needed to get back home to pack and throw Peyton's clothes into the trash bin for the garbage pickup in the morning.

"Reyna, I was a sheltered teenager," Jewel began. "When I went off to college, I ran wild. For the first time I was free from my overprotective father, and although I enrolled in college for an education, my number one objective was to find a man and have fun."

"I could do without the history lesson, but this one might be interesting," Reyna grumbled. "I can't imagine your sanctimonious self looking for a man." Giggles poured from her at the absurd thought.

"My friends and I would dress up and use false IDs to get into the local party spots. One night I met this man. He was so fine, I fell in love instantly. His name was Reynard. Sophistication and class radiated from him, and I wanted what I thought he could offer me. I didn't ask how old he was, because I didn't want him to know how young and inexperienced I was."

Reyna shifted in her seat; this story sounded familiar, but she couldn't place where she'd heard it.

"That night I did everything he wanted. If he wanted to dance, I danced. I'd never tasted alcohol before, but when he offered some, I accepted. When he invited me to his room to talk, I went. I readily accepted his offer to make me his woman, because I wanted to be his. I'd grown up reading fairy tales, and I thought I had found my Prince Charming. I thought since he wanted to sleep with me, he loved me. Love and lust look the same when alcohol is involved."

"I know what you mean," Reyna interjected, thinking of the night she lost her virginity. "I mean, I've heard that before," she added, recovering. There was no way she'd admit to her mother that she fell victim to that stupid way of thinking too.

Jewel's head tilted to the side, like she was analyzing what her daughter had said.

Reyna gestured with her hands. "Keep going." Jewel now had Reyna's full attention. She had tuned out everything and everyone around her. Even the pizza pie had lost its appeal.

"I spent the night with him . . . well, a couple of hours actually. Then he drove me to Rosalie's house since I'd missed dorm curfew." Jewel nodded at Pastor Jennings. "She snuck me inside without her parents knowing."

Reyna smirked. "No wonder you're such good hypocrites together. You've had decades of practice."

Pastor Jennings narrowed her eyes, and Reyna rolled hers.

"At any rate, my life didn't end like a fairy tale. He wasn't Prince Charming, and we didn't get married and live happily ever after. I never saw or heard from him again. I went back to the club every week for three months. I even did a few weeknight drop-ins. No one saw him. To this day I don't know if he's dead or alive. It's nearly impossible to find someone with only a first name."

Reyna gasped. "You mean you slept with a man without knowing his last name?" Not only had Reyna heard this story before, but she'd lived it too.

Jewel's head dropped in shame. "Yes," she whispered.

The pain of heartbreak from decades past sounded fresh to Reyna's ears, and she ached for her mother in the small spot in her heart that bitterness hadn't tarnished. She'd never witnessed transparency in her mother. The fact that she saw herself in her mother agitated her.

"Girl, hold your head up," Pastor Jennings said, encouraging her. "That was a long time ago. We were different people back then. God forgave us a long time ago."

Reyna started to ask Pastor Jennings what deep dark secrets she had, but she didn't want to give the impression she cared.

Jewel collected a fresh tissue from her purse and wiped her face. "That one night with Reynard changed my life in more ways than one." She held eye contact with her daughter. "I got pregnant." Her voice quivered as the words poured out.

Reyna's jaw dropped.

"That's why I tried so hard to find him. I was carrying his child. I held on to the fantasy that if he knew about the baby, he'd do the right thing and take care of us, but I couldn't find him. My family was so angry with me, they refused to support me. I had to quit school and get on public assistance to feed myself and the baby."

"Wow. That's some deep stuff," Reyna said after gulping down the remaining diet Pepsi. The restaurant was filled to capacity, yet Reyna swore if she dropped a pin on the table, she'd hear it crash against the wood.

Reyna observed the nervous glances her mother and Pastor Jennings exchanged, and realized a vital and important piece of the story had been omitted. "What happened to the baby?"

Jewel covered her daughter's hand with hers. "Reyna, you're that baby. I named you after him. Rosalie told me I was crazy, but at the time I had this foolish hope that he'd come back and we'd be a family."

Reyna's head shook violently. She needed to release the vise grip vodka had on her thinking faculties. "I'm a little high right now. What's your excuse?"

"What do you mean?"

"What medication are you on? Prozac? Xanax? Whatever it is, leave it alone. That stuff has you all twisted. You can't get your baby daddies right. My daddy's name is David Mills," Reyna answered emphatically.

Jewel's head shook sideways. "No, baby, the truth is David Mills was your stepfather. Reynard is your real father."

Whatever buzz she had left fizzled with Jewel's confession. He'd abandoned her, yet Reyna loved her father and blamed her mother for driving him away. Her heart ached for him daily. "What are you saying, Jewel?"

"Let me explain. You were two years old when I met David Mills. We were good friends, but I didn't love him. He had a decent job, a car, and was willing to raise you as his own. He even had me amend your birth certificate to add his name. I agreed to marry him because I didn't think I could do better. I didn't trust my heart, and I no longer believed in fairy tales. Real life was hard. I was barely putting food on the table. I needed what he offered, and he wanted what he thought I could give him.

"David made good on his promises, and he took good care of us until he met the neighbor and fell in love. She gave him what I couldn't and apparently what he needed. Although you believe otherwise, David and

I parted on good terms. I'm happy he found his soul mate. In fact, I envy him. A few hours of fun scarred me for life. Chances are, I'll never experience real love." Jewel leaned close to her daughter. "The one thing I regretted is how he disconnected from you. I begged him not to, but he said it was best for all parties involved. Actually, I think his new wife influenced that decision."

The high was officially gone. Reyna now understood what Peyton meant by messing up someone's high. Jewel's admission had dragged her ten degrees lower than her already depressed state. She no longer knew who she was; Jewel had stripped her of her identity. The father she loved didn't love her. The man whom she was named after didn't know she existed, and never would.

"Is that why you hate me so much?" The question flowed from a sea of bitterness and resentment. "You've never liked me."

"I swear that's not true," Jewel asserted. "I love you. I'll admit I wasn't ready for motherhood. I was too young. I didn't know how to be a mother. I tried to do right, but you came out looking just like Reynard. Every time I looked at you, I was reminded of what he took from me, what I had lost. I was angry and felt cheated. I didn't know how to relate to you without attacking you, so I had Rosalie help me."

Red spots floated past Reyna's eyes, and her finger pointed at Pastor Jennings. "How did the way she manipulated me help me?" Reyna's shrill tone caught the attention of the table closest to the booth. "Mind your business," she barked when the couple stared at her.

"Baby, please listen."

"Don't you dare call me baby! Most of my life I've been nothing but a whore or a Jezebel to you. Don't change now!"

"Okay, Reyna. I went about it the wrong way, but I didn't want you to end up like me. I saw so many of my untamed characteristics in you, and I was afraid. I didn't know what to do, but you were close to Rosalie, so we sheltered you. I admit, telling you to chase after Kevin was a mistake, but I didn't do it to harm you. I wanted you to have more than I had and not get caught up with someone like your father. I shouldn't have used Rosalie as a substitute mother, but I did. I regret it, but I can't change what's done. Please forgive me. I don't want you to end up pining after someone who is not good for you and only cares about what he can take from you."

Jewel paused to wipe more tears. "I don't want you to be like me—defining yourself through others. I slept with a man I barely knew because I thought he would make me happy and he said I was pretty. I married a man because my father said a respectable lady should have a husband. I'm over fifty and just now learning my value as a woman." Jewel's sobs made the remainder of her explanation unintelligible.

"Reyna, I was wrong for using you to destroy my son's marriage. Please forgive me."

Reyna's head snapped around at Pastor Jennings's request, but she was rendered temporarily speechless as she fought to keep her emotions in check. Why did her mother and her foe have to bring her to a public place to tell her the words she'd longed to hear most of her life? She now had clarity about her mother's attitudes and actions, but did she have the capacity to care? She didn't think so.

The rising room temperature caused beads of sweat to form across her forehead. In minutes, the gel would lose its strength, causing her hair to stick up.

"This is too much. I have to go," she said, standing and running from the table, leaving the pizza behind. She pushed her way through the crowded waiting area with her head down to hide the tears that refused to cease from flowing.

A broad shoulder bumped her. "Sorry, miss. I didn't see you."

"Whatever," she mumbled and continued on.

"Reyna?"

"Reyna?" Mylan's voice echoed Tyson's.

Reyna stopped when Tyson's firm hand gripped her arm from behind. *Oh, crap!* Out of all the people to run into, why did she have to run into Tyson and his new girlfriend? Before today, she hadn't seen him in six months, and back then she looked good. Tonight she looked worse than she did at lunchtime.

She wiggled her arm, and he tightened his grip. "You don't look well. Are you all right?"

Even with Miss Universe on his arm, he wasn't letting her go without an answer. She had to get the embarrassing moment over with, before her mother and Pastor Jennings made it to the door.

"I'll be fine, Mr. Stokes," she said, turning around to face him. "I've had a rough day, but don't worry. Your rent will be on time." She added the last part as payback for how he had introduced her earlier. Tyson denied her the reaction she was hoping for.

"Fine," he answered through clenched teeth. "Have a good evening, Ms. Mills." He released her arm and turned his back to her. The hand that seconds ago had warmed her skin now massaged Mylan's shoulder.

Reyna ran out the door and down the street. If she hurried, she'd make it to the corner liquor store before closing.

Chapter 24

Tyson allowed his eyes to drift from the road to the beautiful woman seated next to him. Even when she was distracted, Mylan's beauty surpassed that of most women. Although they'd enjoyed pleasant conversation during dinner, Mylan's normal jovial personality was missing. She hadn't smiled as much, and she'd kept her hands tucked in her lap. She'd seemed tense ever since the run-in with Reyna. He couldn't imagine she felt threatened. The night of the christening he'd told her unequivocally that whatever he'd had with Reyna was over, no matter what Mother Scott implied.

He didn't mind the distance at the restaurant. He, too, had been thrown off kilter by Reyna's sudden appearance. He'd dismissed her unannounced visit at lunch as a simple ploy to gain something. What, he didn't know, but Reyna extended niceties only when it benefited her. This evening's drama moment was unrehearsed. The tears were real; her appearance was uncharacteristic. He didn't like it, but her emotional and physical state concerned him.

He could only guess about the source of those tears, until he saw her mother and Pastor Jennings bustling out of the restaurant behind her. It took all his willpower not to follow them, and truthfully, he would have if Mylan hadn't been with him.

Tyson lightly applied the brakes at the stoplight, then turned his body to study Mylan more carefully.

Why wasn't this beautiful saved woman enough to keep Reyna Mills out of his mind? They'd been dating close to five months, and yet he couldn't bring himself to commit. He'd planned to have the "status" talk at dinner, but bumping into Reyna changed that. He'd sat, eaten, and talked with Mylan, but it was Reyna's tears that had captivated his attention.

As he crossed the intersection, the last conversation he had had with his father replayed in his mind. He'd summoned the courage to ask the judge if he loved his mother when they married. His answer both saddened and surprised him.

"I loved the idea and meaning of marriage," his father had said. "I wanted a family, and your mother was willing to give me that. For that I had the highest respect for her. Then, after you were born, I fell in love with her. Actually, I think I loved her all along but was afraid to open up. She's my best friend. She understands me and accepts my many faults. We may not be as outwardly affectionate as most, but your mother and I love one another very much. She's quite a hottie."

Tyson snickered, recalling that statement. He didn't know *hottie* was in his father's vocabulary. Could he expect the same outcome? His gut told him he would end up with less than amicable results.

He pulled into Mylan's driveway and turned off the engine.

"Wait a minute." Mylan touched his shoulder before his hand reached the latch. "We need to talk."

They did need to talk, but his mind was too cluttered to have a serious conversation. However, the dread in her voice made him reconsider.

"What is it, sweetheart?"

As a lawyer, he was trained to read a person's body language. Mylan shifted in her seat, and after fidgeting with her hands, she folded them in her lap. She looked at him but avoided eye contact. He came to one conclusion: he wasn't going to like what she had to say.

"I learned a lot today, or maybe I finally accepted the truth. Now I know why you've been so hesitant about taking our friendship to the next level." Her voice was soft, but firm.

His brow furrowed. "What do you mean? I thought we agreed to take our time and get to know one another."

"It's been almost five months. We could date for five years and it wouldn't matter," she said sadly.

"I don't understand." Tyson refused to evaluate the statement for its truth. He liked Mylan.

Mylan finally made eye contact, but he had a gut feeling again that he wasn't going to like what she had to say.

"Do you like me?"

That was a no-brainer. "Of course I like you. I like how caring and attentive you are. I like how you challenge me with your intellect. I enjoy hearing you pray and watching you praise God. I like how you mesmerize me with your beauty." He added a wink with the last statement, but unlike previous times, she didn't blush.

"That's the problem, Tyson."

"I don't understand."

Her eyes seemed to read his soul when she said, "You like me, but you *love* her."

"Who?"

"Reyna, Ms. Mills, and whatever other name she goes by."

Tyson's equanimity vanished, and he pounded the steering wheel. "Would everyone stop saying that? I'm tired of hearing that. It's not true. I told you, whatever Reyna and I had or didn't have is over."

Mylan waited until the huffing and puffing ended before continuing. "You did say that, and I believed you, until today. At your office today, you introduced Reyna as Ms. Mills, your tenant. I thought that was odd, because I discerned her hurt when you kissed me. Then tonight your eyes burned with love and concern, but it wasn't for me. It was for her. I believe with all my heart if you'd been alone, you would have gone after her."

"That's not true!" Out of habit those three words tumbled from his mouth, and for the first time he considered maybe they weren't true.

"You may not want it to be true, but it is. Everyone isn't wrong. You love her. Please hear me out," she said when he opened his mouth to protest.

Reluctantly, he nodded for her to continue with her off-base assessment. At one time he did love Reyna, but she'd made it clear she didn't want him, and he'd moved on.

"If Reyna is truly part of your past, why didn't you properly introduce us this afternoon? Why didn't you tell me the night of the christening that she lived in your property? Why is she there in the first place?"

"You have it all wrong. Reyna was a friend who needed help, and I had a vacant town house. I was just helping her get on her feet," he explained.

"If you say that long enough, you just might believe it. You're a prominent lawyer with connections. I'm sure several of your colleagues, or even Kevin, could have offered her a rental. Somehow, I don't think that thought crossed your mind."

Defeated, Tyson let his head fall back against the headrest. Mylan had read him well. It had never occurred to him to push Reyna off on someone else. Kevin owned a unit in the same subdivision, and at the time, it was also vacant. Truth was, at the time he wanted to provide for Reyna.

"I don't know what happened between you and Reyna, but whatever is, the two of you need to talk. She loves you, Tyson. I saw it in her eyes."

"No she doesn't." He voiced the words even as hope sprang in his heart.

Relief washed over him in the still silence that followed. This was an abrupt end for him and Mylan, yet he didn't harbor regrets for what could have been. Mylan would make someone an excellent wife; that person just wouldn't be him.

"I didn't mean to mislead you," he said, apologizing. "Sorry if I hurt you."

The smile didn't quite reach her eyes. "No hard feelings. You didn't promise me forever. In fact, you didn't promise me anything," she replied. "You can do one thing for me, though," she added after a brief pause. "Break the news to your mother that I will not be her daughter-in-law when I go out of town next week."

"I have a better idea. Let's send her a text."

They shared a laugh, but Tyson's heart ached. He was back at square one, pining for a love that would never be.

Chapter 25

With the brown paper bag clutched close to her chest, Reyna ran through the subdivision, nearly falling twice from blurred vision caused by the night sky and tears that refused to stop. In a matter of minutes she'd been stripped of her identity and her life. She didn't know her last name or whose eyes and mouth she'd inherited. The hope she'd clung to for years of a father's love had been shattered. All her life she'd tried to fill a role that turned out to be nothing but a manufactured lie. David Mills didn't care, probably never had. He'd just said the right words to get her mother.

Mother. A guttural groan escaped her lips as thoughts of Jewel crashed through her mind. Her mother wouldn't leave her alone. After Reyna ditched her back at the restaurant, Jewel called her cell phone three times before Reyna turned it off. When she left Jewel's house, Reyna wanted nothing to do with her or her likeness. Tonight she had discovered the apple didn't fall far from the tree when it came to mother and daughter. In the midst of trying to do her own thing—live life the way she wanted—she'd repeated the cycle of losing self-worth. She'd become dependent on a man to define her and to make her happy, and in the process she'd transformed into a depressed and lonely drunk.

The one bright light at the end of the tunnel was her job. She wasn't crazy about it, but at least she had one. There her value was recognized, although envy prevented her from completely receiving Paige's compliments. She would report bright and early Monday morning. During the seventy-two hours between now and then, she planned to drink until she passed out, and then start all over again at the first sign of consciousness.

The foul odor attacked her the second she stepped into the town house. *Peyton.* She sat the bag on the kitchen countertop, then decided to throw out the trash before bingeing.

"Pack your stuff, and get out of my house!" she yelled.

"Huh?"

What little patience she had evaporated with his "deer caught in the headlights" response. She stomped over to where he rested on the leather sofa he'd ruined by spilling soda and liquor on it and not bothering to clean it up.

She leaned in his ear and screamed, "Pack your bag, and get your smelly behind out of my house. Now!" She held out her hand. "Give me my key."

Either Peyton sobered or he realized Reyna had reached a point of no return. He sat up straight and pulled his hair into a ponytail.

"Where am I supposed to go?" he asked with the sincerity of a child. "I don't have any relatives here."

Truth or lie, she didn't know, but more importantly, she didn't care. "That's not my problem. Go to a shelter. Check into rehab. Jump off the bridge. I don't care. I'm through with your lying, cheating, stealing, and stinky behind."

Peyton threw his hands in the air. "You're still mad about Laci, aren't you? Stop trippin'. I told you, we're just friends."

Reyna's neck rolled rhythmically. "Do I look that stupid to you?"

He smirked. "You said it, not me."

"I'll give you that one. You are right. I was stupid for falling for you. You're nothing but a fake. A drugged-out cokehead impersonating a real man."

Peyton's cheeks flushed red, and the smirk vanished.

Empowered by hurt and regret, Reyna unleashed a string of expletives so colorful, Peyton's eyes bucked. "If you had a pot to piss in, you'd have to use my window to throw it out. Since the day I met you, all you've done is take from me. If you thought I'd fall for it, you would have sold *me* to support your habit. You talked about my measly job. At least I have one. All you own are the clothes on your back and an extra pair of dirty drawers. The most valuable things you have are the glass mirror and the pipe you use to do stupid coke with. Now, give me my key and get out!"

"All right. All right." His hands fell in surrender. "You're right. I don't have nothing. I don't even have enough money to buy a burger from the value menu at McDonald's, but please don't put me out tonight. I don't have anywhere to go. Give me the weekend to find a new hustle."

Reyna's head snapped. "Hustle? So you admit being with me was nothing but a hustle to you?"

With shrugged shoulders, he gave an honest answer. "My last mark found religion and checked into rehab, and then you appeared. Actually, I'd planned to work a real nine-to-five for a while, but then you showed up, appearing financially stable, but emotionally needy. It was the perfect combination. I couldn't resist." Peyton walked toward her. "If you really want me to go, I will, but give me a few days to make arrangements. I'll be gone by Monday, Tuesday at the latest."

Reyna had finally succeeded after months of trying to pry the truth out of Peyton. Only now she wished he would lie. Too much truth in such a short period of time shattered every wall of denial and fantasy she'd created. With every labored breath, she felt bravado and strength seeped from her as the real world and the one she'd created ran a collision course. A slide show of abandonment and neglect was projected in her mind from memory at such a rapid pace, Reyna slammed her eyes shut to slow down the display. The image of David Mills driving away from their home while she sat on the porch, begging him to come back, gave way to the day she saw him in the grocery store with his new, younger and prettier daughter. "Daddy's little princess," he'd called the little girl, and he'd barely spoken to Reyna.

Peyton's mouth continued moving. Reyna assumed he was still pleading his case. With all the images and voices inside her head, she couldn't be sure. It was too much to handle. With what little pride she had left, Reyna picked up the paper bag containing her happy juice without bothering to get a glass.

"Tuesday. That's it," she said, choking back tears, then with wobbly legs retreated to her bedroom.

Hours later, sprawled across her bed, Reyna battled to come out of a drunken coma-like state. Drinking the vodka straight had served its purpose. Old images no longer decorated her mind, but voices could still be heard.

"Reyna," someone said, shaking her. "Turn over."

Reyna turned on her back. "What?" she moaned without opening her eyes.

"Good girl," the voice said.

"Daddy, is that you?" she said, thinking she had sat up and was looking out into the hallway, when in actuality she lay flat on her back with her arms spread wide. She heard a snicker.

"Daddy's right here," the voice said.

Soft hands moved up her legs, and hot, stale breath whirled around her face. "No." Her head jerked violently as she fought to wake up. She recognized that voice. It belonged to Peyton. Those hands didn't; they were too soft. With the little remaining strength she had, Reyna lurch upward. The room spun too fast. She slammed her eyes shut to allow time for Earth to slow to its normal rate of speed, but not before noticing Peyton lying on her bed beside her and Laci perched at the bottom. Both were naked.

The spinning ceased, and Reyna spewed every curse word she'd ever heard at the two sex-crazed drug addicts. She even made up some new ones.

She kicked Laci in the stomach. "I'm high, but I ain't that high. Get away from me. You nasty—"

"Calm down," Peyton yelled.

Reyna jumped from the bed and unleashed another string of colorful words at Peyton, then reached underneath the bed.

Both Peyton and Laci jumped from the bed when Reyna rose up, swinging the poker. She swung the weapon and made a hole in the wall above Peyton's head.

Laci screamed.

Peyton's eyes bulged; he wasn't high anymore, and his libido had vanished. "You crazy—"

"I'll show you crazy." Reyna raised the poker, and both Peyton and Laci ran out of the room.

When she reached the living room, Laci was gathering her clothes from the floor, but she abandoned the quest when Reyna waved the poker at her. Laci screamed and ran out of the town house, naked.

"Laci, wait!" Peyton, with his pants at his ankles, hurriedly pick up her clothes and hopped out the door behind her.

Waving the poker in the air and cursing, Reyna ran onto the porch, just in time to see Peyton and Laci climb into a dark minivan and drive off.

Bright golden-orange rays caused her to squint, and for the first time she realized it was early morning. She'd managed to sleep through the night, but the hell and the pit of darkness her life had become lingered.

Her sense of touch returned as her bare feet hit the cold cement. Shivers ran down her arm, reminding her she'd run outside in only a nightshirt. Soft giggles escaped as she lowered the poker and went inside. As she leaned against the locked door, she had visions of Peyton and Laci running away in their birthday suits, and her laughter erupted. It was hilarious, yet her laughter transformed into hard sobs as reality once again reared its ugly head. At least Peyton and Laci were able to escape imminent danger. Nothing could deliver her from her torment.

Chapter 26

Monday morning Reyna literally stumbled into the real estate office two hours late, reeking of alcohol and discombobulated.

Her seventy-two-hour sabbatical from the world officially ended when her alarm sounded this morning; however, it took her another hour to get up and crawl from the bed to the bathroom, where she spent thirty minutes slouched over the toilet bowl. By the time she reached the bus stop, the express commuter line service had ended. The trip took twice as long and tested how much mental control she had over her body. Every bump teased her bladder, and her mouth filled with saliva from trying to hold back vomit. The second her feet hit the concrete, the volcano erupted and spilled on her jacket.

"I can't blame this on cramps," she said with a laugh and staggered toward the real estate office.

She avoided the stares with dark glasses, but she heard the murmuring. She didn't care; her main focus was on concocting a lie convincing enough to prevent Paige from firing her. Once at her workstation, she removed her jacket, but she didn't have a chance to sit down.

"Oh, my God! Reyna, what happened to you?" Paige stood in the entranceway, fanning her nose. "What's that smell?"

Reyna rolled her eyes. "I can't smell that bad," she slurred. "I didn't have time to shower, but I took a 'ho' bath. You know, washed up at the sink," she added when Paige's face contorted.

"Reyna, you're drunk," Paige declared.

"No, I'm not," she said in her defense. "I haven't had a drink in at least three or four hours. I'm perfectly sober."

"Really?" Paige folded her arms. "Then where are your clothes?"

"What do you mean? I may not dress like you, but . . ." The words evaporated when Reyna examined her attire.

In her hangover state, she'd forgotten to put on her dress. She'd traveled to work in a slip, a jacket, and four-inch heels. She'd also neglected to comb her hair.

Reyna couldn't think of one lie good enough to justify her actions and appearance, but she needed this job. It was all she had left, the one bright spot in her life.

"Please don't fire me," she begged. "I had a rough weekend. This will never happen again, I promise. Please, I need this job." Unrehearsed tears rolled down her cheeks.

"Put your jacket back on," Paige ordered in a tone that sent chills down Reyna's bare arms.

Reyna did as she was told.

"Come with me to my office."

Reyna followed behind Paige, just slightly more stable than when she'd arrived.

"Sit down." Paige told her after they entered her office, and closed the door behind them. "Who would you like for me to call to come pick you up?"

"Are you firing me?" Reyna had to know. "Please give me another chance. I don't have anything left."

Paige walked around and sat at her desk. "If you force me to answer that question now, it won't be good for you. What I am going to do is give you the remainder of the week off without pay."

Reyna gasped; she needed the money. "Please—"

Paige raised an eyebrow. "That's the best I can do. Now, who would you like for me to call?"

There wasn't anyone Reyna could think of to call that she hadn't alienated. She was still on good terms with Kevin but hadn't spoken to him in months and hadn't bothered to congratulate him on the birth of his son. Besides, she couldn't let him know she was an alcoholic after she dogged Marlissa for being one years ago. She didn't know Mother Scott's or First Lady Drake's phone numbers. There was only one person to call.

"My mother, Jewel Mills," she answered, then buried her face in the palms of her hands and wept.

The lies Reyna concocted to tell Jewel while waiting in Paige's office were for naught. After Paige escorted her out the back door, Reyna hopped into her mother's car, prepared to justify her behavior. To her surprise, the only question Jewel asked involved directions to Reyna's house, which she refused to give.

"Take me home. I mean, to your house."

Reyna didn't want to go to her childhood home but couldn't risk her mother running into Peyton and his addicted friend. She hadn't seen him since the fiasco two days ago, but that didn't mean he hadn't been back. She'd slept with her bedroom door locked. His deadline to move out wasn't until tomorrow, so there was a good chance he'd be lurking around.

"No problem," Jewel responded. "You still have some clothes in your old room."

Reyna thought she saw a slight smile crease Jewel's face, but too emotionally spent, she brushed it off. If

Jewel had grand ideas of a reunion, she was sadly mistaken. She just needed time to sleep off the high, and then she'd be gone.

When Jewel started singing along with the choir on the gospel radio station, Reyna reclined the seat and closed her eyes. The late Walter Hawkins and the southern mass choir were encouraging an old soldier to hold on. The old lyrics mirrored her present life. She was beyond discouraged, and her heart constantly ached, but unlike in the song, she didn't have anything or anyone to hold on to.

Jewel barely had turned off the ignition when Reyna jumped out of the car and ran to the front door. Then she had to wait for her mother. She'd forgotten she no longer possessed a key.

"After you get cleaned up, I'll make you some breakfast," Jewel offered once they were inside.

Reyna shook her head. "Maybe later. I just want to sleep." She postured for an argument, but Jewel didn't give her one.

"Okay. Well, you know where everything is."

Reyna made the trek to her old bedroom with unexpected anticipation. Although she enjoyed the comforts of a king-sized bed on a nightly basis, her old full-size mattress promised her the peaceful rest her body desperately needed.

She stepped inside and exhaled. Her room was exactly as she'd left it six months ago. She threw her jacket on the floor, slipped off the heels, and let the slip pool at her feet. She paused to feel the rough carpet between her toes before trotting off to the shower. The hot beads soothed her tired muscles but failed to wash her problems away. Later, after slipping on a T-shirt and leggings, Reyna drifted off to sleep, humming the beat to the song she'd heard in the car.

Chapter 27

"It's good to see you back among the living," Jewel said when Reyna walked into the kitchen the next morning.

"You should have woken me up. I can't sleep my life away," Reyna grumbled, although she felt rejuvenated after sleeping twenty hours straight.

"No, baby, you needed the rest." Jewel set the coffee cup down. "You look good. Let me fix breakfast. I bet you're starving."

"I can eat a horse," Reyna said, chuckling, then poured a glass of apple juice. She observed her mother moving around the kitchen and noticed something was missing. "Where's Pastor Jennings?" The two usually had coffee together after morning meditation.

Jewel stopped mixing flour and eggs and faced Reyna. "I told her not to come today. You're my daughter, and it's time I started taking care of you."

"It's a little late for that, don't you think?" Reyna snickered, although the words touched her. "I can take care of myself."

"Apparently not," Jewel smarted back and then smiled. "It's never too late to change. We've all made mistakes, but with God's help, our mistakes can turn into ministry."

She watched her mother spray the griddle and flip bacon and wondered if it was all so simple. What ministry could possibly come out of her mistakes? Not that she wanted to jump back on the Jesus train. She'd created her mess, and she'd clean it up somehow.

"Today it's just me and you," her mother continued with her back to Reyna. "But Tyson will be back this afternoon, after court."

Reyna choked on the apple juice. "Tyson's coming here? What do you mean, back?"

Jewel casually patted her back and continued cooking. "He stopped by to check on you last night, along with them pushy prayer warriors from his church. Kevin and Marlissa were here too. We all stood around your bed and prayed over you. I'm surprised all that noise didn't wake you up."

"You told them what happened? I'll never live this down. Thanks a lot, Jewel," Reyna sneered. "At least now I know why my head felt oily this morning."

"That's enough," Jewel declared, then paused. "Reyna, they love you. I love you. We all only want what's best for you."

"Whatever." Reyna waved away the concern. "How could you let him see me like this? Was his girlfriend with him?"

Jewel flipped the pancakes and poured eggs into a skillet. "I assume you're talking about Tyson. No. He stayed late into the night and didn't mention a girlfriend to me."

Relief washed over her. Tyson had seen her bruised and battered before, but she'd never live down the humiliation if Miss Knockout witnessed her drunken stupor.

"Baby, sit down and eat. Then you can go back to bed if you like." Jewel placed a plate containing four hot pancakes, four bacon strips, and three scrambled eggs in front of her. "Go on and eat. I already blessed the food, since I knew you wouldn't," Jewel said, sitting back down.

Reyna ate in silence, except for an occasional moan of pleasure. Her mother had many faults, but she made the best pancakes. She closed her eyes and licked her lips. "These are so good."

"I'm glad I can do something you like. Stop by my room for a minute when you're done." Jewel's voice broke, and she left the kitchen.

In no hurry to spend quality time with her mother, Reyna cleaned her plate at a snail's pace. After washing the breakfast dishes, Reyna searched the medicine cabinets for cough medicine or prescription drugs, just in case her mother dropped another bombshell. Unfortunately for her, the strongest medicine Jewel stocked was Imodium A-D.

Reyna found her mother sitting Indian-style on her bed, looking through old photo albums, which she didn't recognize.

Jewel patted the space next to her. "Come in and have a seat. I want to show you something."

"Great, another history lesson," she mumbled before entering the cluttered room and sitting on the bed. "What's that?" she said, showing interest.

"These are pictures of a much younger me," Jewel responded without looking up. "I thought I was hot stuff back in the day." She turned the album so her daughter could see.

"Hot? You were flaming!" Reyna hollered. "I can't believe you wore miniskirts and makeup." Reyna grabbed the album and turned the page. She pointed to a picture of a much younger Jewel and Rosalie Jennings. "Is that a bustier?" Reyna studied her mother's image more closely. "And a tattoo? You have a tattoo?" The idea that her holier-than-thou mother got tatted up seemed absurd. "I don't believe it."

Jewel unhooked the top button on her blouse. "Want to see? It hangs a lot lower than it used to, but the rose is still there."

"That's okay. I'll take your word for it." Viewing her mother's wrinkled breast to prove a point didn't appeal to her. She continued turning pages. "Oh my," she gasped. "I've seen it all." Reyna pointed to a picture of Jewel in lingerie, hanging from a pole. Her eyes pierced her mother, as she waited for an explanation.

"I told you, I ran buck wild after I left my daddy's house. It was all about me, and I did everything I wanted to do," Jewel explained. "I drank and smoked reefers too. I did anything to be accepted and loved—"

"I don't understand," Reyna interrupted. It didn't make sense to her. "You came from a stable family. Why were you looking for love?"

Jewel reached for a tissue from the nightstand. "My family was stable, and both Mom and Dad loved us, but they weren't good at expressing it. Daddy always complained about the things I did wrong, but never encouraged or validated me when I did well. My father didn't tell me he loved me until cancer had nearly eaten him up. I grew up thinking something was wrong with me. When I left home, I went on a quest to find the love I'd missed."

Reyna didn't have the strength to stop the tears that rolled down her cheeks. She let them fall and gather at the base of her chin before accepting the tissue Jewel offered.

Jewel cupped her daughter's face and held eye contact and pleaded, "Let me help you, baby. I don't know exactly what you're involved in, but I know you're in over your head. I sheltered you, and you are no match for the enemy, especially with the grudge you have against God. The enemy is dragging you down, and he's not going to stop until he completely destroys you. Please talk to me. The woman I picked up yesterday is not the beautiful woman I gave birth to. You are so much more than a drunk."

Reyna's steady breaths turned into gasps as sobs obstructed her air supply. Breaking down in front of the woman she'd conditioned herself to hate was the last thing she wanted to do, but Jewel had transformed into what Reyna desperately needed: a mother who knew her child. Her mouth moved, but the words lodged in her throat.

"It's all right, baby," Jewel coaxed. "You can tell me. I promise I won't judge you."

Reyna didn't know if she could trust her mother or not, but her burdens had become unbearable. Even if Jewel wasn't sincere, at least Reyna wouldn't be carrying the load in silence.

She collapsed against Jewel's shoulder and poured out the story of the past six months of her life, including the night she lost her virginity. She revealed everything: the physical and verbal abuse, chopping her car, and the seduction scene two nights ago. The details of Peyton's courting and how his subsequent drug use led her to drinking were the most embarrassing, but how she allowed him to destroy Tyson's property hurt the most. She put it all out there, even admitting that she actually cared about Tyson but had pushed him away.

Jewel held her and listened without interruption, wiping away her own tears and interceding in prayer for her daughter.

"My life is a mess, and I'm about to lose my job. I can't make things right with Tyson if I don't have a job."

The tears continued to fall, but Reyna's spirit felt lighter now that she had admitted the truth.

"Where is Peyton now? Is he still living with you?"

Reyna's head bobbed against her chest. "He's moving out today."

"Well, that's one less thing to worry about."

With her emotions empty, for the first time ever that she could recall, Reyna fell asleep in her mother's arms.

Chapter 28

Reyna stopped dead in her tracks, turned, ran to her old bedroom, and closed the door. She'd heard the voice, his voice. Tyson was there, in her mother's living room, discussing the Bible. Her mother had said he was coming by, and although she wanted to see him, she wasn't ready to see him. She needed time to come up with a plan to put her life in order.

She leaned against the closed door and caught her reflection in the dresser mirror. She gasped; Tyson couldn't see her like this. Not with her hair sticking up every which way. He'd seen her plenty of times without makeup. In fact, he preferred her not to wear it. Never had he seen her in tattered leggings and a bleach-stained T-shirt.

She rummaged through the drawers and closet in search of something, anything, she'd left behind to piece together an outfit. She found a long blue jean skirt, a remnant from her "holy" days, and a brown sweater top that tied on the side. The outfit was bland, but it would have to work with the black sandaled heels she'd been wearing when her mother picked her up at the real estate office. After changing, she took a scarf from her mother's room and wrapped it around her head like an African head wrap. Just before slipping into the heels, she applied baby powder to prevent her feet from sweating.

She closed Jewel's bedroom door without checking the mirror. She knew the look didn't make a fashion statement, but this was the best she could do with limited resources.

When Reyna entered the living room, Tyson stopped mid-sentence in the conversation he was having with Jewel. "Hey, beautiful," he said, standing to his feet.

Reyna snickered, and said, "You're either blind or have cataracts if you think I'm beautiful in this getup."

Jewel quietly watched Tyson walk over to her daughter and rest his hands on her shoulders.

"This is a vast improvement from the drool and snot you had last night. Did you know you sleep with your mouth open?" Tyson said.

Reyna hadn't expected the merriment coming from her anal friend. The jeans and loafers were totally out of character. *Mylan must be good for you,* she thought, but replied, "How does Malee feel about you spending all your time with a crazed tenant?"

"Jealous, are we?" He chuckled and then pulled her in for an embrace. "Are you all right? I was worried sick about you after Paige called."

Reyna didn't want to be embraced, but at that moment she needed his comfort. Besides, he smelled good. She had expected his arms to warm her on the outside, but she hadn't anticipated the throbbing in her heart when his muscular arms enclosed her.

"I'm so sorry for not being there for you," he said after releasing her too soon. "When you showed up at the office, I knew something wasn't right. I should have made time for you. I should have followed you at the restaurant."

Tyson's sincerity, reflected in those hazel eyes, drew her in like a magnet. She wondered how apologetic he'd be once he saw the condition of the town house.

"And ruin Mah-jong's surprise picnic and dinner? I don't think that would have worked out well for you. That girl looks like she knows karate," Reyna said to lighten the mood. She didn't want him taking responsibility for the mess she'd created. "Seriously, she's beautiful," she added when he smiled. "You look good together."

Tyson opened his mouth as if to say something but didn't, and her heart sank. Not that she actually expected him to tell her the relationship was over, but it would have been nice.

"Reyna, you've been cooped up in this house all day. Tyson, why don't you take her out for some fresh air?" Jewel suggested from the couch. "Since she's all dressed up and everything."

Reyna felt like kissing her mother for butting into her business. A second longer and Reyna would have been in tears for what could have been.

"That's a good idea," Reyna answered, clearing her throat. "Let me get my purse." She turned to retreat to her old room, but Tyson stopped her.

"Sweetheart, are you sure you're up to it?"

I am so stupid. What have I done? her head screamed when she looked up at him. Whether he knew it or not, Tyson's eyes reflected his emotions. When he was angry, charcoal flecks danced around his pupils. Happiness presented amber and light brown hues. She'd never witnessed the dark green hue now boring down on her, but her intuition told her it was love. Tyson really cared. Why couldn't I read Peyton like that? she wondered.

Because you didn't want to, her conscience answered back.

"I think some air will do me some good. Besides, there's something I need to tell you," she said, referring to the news of her real father. "I'm fine," she assured him.

Jewel followed her down the hall to her bedroom, whispering, "Tell him the truth, the whole truth. It'll set you free."

Reyna sat on a bench beside Tyson at Lake Temescal in the Oakland Hills. The secluded tranquility was just what she needed to lift her spirits. Twice on the drive over depression had nearly consumed her. Ironically, both times when she felt herself going under, Tyson had said something to distract her.

"So, I guess Paige told you everything," Reyna finally said after watching a fisherman reel in a medium-sized catfish.

Tyson extended his hand, and she accepted it. "All Paige said was that you weren't yourself and that I should check on you as soon as possible. Your mother filled in the blanks. What I want to know from you is what's driving you to drink." Her hand shook uncontrollably, and he drew closer to her. "Reyna, what is it?"

It took her over twenty minutes to get it out, but she relayed the circumstances surrounding her conception without breaking down. "All this time I've been grieving for the wrong man. That's the story of my life—going after men who don't want me."

He squeezed her hand. "I'm sorry you had to suffer that, but at least now you know the truth."

"The truth hurts too much. At least the lie gave me hope," she replied and snickered, although she failed to see the humor.

"It won't always hurt. Your earthly father may not know you exist, but your Heavenly Father knows where you are. He knows everything about you, and He loves you unconditionally."

She snatched her hand away, but not as forcefully as in the past. "Please, not now. I can't deal with God and 'em right now."

A bird hunting for food captured their attention in the silence that followed.

"You didn't find out until that evening at Zachary's. What did you come to my office to tell me?"

Leave it to a lawyer to pay attention to details. Reyna changed the subject. "Manglee must really have you twisted if she got you to come out of those tailored suits and into jeans. Don't think I didn't notice those khakis the other day. That woman deserves sainthood for changing you."

"First of all," he began with a bit of amusement, "it's Mylan, but you already know that."

Reyna playfully rolled her eyes and smacked her lips.

"She didn't change me. I'm still the same person. The only difference is I'm finally comfortable in my own skin. Mylan had nothing to do with the changes you've mentioned. You can thank the Honorable Fredrick Stokes for that."

"I don't understand."

"I almost feel guilty about sharing this now, considering what you're going through," he said, digressing. "I'm sorry if this upsets you, but my father and I have established a relationship. We're actually friends."

Reyna took note of the smile playing around his beard and feigned happiness with a smile of her own while he shared the details of their reconciliation. "That's wonderful. I'm happy for you."

"We talk daily and hang out often. Mylan and I even went on a double date with my parents to the symphony."

The smile faded. She'd met his parents only once, at Kevin and Marlissa's vow renewal. They were cordial, at the very least.

"I'm happy for you. Miss Mylan is just perfect. She'll make you a good wife," she lied. "What?" she asked when the charcoal flecks flashed.

"Honesty is important to me in any kind of relationship."

Her abdominal muscles tightened involuntarily.

"You don't mean that, but you're right. Mylan will make the right man an excellent wife someday, but I'm not that man," he revealed. "Don't pretend like you're disappointed," he added when she gasped, "because you're not."

She closed her mouth and looked away and held on to the bench to keep from jumping up and doing a celebratory dance.

"I know the suspense is killing you. Go on and ask me how I can be so sure she's not the one for me."

Reyna's determination to prove him wrong lasted less than thirty seconds. Her fists pounded her lap. "Ugh! I hate it when you're right." She faced him. "What happened?"

"She broke up with me after Zachary's."

"She broke up with you?" Reyna thought the idea ridiculous, yet she'd been foolish enough not to give the man a chance. "Why would she do that?"

Tyson's facial expression didn't change, but she could tell a war raged in his head. His eye color changed twice.

"She ended the relationship once she realized my heart wasn't in it."

"You seemed pretty captivated to me. You kicked me to the curb, negated me down to an appointment slot. Not that I'm jealous or anything, but when she walked

in, you started lip-locking like I wasn't in the room."
She thought he'd find humor in her comment, but his
anal side resurfaced.

"It was just a peck, and you don't really want to go
there. I never kicked you to the curb. You sat yourself
there. All I have ever tried to do is help you, but . . ." He
let the statement hang.

"Ouch!" She believed Tyson would never hit her, but
he was an expert at slapping her in the face by being
blunt. "I'm sorry. I shouldn't have pushed you away,"
she finally admitted to him. "I made a mistake." She
expected him to confirm her assertion, but he didn't.

"Reyna, do you trust me?"

"Of course I do."

"Then tell me what's going on. I know you. It's more
than the news about your father. I can see it in your
eyes. You came to my office to tell me something. What
is it?"

She turned away, but gentle hands touched her chin
and steered her head back.

"Please tell me. I can handle anything as long as
you're truthful."

Reyna opened her mouth and bit her lip several times
as she struggled with right and wrong. Sure, telling
Tyson about Peyton was the right thing to do, but if he
turned on her, that would be wrong. And he would turn
on her, once she revealed how she betrayed the trust
he'd placed in her when he offered his home. Peyton
had done the damage, but she'd allowed it to go on far
too long. And just how was she supposed to tell him that
she'd probably lost the job he helped her find and that
she was now broke and could no longer afford the below
market rent he offered. If only she'd told him that day
at his office, they could have worked out a repayment
agreement.

"Can we eat first?" The words trickled out more like a plea than a question.

In resignation, Tyson released her and hung his head. Reyna bowed her head also and prayed he wouldn't give up on her. When Reyna realized what she was doing, her head snapped back up. Determined not to beg God for anything, she turned her attention to the waterfall.

"What do you have a taste for?" he asked after a prolonged silence.

"Well," she said, scooting closer to him, "if it's not too much trouble, I'd love one of your famous Philly cheesesteak sandwiches and homemade fries." She paused. "Please," she added when he continued to stare. "I'll peel the potatoes and cut the peppers and onions."

A smile lacking brilliance creased his beard. "If that's what it takes to get you to talk, no problem. We'll have to stop at the store first for groceries to take back to your mother's house. Or, if you want to eat in the comfort of home, we can cook at your place."

"No," she blurted. "I mean, I'm not ready to go back to Mother's just yet. Let's go to your place and have dinner on the patio. The weather is perfect, and I like watching you move around that gourmet kitchen."

It sounded lame, but that was the best she could come up with to keep him away from the town house.

Tyson's hazel eyes squinted, then relaxed. "Fine, but you should call your mother and let her know you'll be out late."

Reyna snickered and rolled her eyes. "As long as I'm with you, she doesn't care if I ever come back."

Chapter 29

"Yum, this is so good!" Reyna declared, with strings of melted provolone and Muenster cheese hanging from her chin. "This meat is so tender, I could eat this every day." Not bothering with a napkin, Reyna used her fingers to peel the gooey delight from her chin, then savored it before devouring another bite of the sandwich.

Tyson shook his head at the irony of it all. He and Reyna had worked together on every aspect of preparing dinner, from grocery shopping to setting the patio table. Although she'd been inside his home only a handful of times, Reyna had moved around his kitchen with ease, storing food in cabinets and the pantry and prepping food. They'd worked in sync, with little conversation required. She'd questioned him only when she couldn't locate the casual dinnerware. "I should have known," she'd said when he informed her he didn't own any, but if she would select a set, he'd purchase it. She'd smiled and proceeded to set the patio table with china.

Judging by the peaceful atmosphere, it was as if they'd always been together, but they weren't together, and Tyson doubted they ever would be.

All weekend his heart and mind had battled over his feelings for Reyna. His heart embodied the love he possessed for her, but logical thinking told him to move on. In church on Sunday he'd prayed for direction with

Reyna—something he'd stopped doing months ago—
but he didn't get an answer right then.

He took Paige's urgent call Monday morning as a
sign, of what, he wasn't sure. Then Jewel had called,
and everything became clear. He had to help Reyna,
but he hadn't figured out how. Although now she was
more receptive to him, she was still pushing him away.
Mylan's discernment of Reyna's feelings for him, combined with Reyna's fit of jealousy, had left him with
a minuscule amount of hope. However, Reyna had
crushed those hopes when she refused to level with
him.

The Reyna seated across from him, licking cheese
from her fingers, wasn't the same headstrong, know-
it-all woman he'd chased down Kevin's hill six months
ago. He often wondered if anyone else had noticed
the natural glow on her face. Whenever she entered a
room, she brought sunshine. The thick layer of makeup
she insisted on wearing dimmed the illumination for
him, but she still radiated.

Today, without makeup, her natural beauty ap-
pealed to him, but the glow had vanished. He had noticed the second she entered the living room at Jewel's
house, and every time he had looked at her since. She
smiled and laughed with him, but depression clouds
and rainstorms blocked her sunshine. Her vibrancy
and drive were depleted. Fresh emotional wounds
commingled with old ones had built a fortress to keep
her spirit bound. Something or someone had devalued
her and had caused her to lose self-confidence and to
find solace in a bottle. Before driving her back home,
he planned to use every litigation tactic he had to make
her talk.

"Would you like me to make you another one?" he
offered after she'd taken the last bite of her sandwich.

"No, but I'll trade you a fry for a bite of yours," she said, waving a fry in his face.

He slid his plate over. "You don't have to bribe me for anything. Just ask for what you want, and it's yours."

Her left hand shook slightly, and her eyes blinked rapidly. Something else new that he noticed. She seemed nervous and fearful, but she put up a good front.

"I see your anality is back," she teased and slid the potato into her mouth, then reached for the remaining half of his sandwich.

He allowed her to eat in peace, but the second she washed the last bite down with lemonade, the interrogation began.

"Leave them," he instructed when she stood to clear the table. "I'll do them later, or the housekeeper will take care of it in the morning." He stood and reached for her hand. "We need to talk." He didn't miss the fear masking her face when she timidly accepted his hand and followed him inside to the den. Instead of sitting side by side with her on the sofa, he directed her to the lounge chair. Wanting to concentrate on her every word and move, he sat on the ottoman in front of her. He waited for her to begin. After several minutes of watching her play with the belt on her sweater, he initiated the conversation.

"Reyna, sweetheart, talk to me," he said in his most nonthreatening tone. "What's going on? You know you can tell me anything, and I promise I won't judge you. I know you think I have in the past, but that wasn't judgment. I spoke out of frustration because I wanted so much more for you than what you were settling for. I wanted . . ." He stopped before he turned the focus away from the present. "Just tell me why you came to my office. What did you want to tell me?"

She ceased playing with the belt and wrung her hands. "Can I have some tissues?"

"Don't move," he said and backed off the ottoman. Hope stirred when he returned from the bathroom and found her still there.

She accepted the Kleenex box from him but waited until he had repositioned himself on the ottoman before she spoke.

"My life is a mess, and I don't know what to do about it. You were right. It's more than my mother's confession about my real father. It's strange, but that may have brought us closer together."

Tyson started to ask how but didn't want to interrupt her now that she had opened up.

"Since I last saw you, I've made some bad decisions. I was so determined to prove my mother, you, Pastor Jennings, and everybody else wrong, I dwelled in a fantasy world I created with people that weren't real. I gambled, and I lost everything, including part of myself." Her voice lowered to a whisper. "Drinking numbs the pain and gives me an escape. When I'm drunk, I don't have to face the truth that I don't have anything. I lost it all. My car is gone, and my credit cards are maxed out. I'm sure Paige is going to fire me, and soon you'll evict me, because I can't pay you."

"Hold on," he said, lifting her chin. "I don't know about Paige, but I'm not going to evict you." At least he could ease one of her worries. "You can stay in the town house as long as you want rent free."

"No, I already owe you more than I can pay," she blurted, then quickly added, "I mean, you were already taking a loss by charging below market rent."

He massaged her shaking hands. "Relax. The town house is paid for. I use the rent to cover the taxes and HOA fees. The rest I save. Stay as long as you need to."

"Thank you," she mouthed. Sniffles accompanied the tears that trailed down her cheeks, and she allowed him to wipe the tears away with a tissue.

Tyson needed more details. "Is the white guy you were hugged up with at Skates one of the fake people you're referring to?" *Bull's-eye,* he thought when her jaw dropped and her breath caught in her throat. He didn't miss the fear in her eyes, either.

"How d-did you f-find out about Peyton?" she stuttered.

"Peyton. So that's his name." Tyson kept the invidious comments that surfaced in his mind to himself. "I didn't find out anything. The night my father and I connected, we ate dinner at Skates. I saw the two of you there, but you were too busy giving him a lap dance to notice me."

"I did no such thing," she said in her own defense. "I've been liberated, but not to the point of—"

"Okay," he interrupted, not wanting her to get off track. "You weren't lap dancing, but you were practically sitting on his lap. So is he part of your fantasy world?"

"Yes." Her head dropped. "He earned the top awards for best actor and director."

His heart constricted as images of the horrible things the man might have done to Reyna flashed before him. Even at a distance the man had looked shady to him.

"Are you still seeing him?" He had to know. "Is he still part of your life, fantasy or real?"

Her head shook laterally several times before the answer came forth. "No. I'm done."

"Are you seeing anyone else?"

"No."

Tyson released the breath he'd been holding. At least there wasn't a third party involved; still, he couldn't

shake the feeling that Reyna was holding something
back.

"How did you feel about me before that night?" she
asked.

The question caught him by surprise, and he was uncertain how to answer. "What do you mean?"

She leaned forward and for the first time made eye
contact. "Level with me. What were your real feelings for me? We were once close friends. I know you
cared about me, but to what extent? In the past you
dropped hints, but you said nothing concrete. I probably wouldn't have listened back then, but I'm listening
now. How much did you care?"

He leaned forward with his elbows perched on his
knees, contemplating how to respond. How could he
answer the question without revealing how much he
still cared? On a regular basis he trained clients on
how to answer questions without giving up too much
information. The time had come for him to follow his
own advice.

"I cared a lot. When I walked into the restaurant that
night, I was in love with you."

She gasped and covered her mouth, then fell back in
the chair.

"However, when I exited, I accepted that you didn't
see me that way and would never feel the same. That
night I started the process of releasing you from my
heart." He released a sigh of relief, thinking he'd dodged
a bullet.

"What about now? How do you feel now? Were you
successful in removing me from your heart?" She held
her open palms up. "Think about it before you answer,
and please don't lie to me. I don't trust my own judgment anymore, and I'm leery of most people. I don't

trust my mind or heart to decipher what's real from what's fantasy. People have lied to me and have fed me pipe dreams so they could take from me, but with you it's different. Everyone else takes from me, but not you. You freely give to me, knowing I can't give you anything in return." The tears and shaking returned. "Please, tell me how you feel. If you care about me, tell me. I need to hear it. Tell me. I'm listening, and I'll believe you. I just need to know, as messed up as I am, that I'm worth loving. That I'm not worthless and stupid—"

"Stop! You're not stupid." His heart couldn't take any more. The self-preservation wall tumbled down, and he fell from the ottoman to his knees, collecting her hands.

"It didn't work," he admitted audibly for the first time. "As hard as I tried, it wouldn't go away. Mylan's good looks and sensitivity couldn't touch what I feel for you. Thank God she had enough sense to send me packing before I ruined our lives by substituting her for you." He squeezed her hands. "I do love you, but in all honestly, it feels like a death sentence, because you won't let me love you. You would rather manipulate and reject me than open up to me. You insist on settling for mediocrity when you can have and be so much more. You're a daughter of the king, and you deserve the best, but you refuse to receive the gift the Father wants to give you through Him and through me."

He closed his eyes and emptied his lungs. The burden of internalizing the pain her rejection had caused weighed heavier on him than he'd thought. Her serene countenance surprised him, but not as much as the touch of her fingertips caressing his beard.

"People change," she whispered before pressing her lips against his.

If his confession hadn't left him open and vulnerable, Tyson would have broken the sensual exchange. Instead, he pulled her closer and deepened the kiss, and when she gripped his head and pressed him closer to her, he returned the favor by releasing the scarf concealing her unkempt hair.

"Don't," she moaned against his lips when he pulled at the scarf. "I look a mess."

"You're beautiful with or without chemicals," he mumbled against her neck as the scarf cascaded to the floor. He assumed the truthful words pleased Reyna, because her tongue slid deeper into his mouth and her hands tugged at the buttons on his shirt. He cried out when her soft fingertips found and massaged his pectorals, and he lost control.

When Tyson finally regained control of his mind and body, Reyna lay beneath him in his bed, moving in sync.

Reyna imagined she resembled a mental ward escapee, lying there giggling and crying at the same time, with her "overdue for a perm" hair standing all over her head. What was she to do? Euphoria and bliss saturated her being, and for the first time she knew what it felt like to be loved by a man. Tyson did love her and not just with words. With his thorough lovemaking, he'd cherished her and touched her soul, giving her the gift of womanhood.

"Are you sorry?" He asked the question while kissing away both her happy and regretful tears.

"Sorry that I didn't save myself for you," she answered honestly. Chase and Peyton didn't deserve her. "Are you sorry? I mean, what we did is contrary to your lifestyle. I'm not very good at it, but hopefully, I wasn't too bad." She let out softer nervous giggles in anticipation of his answer.

The dark green hue returned to his eyes and a warm smile parted his beard, causing her heart to jolt.

"No, sweetheart, I'm not sorry. I love you, and you're perfect for me." He leaned down and brushed her lips with his own. "But I can't condone what we did. As wonderful as it was, the act was contrary to God's will, and I failed to protect you. Are you on the pill?"

The giggles ceased. She wasn't on the pill, and her supply of condoms was at home. "No."

He rolled onto his back and mumbled something Reyna interpreted as a desperate prayer. Fresh tears threatened to fall as she felt him withdrawing from her emotionally. She bit her lip and prepared for the worst.

He braced himself on his elbow and turned her chin toward him. "Please forgive me for placing you in this predicament. If I impregnated you, promise me you'll have the baby, even if you don't want it. All you have to do is have it, and I'll take it from there," he pleaded. "Promise you won't have an abortion, even if you don't want me."

From his desperate plea, Reyna sensed Tyson had his own demons to contend with. "If it comes to that, of course, I'll have your baby." For her the request was a no-brainer. Relief washed over his countenance, and she stroked his beard with the back of her hand. "Just so you know, I do want you in my life and not only as my friend, but . . ." She paused to search for the right words.

"But there's still more you need to tell me," he said, finishing for her.

She nodded. "There is. And I will tell you very soon. I just need to take care of some details first," she said, thinking she needed to make sure Peyton had left the premises before giving Tyson the grand tour of the depressed remnants of his town house. "There's still that issue of being unequally yoked. I'm not sure if I'm ready to go back to religion and legalism."

He snuggled closer. "Considering I just finished committing fornication and would probably do it again if I had a condom . . ."

She jarred his side.

"Hey, I'm just being honest." He chuckled, then sobered. "I may not be the best witness right now, but try to receive what I'm saying. God doesn't desire the religion or legalism you grew up in. What He wants from us is a relationship. God is a loving father who loves us past our faults. Although I'm disappointed in myself, my actions tonight didn't surprise Him. He's not pleased, but He loves me and is waiting to extend grace and mercy. God loves Him some Reyna Mills. There is nothing you can do to make Him stop loving you, because there is nothing you did to make Him start loving you. There isn't a sin He won't forgive you for. You'll run out of sins before He runs out of grace and mercy."

He lifted her chin. "I believe God has been speaking to your heart already and your resolve is dissolving."

She buried her face against his chest, refusing to confirm or deny the call.

Chapter 30

Kevin's whistle pierced the solace of Tyson's office after his friend shared relevant details of the previous night. As best friends and accountability partners, when they fell, they confided in one another and restored one another.

"I guess this means the two of you worked through your communication issues," Kevin teased.

"Whatever, man. I feel bad enough. I can do without your jokes."

"I couldn't help it. You were in such denial, I thought you'd never come around. Less than a week ago, you were still talking that 'love comes later' marriage foolishness with Mylan. What happened?"

Tyson smirked. "As always, Reyna's drama happened, and I had to be there for her."

Kevin's eyebrow shifted. "Really? You just had to be the one?"

"Man, you saw how messed up she was the other night at her mother's house, so fragile and helpless."

Kevin helped himself to Tyson's supply of Reese's. "The purpose of these sessions is for restoration. That can't happen if the party in question isn't truthful. Attorney Stokes, do I need to remind you, you're under oath?"

Tyson threw up his hands. "All right. When she came to my office, I knew then I wasn't over her. Okay, I was relieved when Mylan dumped me. I love Reyna, and I *wanted* to be there for her. I wanted to make love to her. I just didn't mean for it to happen this way."

Kevin tossed the candy wrapper into the trash and reached for another peanut butter cup. "I assume you confessed your love before you hit the sheets?"

"I'm not like you," Tyson answered, referring to when Kevin had held Marlissa in limbo.

Kevin shrugged off the jab for the stall tactic it was.

"That's what got me in trouble. She asked me how I felt, and I started singing like a canary," Tyson revealed. The two laughed. "Man, she had me so messed up, I didn't even think about a condom. It wasn't like I had one lying around, anyway."

Kevin stopped laughing and whistled again. "Whoa, man. No condom?"

"It gets worse." Tyson went on to explain how he had begged Reyna not to abort his child if she got pregnant.

Kevin sat contemplatively. "What's next? Does she share your feelings?"

With everything in him, Tyson wanted to answer in the affirmative. He wanted Reyna to love him so much. This morning he convinced himself she did, although she hadn't expressed the sentiment. She had admitted she desired more than friendship.

"I believe she does, but she doesn't trust herself. Plus, she's hiding something from me. This latest episode has depleted her self-esteem and confidence." He saw that Kevin was staring at him. "I know. Sleeping with her didn't help," he interjected when Kevin opened his mouth. "In fact, it may have caused more harm than good," he admitted sadly. "But she needed me. No. I needed her. Actually, we needed each other."

Kevin stood and extended his hand. "Both of you need the Father's help."

Tyson bowed his head and joined his friend in intercession.

More than giggles bubbled out of Reyna as she drove into the subdivision; she was also singing "Baby, it's you." She couldn't remember the last time a happy tune had flowed from her without the aid of alcohol. She was high, all right, but she'd traded in her old boyfriend vodka for a king-sized order of TFS: Tyson Fitzgerald Stokes. Like the words to Beyoncé's song on the radio, Tyson put her "love on top."

What she had been longing for was right in her face. If only she'd listened to Tyson that day on the hill, she wouldn't have wasted her energy and resources on a loser like Peyton. She'd long ago acknowledged that she didn't love Peyton, never had, but had craved the attention. She didn't wish Peyton well, just gone.

Reyna parked Tyson's old BMW in the driveway and turned off the engine—glad she had accepted his offer to use it as a loaner until she could purchase a new car. Actually, he had offered to buy her a car, but she had flatly refused. Before leaving for the office, he'd packed her a Philly cheesesteak to go, which she ate for breakfast, then kissed her forehead.

She exited the vehicle. "God, I love that man," she squealed as the sudden awareness cleared a path to a hidden truth. "Oh, my God, I love him," she repeated countless times while hugging her body. "I've loved him for a long time." She bubbled over with joy. "And he loves me," she sang before skipping to the front door.

She paused before unlocking the front door and looked upward. She hadn't seen Peyton since chasing him and Laci with the poker. "Okay, God and 'em, I'm trying to do the right thing. I'd appreciate it if the dope fiend is gone."

With caution she entered the town house. Quiet and a musty odor greeted her, but no Peyton. "Thank y'all," she said, looking upward.

Relief and joy settled over her completely once she walked through every room and found no sign of Peyton or his handful of belongings. His travel bags were gone, and so were Tyson's coffee table and Persian rugs. The remaining artwork and wall coverings were also gone. He did leave a sink full of dirty dishes and an empty refrigerator as souvenirs.

Too happy to dwell on Peyton's antics, she simply sprayed air freshener throughout the house and cracked open some windows. It was Wednesday, the day to start a new chapter in her life. She started by tidying up what remained of the furnishings and making a list of damaged and missing items. She abandoned the notion that she could ever compensate Tyson, even if they settled on a twenty-year plan. Peyton had stolen or damaged over one hundred thousand dollars in merchandise, in addition to punching several holes in the walls.

By noon she was ready for a long hot bubble bath—a luxury she hadn't indulged in since the drinking increased. Afraid she'd fall asleep in the tub and drown while under the influence, she'd opted for showers.

Inside the master bathroom, she ran bathwater and poured in jasmine-scented bubble bath. She noticed the lit message light on the answering machine on the way from the master bathroom to the laundry hamper. She stopped and pressed the play button, hoping to hear Tyson's voice. Neither of the two messages were from him, but they gave her more reasons to celebrate.

"Reyna, it's me, your mother. Just calling to see how the night went. If you need me, call me."

Reyna had called Jewel on the way from shopping with Tyson to say he would take her home after dinner. She'd lied, because that's what Tyson offered, but she hadn't planned to spend the night in Tyson's arms. When she'd made the call, she had every intention of having Tyson take her back to Jewel's, and then having Jewel take her home—anything to keep Peyton and Tyson from crossing paths.

She deleted the message and waited for the next message.

"Hello, Reyna. This is Paige. I hope you're feeling better. I've been praying for you. The entire office has. I have decided not to terminate you on one condition." There was a pause. "I want you to enroll in an alcohol treatment program. Once you provide proof of enrollment, I'll allow you time off to attend classes, meetings, and counseling sessions. See you on Monday. Take care."

Reyna fell back onto the bed, kicking and screaming, "Thank you! God and 'em, y'all is all right with me today!"

Instead of deleting the message, she saved it to play back later for Tyson.

The bubble bath wasn't nearly as soothing as in times past. Too many thoughts of Tyson and how he'd bared his soul and made love to her disturbed the aromatherapy's calming effects. She wanted him in the tub with her for a repeat performance. After ten minutes, she rinsed off and put an end to her frustration.

For the first time in weeks, Reyna admired the image in the mirror. She was beautiful—half-processed hair and all. Reyna danced in the mirror as Beyoncé's beat filled her. "Baby, it's you," she sang while moisturizing her skin with jasmine body butter. She continued singing after slipping into her bathrobe and collecting more clothes for the laundry. When she checked the jean skirt pockets, the singing stopped, along with her heart. Inside the left pocket was a ten-thousand-dollar check from Tyson.

Sudden dread and shame engulfed and crippled her spirit as the revelation that she'd been used once again sucked the life from her. Although generous, Tyson had never given her money, and according to her reasoning, the only reason for him to secretly stuff money into her pocket now was to pay for services rendered—like Chase had. She didn't have the strength to stop the tears from falling, but she did, however, have more than enough anger and pride left to curse Tyson out. She stomped over and placed the check on the nightstand and then picked up the cordless phone with the intention of doing just that.

"Hey, sweetheart," he greeted when he answered his personal cell phone. "I was just thinking about you. I hope your day is going well."

She stalled; most of her bravado evaporated as his concern reached through the phone line and soothed her aching heart.

"Reyna, are you there?"

"No matter what you think, I'm not some trick," she blurted. "You can keep your money and your car."

"Whoa! Hold on. Where is this coming from?"

"I found your little check. You could have at least left it on the nightstand, instead of hiding how little you think of me in my pocket. I guess I wasn't so perfect for you, after all." She stopped before the depth of her pain poured out.

She heard heavy breathing on the other end and envisioned his face inflamed with a red hue and charcoal specks dancing in his eyes.

"Sweetheart," he said, his voice calm, "last night you said you were broke and had lost everything. The check isn't for services rendered. It's to help you get back on your feet. I tucked it into your pocket because you're too prideful to accept it outright. I care about you too much to let you struggle when I have the resources to help, but if accepting money from me offends you that much, tear up the check."

"Ouch," she mouthed.

"And for the record, sweetheart, there isn't a price tag big enough for what we shared last night."

Happy tears returned as she silently scolded herself for grouping him with a lying adulterer.

"Sorry for jumping to conclusions," she squealed into the phone. "I like that."

"You like what? The check?" He sounded confused.

"Hearing you call me sweetheart," she explained. "It sounds nice coming from you."

"Woman, you're an enigma I'll never figure out," he said after a moment.

Reyna sat on the bed. "But you love me, right?"

"Yes, I do. And this is one of those death sentence moments."

She laughed. "Thank you. You are so good to me."

"Not as good as I'd like to be."

She heard shuffling in the background.

"Sweetheart, I have to go. I'm scheduled for court in thirty minutes. Talk to you later."

"Wait," she yelled into the phone. "Can you come by this evening? We need to talk." *It can't get any worse. Might as well get it all out now,* she thought.

"Are we going to have the discussion we need to have, or are you going to put up another smoke screen?"

"I promise to put all the cards on the table. You should eat before you get here. More than likely you'll be angry and lose your appetite once I you hear what I have to say," she said nervously.

"Sweetheart, as long as we're honest with one another, we can work through anything."

She sat motionless, pondering those words long after ending the call, until she heard a noise from the hallway. Before she could stand, Peyton appeared at the threshold, holding her purse.

Chapter 31

Peyton barged into the bedroom and stomped over to the bed. "Where have you been? I've been waiting two days for you. Whose car is that outside?"

His faded jeans and T-shirt were dirty, and his breath reeked. She rolled her eyes and scooted away from him. "The better question is, what are *you* doing here? Yesterday was your deadline. Now, give me my key and leave." She pointed toward the door.

"And just where am I supposed to go?" he asked sarcastically.

"That's not my problem," she smarted. "You're a grown man. Figure it out. What happened to your girlfriend, Laci?" she smirked. "See if she'll let you live in her minivan for a while."

"I don't have time for your stupid comedy routine. I need some money. Laci's husband got suspicious and cut off her cash flow."

"Smart man."

"I've been waiting for your sorry behind to get back here because I need some stuff. Where's the money?" he barked after throwing the empty purse on the bed. "Ain't nothing in there, but I know you got some money somewhere."

Reyna leaned over and reached under the bed but didn't feel what she needed.

"Looking for something? You got me the first time, but I'm not as stupid as you. I got rid of your little weapon. Now, where is the money?"

The sinister smile he offered her made the hair on the back of her neck stand up. She swallowed her fear and jumped up in his face. "Idiot, I don't have any money. You and your cokehead girlfriend snorted every dime I had."

"Whose BMW is that?" he barked again.

"Mine," she lied. "Now, get out before I call the police."

"You ain't calling nobody!" He grabbed the phone from the nightstand and threw it across the room. "Hey, what's this?"

Reyna watched in dread as Tyson's check floated to the floor.

"You little liar," he said after picking up the check. "If I didn't need you to cash this check, I'd ring your neck. I knew you were holding out. That's his car outside, too."

Reyna opened her mouth to refute his charge, but Peyton raised his hand to striking position and she backed down.

"Before you lie again, I already checked the glove compartment. The car is registered to the same T. F. Stokes. You little slut. You couldn't wait for me to leave before starting to kick it with another dude. At least you got some money out of it. You paid me to be with you." His laugh sounded more like a howl. "Get your sorry behind up and get dressed so I can get my money."

Reyna shook her head as if to clear it. She couldn't have heard him correctly. Did this fool really think he was going to get another dime out of her? She tightened the belt on her robe and planted her fists at her waist. "I may not be the sharpest pencil in the box, but you're dumber than dumb if you think I'm going to waltz into a bank and hand you ten thousand dollars to stick up your nose." She snatched the check from him and ripped it in half. The last thing she heard before Peyton's backhand sent her tumbling to the floor was him likening her to a stupid female dog.

"I should have snapped your neck." His voice took on an evil hoarseness she hadn't heard before.

Slightly dazed, Reyna pulled up her legs and crawled across the bedroom toward the door to get away from him. If she could get down the stairs, she'd make it out the front door. Her knees didn't carry her fast enough, and Peyton caught her from behind and pulled her up by her hair.

"Who do you think you are, messing with my money like that? I need my stuff." He turned her so she faced him. "Call and tell him to get over here with more money, or we'll pick it up."

Excruciating pain pierced her head and his halitosis nauseated her, but she'd die before placing Tyson in danger. An adrenaline rush fueled her fear, and she used every ounce of energy to get her point across. "No! Beat me if you want, but I'm not calling anyone, and I'm not going anywhere. I will not allow your worthless behind to take—"

"So you think I'm worthless? You think you're better than me now?" He dragged her back to the bed and threw her facedown on it. "I'll show you what worthless feels like," he growled, then parted her legs and grabbed her in a choke hold from behind.

He sodomized her before she could mentally escape to Disneyland. Agonizing pain tore through her body, but she refused to give him the satisfaction of seeing her shed another tear for him. "God, please," she whimpered and bit her tongue to keep from crying out.

After causing as much pain as possible, Peyton pulled away, flipped her over on her back, and continued stripping her of her dignity while cursing and demeaning her until he relieved himself and climbed off of her.

Throughout the ordeal Reyna didn't mumble a word, but internally cries of despair poured from her heart. She had nothing left as new emotional wounds mingled with old ones and crushed her spirit. Determined not to cry, she sucked back the lump at the back of her throat, slid off the bed, and retied the belt on her bathrobe, which had come untied during the altercation. "I will not cry. I will not cry," she whispered as she somberly walked out of the bedroom, leaving Peyton at the dresser, trying to salvage the check with tape.

Mechanically, she walked into the kitchen and reunited with an old faithful friend. She gulped vodka straight from the bottle until her head throbbed so much, she could no longer hold it up. She staggered over and collapsed on the couch and willed herself to die. If she drank fast enough, just maybe she'd be lucky enough to die from alcohol poisoning.

Two swigs later she noticed the second cordless phone handset stuffed between the cushions. Without looking at the keypad, Reyna punched in the numbers that at one time she'd tried hard to forget.

Jewel answered on the third ring. "Hello."

She took another swig before answering. "Ma," she breathed into the phone.

"Reyna? What's wrong?"

She heard the worry in Jewel's voice and regretted making the call. She didn't even know why she'd made the call in the first place.

"Reyna!" Jewel yelled into the phone. "Are you all right?"

Tremors rocked her as she fought to maintain her composure. "No, Mother. I'm not all right."

"What—"

Before Jewel finished the question, Peyton came up from behind. "You trying to call the police on me?" he accused and snatched the phone. "I already have two strikes. I'll kill you before I let you do that."

Too much information too late, she thought between gulps of Vodka but didn't speak it. "That was my mother, you moron."

"Look." He held up the restored check. "This just might work. The account number is still intact. You can tell them, you accidently ripped it and taped it together so you wouldn't lose the pieces. Go get dressed so we can make it to the bank before closing."

She wiped her mouth with the back of her hand. "I'm not going anywhere, physically," she answered, hoping to die soon.

"Get your stupid—" The doorbell interrupted Peyton's tirade. "Are you expecting someone?" He eyed her suspiciously, then stomped to the door.

"No," she answered and raised the bottle again. Before the rim reached her lips, Tyson's voice emerged from the foyer.

Chapter 32

"What are you doing here?" she heard Tyson ask. The earlier trauma had caused her to forget she'd asked him to come over.

"I live here," Peyton smarted. "The question is, who are you, and what are you doing at my house?"

The anesthetic missed her lips, and the lukewarm liquid ran her down her chest. The bottle slipped from her fingertips and crashed to floor. Fear gripped her and pounded her chest. She jumped up and started for the door; she had to protect Tyson from this maniac. She'd never forgive herself if Tyson got hurt because of her foolishness. The throbbing in her head made her dizzy and caused her to stumble the remaining distance.

"Your house? You live here?" Tyson spat the questions just as Reyna stumbled around the corner, leaning against the wall for support. His attention turned to Reyna, and he ceased speaking.

The look of disgust and repulsion on his face sapped what little strength she had. The man who loved her came bearing roses and food, and she greeted him with chaos. "It's not what you think," she whispered.

"Forget what I'm thinking," he said, more coldly than she'd ever heard him speak. "You should be more concerned with what I see."

It dawned on her then that she was naked under the bathrobe and reeked of alcohol. Peyton was shirtless, and his pants were unbuttoned.

"You were right, Reyna. Now that I've seen what you couldn't tell me yourself, I have lost my appetite." Tyson brushed past both of them and went into the kitchen and literally dumped the roses and food into the trash.

"Hey, you can't just walk up in my house," Peyton warned.

Tyson turned back to Reyna. "Aren't you going to introduce me to your boyfriend?"

It was a dare that Reyna shied away from. "It's not what you think," she repeated, avoiding eye contact.

Tyson faced Peyton. "It's Peyton, right? I'm Tyson Stokes, the landlord."

"Oh, God," Reyna groaned when Peyton's blue eyes danced with excitement. There was no way she could stop him from distorting everything, now that he knew the source of her sudden wealth.

"I wasn't aware you lived here, since Reyna never added you to the lease. How long have you lived in *my* house?" Tyson pressed on, much to Reyna's discomfort. "Are you employed?"

"What difference does it make? She pays the rent on time. So what? A few things are missing, but it's nothing your insurance won't cover," Peyton spat and then turned to Reyna. "Why didn't you tell me you were banging the landlord too? We could have been living rent free." He pointed at Tyson's wrist. "I told you the stuff I sold was no big deal. Look at that Rolex. He can afford it."

Tyson turned to Reyna. "What is he talking about?"

"I wanted to tell you," she slurred.

Filled with dread, Reyna watched Tyson walk around the main floor of what was once his home, as if seeing it for the first time. He touched the spot where an original painting had once hung, and inserted his fist into a hole in the wall. He went downstairs to his old office alone, and after what seemed like an eternity to Reyna, he returned and stood in the middle of the living room. Reyna waited for him to yell or scream, but he didn't say a word. Just stared at her through charcoal flecks.

Peyton interrupted the silent communication. "Since you're here, can you write out another check?" He held out the original one. "This one got torn by mistake."

"Either you're on something or you're the dumbest person in the world. Get that out of my face before you lose your arm," Tyson warned.

Reyna laughed as Peyton retreated like a scared puppy, a small vindication for what he'd done to her. The victory didn't last.

Tyson turned to her. "I could have forgiven you for anything if you had just been honest with me."

"I was going to tell you what Peyton did. That's why I wanted you to come over," she answered, stumbling over her words. "Then he showed up, and he—"

He pointed at Peyton and for the first time unleashed his anger on her. "This is not about that loser. This is about you and me. I gave you my heart and compromised my beliefs for you. And less than twenty-four hours later you're screwing someone else. I specifically asked you if you were involved with him, and not once did you mention you were living together and destroying my house."

She collapsed on the couch. "I promise I'll pay you back, somehow."

"Those are just things, Reyna! They can be replaced. You can't repay what I've invested in you." He pointed at his chest. "I believed in you when no one else did. I was there when no one else would come. I went out on a limb for you. I gave you everything, and you didn't have the decency to level with me."

She rocked back and forth. *I'm not going to cry.*

"I've never begged a woman to be with me, and it'll be a cold day in hell before I beg a coldhearted and self-centered woman like you again for a morsel of affection. I'm done."

"I thought you loved me." The words dripped out before she could stop them.

"Love," he smirked. "You don't know the definition of the word. Consider this your thirty-day notice. I want you and your trailer-trash boyfriend out of my house. I'll have the car picked up tomorrow. Outside of turning in your keys, I don't ever want to see or hear from you again." He turned to leave, then paused as if he'd remembered something. "Good-bye, Reyna."

She expected a door slam, but it never came. She heaved and shook but forbade tears to fall. *I'm not going to cry.* She rocked faster and gripped her stomach when she heard his tires screech, taking her heart with him. The expanding ache in her heart overpowered the throbbing in her head. *I'm not going to cry.*

Tyson was wrong; she did know the definition of *love.* He'd shown it to her and then broken her heart by not believing her. Sure, it looked bad, but Tyson should have known she wouldn't willingly be with another man after him. Even semi-drunk, she could see something was wrong with the scene he'd walked in on. Then again, she had been living with Peyton for almost four months and knew his antics.

"Give me the keys to the car. I have a run to make," Peyton demanded while standing over her.

Reyna rolled her eyes. "Get out of my face. I'm not giving you anything." Peyton had taken the last thing of value from her. Besides, she couldn't remember where she'd left the keys.

He yanked her up by her throat. "Give me the keys before I snap your neck."

A loud, quick boom blasted Reyna's eardrums and sent Peyton to the floor.

"That was a warning shot, but I promise you the next one won't miss."

Reyna whirled around, too stunned to speak. The sight of her mother cocking a gun left her speechless, and so did the crew standing in the doorway with her. Pastor Jennings held a baseball bat in striking position, Mother Scott brandished a switchblade, and First Lady Drake waved a pipe wrench. All of them had a shiny look, like they'd been smeared with Vaseline.

By the time Peyton got his bearings and raised up on his knees, Jewel was standing over him, pointing the barrel of the gun between his temples. "This ain't no toy, and I ain't playing a game. This is a thirty-eight snub-nose. Put your hands on my daughter again, and I'll brand your forehead with all five bullets before you can call on your Maker."

"And on the off chance that she misses, we'll beat you like the thief you are while she reloads," Pastor Jennings cosigned.

Peyton's olive skin burned crimson, but he didn't say a word.

"M-mama," Reyna stuttered. "When did you get a gun?"

"Always had one, baby," Jewel answered without taking her eyes off Peyton. "My grandfather was a marksman. He gave me my first gun for my sixteenth birthday and taught me how to shoot. I can hit a target a quarter mile away." She directed the conversation to Peyton, whose teeth chattered. "You're leaving this house today and never coming back. Either you can walk out or the coroner can roll you out. The choice is yours. You got five minutes to get your junk and get out of here."

"He don't need that long," Mother Scott said, pointing the switchblade. "I can tell he don't own nothing. Two minutes is all he needs to grab his stuff."

"You heard her. Now move!" Jewel ordered. "And you better not take anything that doesn't belong to you."

Peyton jumped up and ran to the hall closet.

Reyna blinked and refocused. She needed to spend more time with her mother; there was so much she didn't know. "How did you know . . . I mean, why did y'all come here?"

Jewel kept her eyes on her target. "I told you to call me if you needed me, and you did. We'd just ended our prayer session and were getting ready to head out to that new Chinese buffet when you called. When I heard him threaten to kill you, we grabbed our girls and headed on over."

"Girls?" Reyna questioned.

"Beulah, Louise, Silvia, and Roxy," the women answered one after the other, referring to their weapon of choice.

"But I never told you where I live."

"Rosalie got that information from Kevin a long time ago. I just let you think I didn't know because that's what you wanted," Jewel said.

Reyna shook her head as if to clear it. She couldn't have heard her mother correctly. "The pastor, the prayer warriors, and the pastor's wife carry weapons?"

"We put on the whole armor of God every day, but every now and then you need some tangible armor to take care of business," Pastor Jennings explained.

"We weren't born prayer warriors," Mother Scott added. "We all have a past, and I know I ain't forgot nothing. Besides, we're doing what Jesus would do. We're about to whip this thief out of this temple."

Reyna wanted to laugh but no longer had the energy. At some point she would ask when the four of them became buddies.

"Thirty seconds," First Lady Drake warned.

Peyton raced into the kitchen and opened the utility closet and pulled out a garbage bag and dumped his clothes inside it. He headed for the door, still shirtless, with the bag over his shoulder.

"Stop," Jewel called from behind. "Leave the key."

Without turning around to face the gun's barrel, Peyton complied. With shaky hands, he removed the key from the ring and set it on the table.

"Reyna, is there anything you want to say to him?" Jewel asked.

"Or do to him," Pastor Jennings added, holding out the bat to her.

Reyna shook her head. "No. I just want him gone." He had taken so much from her, his death wouldn't be enough to make retribution.

"Turn around," Jewel ordered Peyton. "I want you to see my face and Beulah's smile when I say this."

He obeyed.

"For the remainder of your natural life, you better not come within breathing distance of my daughter. If you do, I promise to carve your name on your body with bullets. When I get through, the only identifying marks left will be your fingertips. Do you understand me?"

"Y-y-yes," he stuttered.

"Now, turn around and run, just in case I change my mind and let Beulah loose."

The gang of women stood in the doorway, laughing at Peyton as he ran through the subdivision with that garbage bag over his shoulder.

Reyna watched the scene until she heard someone screaming. A piercing shrill followed by intense wailing echoed throughout the town house. It wasn't until she felt her mother's arms around her and heard the prayer warriors speaking in an unknown language that she realized the horrific sounds were coming from her. "God, help me," she opened her mouth to say, but only cries of agony would come out. Her fists swung and her legs kicked at beings that were visibly present in her mind, but not physically there.

Chapter 33

The sun's brilliance obscured Reyna's vision as the car traveled down Fairmont Drive, away from John George Psychiatric Pavilion. She had no memory of the trip there three days ago. Emergency room doctors had placed her on a 5150 hold and then had had her transported to the county's psych facility after failing to find anything physically wrong with her to explain the constant wailing and combativeness. After three days of probing questions and evaluations, Reyna had arrived at her own diagnosis: she'd lost her mind, along with everything else. Oddly enough, this time she didn't blame anyone but herself.

Spending hours isolated in a small room had a way of bringing out the truth. When she was surrounded by those white walls and that dark linoleum, her pride and denial vanished and the bare truth emerged. Her predicament wasn't Peyton's fault; she'd allowed him to take advantage of her. Her relationship with Tyson didn't end because he didn't believe her; the foundation of the budding relationship had been built on her lies and omissions. It wasn't even Pastor Jennings's fault for manipulating and using her all those years. After Jewel came to her rescue, Reyna could no longer blame her mother for her insecurities. In that cold, sterile room, Reyna came face-to-face with the real perpetrator: herself.

Stubbornness had driven her to make bad choices. In rebellion, she'd deputized herself captain of her ship and master of her soul. She'd allowed hurt to fester and transform into bitterness, which ate away the tenderness of her soul. Pride had blinded her on her quest for independence. The enemy had disillusioned her and beguiled her into believing no one controlled her, that she was in control. Lying flat on her back on the metal-framed slab that served as a bed, with a braid on each side of her head, Reyna accepted that she controlled absolutely nothing.

Pastor Jennings had many warped teachings. Ironically, one of the few biblically sound ones had echoed in Reyna's head all night.

"God will never leave you or forsake you. You'll never get too far, where His hands can't reach down and grab you," her former pastor would say.

Tyson had told her the same thing with different words, but she hadn't wanted to hear it then. She was ready to listen now.

"Would you like to stop and get something to eat?" Jewel asked from the driver's seat. "We could pick up Zachary's to go."

"That's okay. I'll make a sandwich at home."

Home meant back under her mother's roof and in her old bed. She thought it best to make a clean break and not wait to move out of the town house. She'd be going to back to her mother's house in thirty days, anyway.

"You really should eat a decent meal," Jewel insisted.

Reyna detected the worry in her mother's voice. Jewel had good cause to worry. In the last ten days Reyna had lost twelve pounds.

"If you make fried chicken, cabbage, and macaroni and cheese for dinner, I promise to eat two platefuls."

After Jewel saved her life, she didn't want her mother worrying about her.

"You got a deal." With exact precision Jewel made a U-turn and pulled into the grocery store parking lot.

Reyna napped in the car while Jewel shopped. Images in her mind of her seated at Pastor Jennings's table, reciting the sinner's prayer at age seventeen, disturbed her rest but gave her the peace she'd been searching for. She was both physically and spiritually exhausted; instead of resisting, Reyna welcomed the comfort. "Come into my heart, Jesus," she whispered repeatedly until uncontrollable tears cascaded down her cheeks. "I'm sorry, Lord. Come into my heart, Jesus."

Supplication was still being made when Jewel loaded the grocery bags and entered the car.

"I can't do this anymore," Reyna cried, gripping her mother's arm.

Jewel threw her purse on the backseat. "You can't do what anymore, baby?"

"I can't live like this anymore. This is not who I am. I need God. I need to feel His presence again." She collapsed on her mother's shoulder.

Jewel lost track of time in the parking lot as she held her daughter and prayed for her restoration. It didn't matter that the vanilla ice cream she bought to accompany the peach cobbler she'd planned to make would melt. Her child had finally come back home.

"I found one I like," Reyna announced, walking into the kitchen three days later. "I can check in on Friday. It's a little pricey, but I think it's a great fit."

"As long as it works for you, don't worry about the cost."

Reyna kissed Jewel on the cheek. "Thanks, Ma. You won't regret it."

Jewel pulled a paper towel from the rack and dabbed her eyes. "I know I won't. You can do all things with God's help."

Reyna's cheeks flushed at her mother's vote of confidence. It had taken almost thirty-one years for her to realize her mother was a ride-or-die chick.

"I have to start preparing. I hope you don't mind me not helping with dinner."

"Take care of your business, girl. I have some calls to make."

Reyna trotted off to her room and began making preparations for the rest of her life. She didn't doubt the power of God. She believed He'd forgiven her and restored her, and denial no longer ruled her. She acknowledged she had become an alcoholic and needed help beating the addiction. Old issues remained that needed to be dug up. She needed help identifying triggers, and she needed to learn how to properly deal with problems, instead of numbing the pain.

After much prayer, she'd found a faith-based recovery center online. The luxury, state-of-art center, located in the beautiful Santa Cruz Mountains, was small enough to provide an individualized recovery plan and resourceful enough to help her manage her personal and financial problems as well. A ninety-minute drive, the center was far enough from the city for her to focus on getting better without distractions. After a thirty-minute phone assessment, both she and the counselor agreed she was a good match for the program.

She had three days to completely move out of the town house and pack for the ninety-day stay. Utilities had to be turned off, and a change of address request given. Most importantly, she needed to call and plead with Starla to do her hair. Dealing with her hair would be a distraction at the center. Single micro braids would be perfect for the three-month stay. She hadn't spoken to Starla since the incident at Kevin's house months ago, yet, Starla called and welcomed her back into the fold and offered to assist her in any way possible.

Reyna figured the entire crew knew about her re-dedication to the Lord within seconds of Jewel calling Mother Scott, because they all called. Tyson must have known too, but he didn't call. She couldn't dwell on that now; it was time for her to "do her."

Her next order of business was to call Paige and resign from her position. She was grateful to Paige for not firing her, but Tyson had gotten her that job. She thought it best to cut ties and stand on her own two feet. It was time for her to trust in God's provision and not Tyson's resources.

"Ouch!" Reyna screamed and winced when Starla started the first braid two days later. They were sitting on Jewel's front porch to avoid tracking hair in the house.

"Girl, I can't believe you're tender headed. I barely touched you."

"I've never had my hair braided," Reyna said, pouting.

"Stop whining, before I send you to the mountains looking like Simba from *The Lion King*."

Reyna turned and looked upward. "You wouldn't dare?"

"Yes, I would. Now, turn around and hold still," Starla ordered. "I'll give you a Tylenol before I leave."

Reyna gritted her teeth and obeyed. She didn't have a choice; she was scheduled to leave for the center in eighteen hours. She'd completed every task, including mailing the keys for the town house to Tyson's post office box. She still hadn't heard from him and didn't expect to. He'd made it crystal clear: he was done.

"What time is Tyson picking you up?" Starla inquired three rows later.

"He's not. My mother's taking me. We're not a couple, you know," she answered, hoping to prevent further questions about Tyson.

Starla smirked. "Since when does that make a difference?"

"It makes a big difference now," Reyna commented with a hint of sadness. "At any rate, he's not coming."

Starla continued braiding, and Reyna continued wincing.

"What's that you were saying about Tyson not coming?" Starla said a quarter of the way through.

"What?"

Starla held Reyna's head up.

Reyna winced again, not from pain, but from shock. Tyson stepped from his BMW and walked toward the porch. Her breath caught as every deliberate step accentuated his muscular body. She wouldn't consider him tall, but the tailored suit added inches to his stature. The closer he got, the more nervous she became. Was he going to wish her well or spit more painful darts?

"Hey, sis," he said to Starla and gave her a light side hug. "Do you have a minute?" he asked Reyna, without bothering with a greeting. "I need to discuss a private matter with you."

Reyna didn't miss the slight, but her heart still fluttered. "I'm kind of busy right now." She would not place her life on hold again for a man, even if she loved him.

Starla held up her wrist and looked at her watch. "You're right on time. It's time for me to take a break. Be back in ten." By the time Reyna looked up, Starla's back was across the threshold of the front door.

Reyna's shoulders shrugged. "I guess you're in luck."

Tyson's facial expression remained hardened. "Luck has nothing to do with it. This is business."

"I'm listening."

Tyson stood facing her, like she was on the witness stand and he was the cross-examining attorney.

"Do you know how to get in touch with Peyton's family?"

The question caught her off guard. Why would he ask her anything about the man who had destroyed his house?

"I don't know anything about his family, other than they live in Oregon. At least that's what he told me, but that may not be true."

"So you expect me to believe you lived with the man for months and never met or talked to his family?" It was more of an accusation than a question.

"Believe whatever you like. It's the truth. Why don't you ask Peyton yourself?"

"I can't. He's dead," he answered, then folded his arms and stared at her like he was waiting to scrutinize her reaction.

At that moment, Reyna knew God had changed her heart. The hatred she had once felt for her abuser wasn't there. It had been replaced with pity.

"How? What happened?"

"According to police, the husband of the woman he was messing with came home early from a business trip and caught them in bed, doing coke. The husband went ballistic and beat them both with a two-by-four. The wife died immediately, but Peyton died two days later from internal bleeding."

Her hand covered her mouth. "Oh, my God, what a horrible way to die."

"For some unknown reason Peyton had the address to the town house in his pants pocket, which is why the police contacted me, the owner. I wasn't able to give them any more information than they already have. I thought you might know something to assist them in contacting the next of kin."

"Sorry, Tyson, but I don't know anything. As pathetic as it may sound, I didn't know much about the man before I moved him in," she admitted.

"If you remember anything, give this investigator a call," he said, holding out a business card.

"You keep it," she said, shaking her head. "I'm leaving in the morning."

"That's right," he said, like he'd remembered something important. "You're checking into a treatment center. Good luck with that." He replaced the card in his breast pocket and backed way. "Oh, yeah, congratulations on rededicating your life to the Lord," he called over his shoulder. Then he was gone.

A feeble strand of hope bubbled up in Reyna. He might never admit it, but he still cared. His body language might have been aloof and his voice cold, but every time she gazed at him, dark green flecks in his eyes communicated the feelings his heart would never again acknowledge.

Chapter 34

The description and pictures on the Internet didn't do the recovery center justice. What was described as a "luxury rehab treatment center" was in actuality a resort. The single rooms were actually one-bedroom villas with a queen-sized bed with a pillow-top mattress and daily maid service. Meals were prepared three times daily by an in-house chef, and snacks were available twenty-four-seven. Computer and Internet services were available in the media center. The fitness center contained all the latest exercise equipment and a spa, complete with body massages.

Of all the recreational activities offered at the recovery center, Reyna most enjoyed the early morning walks along the two-mile trail that encircled the facility. The immaculate landscaping borrowed from every hue in the spectrum to create a magnificent kaleidoscope of color.

During these daily walks she met with God. On most days she talked about her life and the mistakes she had made, while He listened. Some days she simply walked and cried. She lamented that she would never know who her father was. For comfort, she heard Him speak to her spirit, assuring her that He was her father and that He would never leave her. Reyna admitted being angry at her mother for waiting so long to talk to her and teach her how to be a strong woman. In the process of forgiving her mother, Reyna was also able to forgive Pastor Jennings. Their actions hadn't always been in her best interests, but they loved her. Like her, they weren't taught how to effectively express love on a daily basis, but in a crisis their actions revealed what they couldn't express verbally. The Father, in His gentle way, opened her heart to receive the truth that she, like them, was a product of her environment. To demonstrate forgiveness, Reyna sent an e-mail to her mother and Pastor Jennings stating that she had forgiven them and thanking them for coming to her rescue.

A month into her stay, Reyna finally stopped crying herself to sleep. She couldn't help it; the nights were the hardest, when she felt the most alone. The mountains, beautiful and calming during the day, were dark and cold at night. The night sky there seemed darker than the one back home. When the lights went out at curfew, it got so dark inside her room, Reyna couldn't see her hands in front of her. She couldn't see anything, but the sun's brilliance always welcomed her the next morning, giving her the energy to face the day.

One night, while struggling to fall asleep, she applied the dark-light scenario to her life. Sure, she was in a dark place right now, but if she endured and persevered, the Son would carry her to a brighter day. Determined to succeed, Reyna followed the program to the letter: praying and connecting with her higher power, journaling, meeting daily with a counselor and giving accounts of her thoughts and actions, and learning to replace drinking with positive behavior. In the process, she discovered she had a knack for beading. When Jewel and her gangsta girls came to visit on Family and Friends Day, Reyna sent them each home with a necklace and bracelet set and sets for Starla and Marlissa.

Whenever Tyson drifted into her thoughts, she opted to pray for him instead of pining for what could have been. Unselfishly, she prayed for him to find the right woman to share his life with. After asking God to give her the strength to handle Tyson being committed to someone other than herself, she moved on to another petition. She refused to allow her feelings for him to distract her from receiving the tools to change her life.

A brighter day—a breakthrough—came eight weeks into the program, during a group therapy session conducted by Dr. Candace. While at the recovery center, staff and clients used first names only to protect their confidentiality. There wasn't a set format for group therapy. Any and every topic could be discussed in the sessions as long as every participant followed one rule: no lurking. Everyone had to share truthfully.

Rose, a suburban housewife and mother of two adult children, started the discussion. "I don't know how I became a drug user. I mean, I've thought about it over and over, and I can't figure it out. I have a loving husband and family. Nothing traumatic happened to push me over the edge." She threw her hands up. "I just don't get it. How did I get here?"

"I've been thinking the same thing," Josh said, jumping in. "I was next in line to make partner at the firm. I had it all . . . houses, cars, a boat. I even bought a thoroughbred. Next thing I know, I'm disbarred. I can't remember why I started using in the first place. I think it was a dare."

"Any more comments before I address Rose's and Josh's comments?" Dr. Candace asked.

"I'd like to say something," Reyna said, unsure if she possessed the courage to be transparent. *I can do all things through Christ.* "I know why I became an alcoholic." She eyed Rose and Josh, who looked at her expectantly. "On the surface, it was easy for me to blame my verbally and physically abusive boyfriend for my drinking, and I did for a while. I convinced myself that I needed alcohol to mentally cope with my environment. Eventually, I did more escaping than coping. Since I've been here, and even before I arrived, I've accepted the truth. I became an alcoholic because I didn't know my value."

She paused to let the statement settle in her spirit. This was the first time she had talked openly about having low self-esteem.

"When you don't know the value of something, you'll abuse or misuse it. I didn't know my value as a child of God, as a woman, or as a human being, for that matter. As a result, I abused myself with alcohol and allowed my so-called boyfriend to verbally and physically abuse me. Had I known my worth, I wouldn't have gotten drunk and given my virginity to a stranger. Had I realized I deserve respect and honesty, my ex wouldn't have had the chance to rape me. He never would have moved in with me." Her voice trembled, and she used the back of her hand to wipe her eyes. Although she was working on forgiving Peyton, discussing the vicious attack proved difficult.

She went on. "One sip became three, and an ounce became a pint, because I didn't love myself. I showed up at work in my slip because I devalued myself." She used the tissue Dr. Candace had handed her to dry her eyes. "That's how I became an alcoholic."

"How do you perceive yourself now?" Dr. Candace's question broke the silence that had followed.

"Since I've been here, I've begun learning who I am and what I like. Before I got here, I couldn't tell you one activity I enjoyed doing alone. I defined myself through others and what *they* liked. I thought I needed a physical person to validate me—to make me feel special. I thought I didn't finish school and open up a practice because someone I trusted told me I shouldn't. The truth is, I didn't really believe I'd be successful, and I used their opinion as a reason to drop out with just a year to go." Another truth spoken for the first time.

Reyna continued. "Today I know I'm valuable. I'm not perfect, but I'm worth more than a bottle in a brown paper bag. I've made many mistakes, but there's more good than bad inside me. I may not get it right the first time, but I have the power to complete anything I start."

Rose and Josh looked perplexed, like they were analyzing her words. Reyna prayed God would use her testimony to minister to them. In the meantime, she added them to her expanding prayer list.

Chapter 35

"Son, you couldn't putt the ball if your life depended on it," Judge Stokes teased. "I don't know why you throw away your money every month. You should donate the money to one of your mother's charities. That may help you get back on her good side." Judge Stokes was in a jovial mood, and Tyson was depressed.

"Whatever, Dad. I come here because you're here and I want spend time with you, but if you prefer I not come, I won't." Tyson sat on the golf cart and watched his dad hit the golf ball twenty feet.

Judge Stokes whistled and admired his shot, then joined his son on the golf cart but didn't start the ignition. "You've been in a funk for weeks, actually since you broke up with Mylan. Do you want to tell me what's going on?"

Tyson huffed and folded his arms. The juvenile behavior was uncharacteristic, but he couldn't help it. Once again his life lay in limbo, thanks to Reyna Mills. Checking into that recovery center served two purposes: it helped her get over her issues and it helped him avoid dealing with his. Managing a breakup was easy when the other party wasn't around, but Reyna was scheduled to return home in two weeks.

They weren't an official couple when she betrayed him, but this split was more difficult than the first. He'd experienced contentment in the most intimate way with her, and the experience was everything he'd imagined it would be. He wanted more.

"I'm new at father-and-son bonding, but I think it works better when both parties participate in the conversation," Judge Stokes said, interrupting his pity party.

Despite his best efforts to resist, Tyson chuckled. "Did you say 'funk'? I didn't know that was in your vocabulary."

"At least I got a laugh out of you. Are you going to tell me what's funkin' ya?"

Tyson shook his head. He wasn't being stubborn. He just didn't know how to tell his father he'd screwed up his life again, chasing someone who didn't want him.

Judge Stokes leaned back in the seat and rested an elbow on his son's shoulder. "I'm no expert at male-female relationships, but let me take a stab at this. You broke up with Mylan to be with that Rachal girl, who lived in your place. That didn't work out, so now you're selling the town house."

This time Tyson laughed out loud.

"Well, am I right?" the judge asked expectantly.

"No, but close," Tyson admitted.

"Well, straighten your old man out."

Tyson stared at his father, amazed. At times he found it hard to believe the cool, laid-back man his father had transformed into was the same stoic man who had raised him.

"First of all, I didn't break up with Mylan. She broke up with me. It wouldn't have worked, anyway. It's *Reyna,* not Rachal. No, it didn't work out between us, but that's only partially the reason I'm selling the town house." He spared his father the details of the damage Peyton and Reyna had caused. "Before you ask, yes, I still love her, but I'm sure it's over this time."

"But you don't want it to be," the judge observed. "That's why you're out here, pouting like a five-year-old who's lost his toy. If you love her that much, then go and fix what's wrong."

"What?" Tyson said, leaning forward. "I thought you said, and I quote, 'Marry someone who loves you. She'll make a good home. Love can come later.'"

"I told you, I'm not the relationship guru." The judge slapped his shoulder, but Tyson failed to see the humor. The judge sobered. "Look, son, your mother and I liked Mylan, but this is your life. You have to live it the best way you see fit. If your heart is with Reyna, then that's where the rest of you should be. Your mother and I want you to be happy so we can have some grandkids."

"It's not that simple," Tyson noted. "I know where my heart is, but I don't know where hers is."

Judge Stokes smirked at his son. "When I was in law school, they taught us how to ask questions." He shook his head and started the cart.

"Reyna's away right now."

He shifted the gear into drive. "Is she studying abroad or something?"

Tyson didn't believe in sugarcoating anything. Besides, this was his chance to test the truth of his father's previous statement. "She's away at a treatment center for alcohol abuse."

The cart came to a lurching halt.

When Tyson pulled up to Kevin's house, he was still amused at his father's response to his dilemma. He'd never seen his father so indecisive. The judge had flip-flopped three times on his position before he'd relented. "You gave up Mylan for an alcoholic?" he'd asked at least ten times by the time they'd returned to the parking lot. Condescending and encouraging statements, everything from "Well, if you really love her . . ." to "Have you lost your mind?" had filled the trip back to his parents' estate.

"I've got to start going to church so I can pray for you," his father had said, exiting his car.

Tyson had put his father's worries to rest before he closed the car door. "Dad, you have nothing to worry about. I love Reyna, but we're not meant to be."

Laughter had poured from Tyson when his father looked toward heaven and yelled, "Hallelujah!"

"Hey, sis." He side hugged Marlissa before entering the house. "Where's my godson?" Unable to spend time with Kevin Jr. for two weeks, thanks to back-to-back court cases, he missed him terribly. The energetic baby never failed to sooth his spirit just by gurgling at him.

"He's out back, on the deck. Mother Scott is holding Bible study."

"What?"

"I'm joking. Actually, she's reading Bible stories to him. Kevin's out there to make sure she doesn't start teaching him how to speak in tongues before he learns to say 'Daddy.'"

"He's going to need backup." Tyson laughed, then started for the deck.

Marlissa's firm grip on his forearm stopped him. "Can I speak to you for a minute?"

He noted the concern in her voice and gave her his undivided attention. "What's up?"

"Have you spoken with Reyna lately? She's due home in a couple of weeks."

Just what he didn't need: another reminder of her pending arrival. "I haven't, and I don't plan to. She returned the keys. There's nothing left for us to discuss."

"Sit down and listen to me," she ordered, pointing at a stool at the kitchen counter.

He obeyed and mentally braced for a Marlissa Jennings drama moment. Surely neck rolling and finger wagging would be involved.

She didn't disappoint him.

"I don't know exactly what happened between you and Reyna. I'm sure she did something foul, because that's who the old Reyna was—foul and trifling. She's saved now, and I see a real change in her. You need to cut her some slack. You've been in love with that girl too long not to give her another chance." She leaned in closer. "You know you want to. That's why you sent roses for her birthday last week."

"Which she failed to thank me for," he threw out like a spoiled brat.

She slapped his shoulder. "Did you or did you not tell the girl you didn't want to hear from her again?"

Tyson shook his head. His circle of friends was too small. "You're assuming she cares about me."

She planted her fists at her waist. "And you thought I belonged on a big yellow bus?" She was referring to when she and Kevin were having communication problems. "Look, bro," she said, her voice more calm now, "I know what she's going through. I used to be an alcoholic too, remember?"

He let the rhetorical question hang and waited for her to continue.

"I know what it's like to have so much hurt bottled inside that you'll do anything to numb the pain, even if that means hurting those closest to you. Whatever she did, it wasn't from her heart. It was from a place of fear and pain."

"That's right," Mother Scott cosigned, coming in from outside.

Marlissa stepped back and let her take over.

"Oh, God," he grumbled, throwing his hands in the air. "I didn't come for this."

"She was acting like sinners act." Mother Scott went on a tangent. "I don't know why church folk get mad at sinners for doing what sinners do. They wouldn't be sinners if they didn't sin. Church folk always want sinners to act like them."

"That's not it," he said, trying to interrupt.

"That's part of it." Mother Scott pressed forward like she was the one who had initiated the conversation. "Your biggest problem is you haven't learned how to love unconditionally yet. I told you that months ago, before the mess got started, but you didn't listen to me. I know what really happened, and it's not as black and white as you think. Yes, she lied and deceived you, but there's more to the story." She glared at him. "You know what? You ain't squeaky clean, either. Your flesh done got you in trouble a time or two."

Tyson shifted on the stool.

Mother Scott went on. "You need to stop lying to yourself. You're hurt and angry, but you want to be with that girl. If you didn't want her, you wouldn't be footing the bill with Kevin for her stay at that fancy resort."

Tyson feigned innocence. "Mother, what are you talking about?"

"Don't play with me. Who do you think told Jewel to call you in the first place? She called asking me to pray for the Lord to send her a financial miracle so she could pay for Reyna's recovery. I said, 'What do we need to pray for? We already got Tyson and Kevin, a lawyer and a doctor. A negotiator and a healer.' Y'all just needed to sit down and negotiate how to pay for the healing.'"

Marlissa leaned over the counter, laughing.

Tyson refused to give vent to the merriment bubbling inside for fear he'd start bawling like a baby. Mother Scott had read him correctly. If this wasn't his life, the scenario would be hilarious. Loving Reyna was the thorn in his flesh. He'd sought the Lord more times than he could count, yet the Lord hadn't seen fit to remove Reyna from his heart. Was God's grace truly sufficient?

"I'm going to see my godson," he said and headed once again for the deck.

Later that night, while checking his e-mail, Tyson learned he did indeed have the capacity to love unconditionally.

The subject line simply read: From Reyna.

Before opening the message, he prayed, asking God to open his heart and to direct him on how to deal with her.

> Hello Tyson,
> Thank you for the flowers on my birthday. The yellow roses were beautiful. I know you said you didn't want to hear from me again, but I made you a promise.
> Let me start by saying I'm sorry for lying to you and hurting you. It wasn't on purpose; I'll explain that in a moment. I should have told you the truth about Peyton from the beginning. I should have done many things differently, but I can't change that now. I can only move forward.
> The morning after we spent the night together, I had every intention of telling you everything. That's why I asked you to come over.

Then Peyton showed up. He was supposed to have moved out the day before, but he showed up, begging for money to buy drugs. I refused, and when I ripped your check to keep him from trying to cash it, we fought. In short, he sexually assaulted me, and I got drunk to deal with it. That's what you walked in on, the aftermath. Before that afternoon I hadn't been intimate with Peyton in over two months, since I found him with Laci, the married woman he died with. He wouldn't have touched me again had he not forced himself on me.

What I'm trying to say is, after being with you, I couldn't be with him or anyone else. That night, in your bed for the first time, I experienced what real love is. As delectably sinful as it was, being with you awakened a dormant part of my soul, and I wanted to experience life with only you. I didn't say it then for so many foolish reasons, but I love you and have loved you for a long time.

Now, about that promise. I'm pregnant. Before you get upset and delete this message, I didn't find out until yesterday, when I threw up breakfast for the second day in a row. The facility nurse performed a pregnancy test, and, well, I'm around ten weeks or so, according to dates. I won't string you along or hurt you further by pretending this baby is yours. I don't know who fathered this child, you or Peyton. As you know, we didn't use a condom, and of course, neither did Peyton. The odds are in your favor since we were together first and Peyton was using cocaine. I'm rooting for you. I'll have a paternity test as soon as possible.

I'll be home in two weeks. If the baby is yours, I hope we can put the past behind us and work together. I don't want my child growing up in the same dysfunction I did.

Talk to you soon,
Your baby momma (maybe) LOL
P.S. Sorry for the long message

Tyson read the message three times before picking up the phone and dialing his parents' home.

"Hey, Dad. What's that you and Mom were saying about grandchildren?"

"Bev!" his father yelled after Tyson informed him of Reyna's pregnancy. "We're joining church on Sunday so we can learn how to pray for this boy."

Chapter 36

"Ma, I told you I didn't want a party," Reyna said, pouting. "I just want to enjoy a quiet evening at home. I'm tired," she whined.

Jewel pulled into the driveway. "Relax, baby. *I'm* not having a party."

"No party, huh? Then what's all this?" Reyna waved her arms, indicating the cars lining the street on her mother's block.

Jewel downplayed Reyna's keen observation. "Oh, a few friends must have dropped by while I was gone."

"A few friends? Yeah, right."

Reyna's eyes rolled, but not because of anger or irritation. At that moment she couldn't be happier that a "few friends" had stopped by to welcome her home from the treatment center. No doubt everyone who had aided in her recovery was crammed inside her mother's ranch-style home. Kevin and Marlissa's Mercedes touched bumpers with Leon and Starla's minivan. A Lexus bearing the license plate DRAKE2 sat at the end of the driveway. Pastor Jennings's 1992 Cadillac DeVille was in its normal position— halfway on the curb nearest the living room window so she could look out for thieves. She didn't see Tyson's car.

"Reyna, you're like the prodigal daughter, and everyone's excited you're back. Be nice," Jewel ordered. "We have a small family, but God has blessed us with people who love us and treat us like blood. Don't push them away."

Reyna shook her mother's shoulder. "Oh, Ma, lighten up. I fed you that no party crap to make sure you'd give me one. I can't wait to see everyone." She jumped out of the car and ran into the house. "I'm back!"

Just as she had hoped, the house overflowed with people who loved her and whom she'd grown to love and who were cheering for her.

"Look, Auntie Reyna. We made this for you." Leon and Starla's sons unrolled the WELCOME HOME sign.

Reyna loved the homemade sign, but their name selection touched her heart. Auntie Reyna was officially part of their family. She squatted and hugged them. "Thank you."

"Sis, come here and give me a hug," Kevin said from behind.

Pastor Jennings, Leon, and Marlissa followed suit, offerings hugs and kisses.

"I need to find a church home," Reyna said when Pastor and First Lady Drake greeted her. "I would join Restoration Ministries, but I don't know if I can handle a gangsta first lady," Reyna teased.

"What are you talking about?" Pastor Drake asked, looking bewildered.

"She's just teasing, baby," the first lady assured her husband. Then she whispered in Reyna's ear, "Remind me to teach you not to tell everything," then steered him away.

Reyna doubled over with laughter.

"I don't know what she said, but I'm sure she meant it," Starla commented behind her.

Reyna turned, but before hugging Starla, she noticed her necklace. Starla was wearing the beaded necklace

Reyna had made. She looked around the room again; all the ladies had on one of her designs. Reyna beamed with pride; she'd made something beautiful with her hands, instead of using them for destruction.

"I love you guys, all of you," Reyna told the crowd. "Thank you so much for being there for me. I don't know what I would have done without you—"

"We love you too," Mother Scott interrupted, coming from the kitchen, carrying a glass of milk. "Now, get somewhere and sit down before you tire yourself out. Here. Drink this. You need the calcium for the baby."

Mortified, Reyna gulped the milk down but noticed no one seemed disturbed by Mother Scott's announcement. She handed Mother Scott back the empty glass and sought the guilty party, but Jewel was nowhere to be found. "Chicken," Reyna mumbled.

"So, I guess everyone knows I'm pregnant," she said out loud, wondering how much information her mother had disclosed. She'd shared the complete details of the baby's conception.

"Girl, sit down," Mother Scott ordered, pointing at the one empty chair. Reyna obeyed. "That's old news. We've already selected the baby shower date. Now, tell us your experience at that fancy resort."

God, you are so amazing, Reyna thought. Although she had accepted the pregnancy with optimism, she'd worried about how her friends would receive the news, especially since she was unemployed, unwed, and didn't know whose name belonged on the birth certificate as the baby's father. These people didn't care; they loved her and would love her baby.

After sharing highlights of how the recovery center had changed her life, she dropped her own bombshell.

"As soon as I recover from having the baby, I'm going back to school to finish my master's. It may take me a few years to do it, with finances and tending to a small child, but I am going to finish my graduate degree and open a practice. I'm going to be a family therapist."

The room erupted with praise and cheers. Jewel got so caught up in praise, she danced in the spirit.

"First Lady," Mother Scott said, "Look at how the Lord is blessing and growing our family. You and I barely finished high school, but look what He gave us. A contractor, a doctor, a lawyer, a judge, and now a family therapist. God sho' is good."

"Yes, He is," First Lady Drake affirmed. "Effectual fervent prayer gets results."

"Amen," Reyna started to say, but asked, "Who's going to be a judge?"

"Let me update you on the latest breaking news around here," Kevin said before anyone answered. "Guess who closed down their church and joined Restoration Ministries?"

"What?" Reyna gasped and looked at Pastor Jennings. "I don't believe it. You closed your church? That's a miracle." For years the small congregation had been Pastor Jennings's life and identity.

"I'm a witness to the fact that miracles never cease to happen," replied Pastor Jennings. "After Sunday service two weeks ago, I locked the door, called my Realtor, and placed the building up for sale. Your mother and I joined Restoration Ministries the next Sunday."

"You should have closed that church years ago. You only had ten members, and three of them were bedridden," Mother Scott threw out to the merriment of the group.

"Mother," Pastor Drake warned.

"I'm just saying, Pastor," Mother Scott said in her own defense. "Rosalie, you know we're happy to have you. Now that you're saved for real, you can join the prayer team, but you need to learn how to rightly divide the Word before you teach Bible study."

Reyna shook her head. Never had she imagined that Pastor Rosalie Jennings would meet her match.

"Hello, everybody."

Reyna's breath caught when Tyson entered the house, wearing black jeans with a pullover sweater and carrying a dozen red roses. She attempted to downplay the effect he had on her by pretending she didn't see him.

"Stop frontin'," Starla whispered in her ear. "You know you want to see your baby's daddy."

Reyna threw caution to the wind. "Tyson," she hollered and ran to him, jumping on him and wrapping both arms and legs around him. She buried her head against his neck and sniffled. "You came. I'm so happy to see you. I can't believe you came."

Marlissa relieved him of the roses, allowing him to hold Reyna with both arms.

He brushed his lips against her cheek. "You thought I wouldn't be here? I had to pick up my parents. That's why I'm late."

The sniffles stopped. "Your parents are here?"

"This is a special day. Of course they're here."

In slow motion, Reyna peeked around Tyson's shoulder and looked into faces of the Honorable Judge Stokes and Mrs. Stokes. Thoroughly embarrassed, Reyna slid down Tyson's body to everyone's amusement.

Once she was resting on her feet, Tyson pulled her to his side by hooking her waist with his hand and faced his parents. "Mom, Dad, this is Reyna."

Confused but pleased by Tyson's possessive action, Reyna stuttered. "N-nice to see you again, Your Honor, Mrs. Stokes."

Judges Stokes patted her shoulder. "We're practically family, so no need to be so formal. Judge is fine."

"Reyna, I'm sorry, I can't recall meeting you before, but I look forward to getting to know you. Please call me Bev."

"Okay," Reyna answered pensively, still stuck on the judge's remark about being family.

"Now that Tyson's here, we can get this show on the road," Jewel announced from the kitchen doorway. "Reyna, sit down so the man can handle his business."

"What business?" Reyna wanted to know, but no one answered.

"Come on, sweetheart. Have a seat," Tyson coaxed.

His mother walked alongside Reyna back into the living room. "How are you feeling? I hope the morning sickness isn't too bad. I suffered horribly with Tyson."

"I'm surprised he told you about my pregnancy," Reyna replied.

"Of course he did. The judge and I are dying for grandchildren. I'd kill him if he kept something like this from me. Your mother and her friends and I have already planned the baby shower. The only thing left for you to do is select the color scheme."

The air seeped from Reyna's lungs as she sank into a chair. What was going on? Tyson's parents were under the impression the child she carried was their grandchild, and so was everyone else. She glared at her mother for an explanation, but Jewel smiled like all was right with the world. This was not right; she couldn't deceive them. What about Tyson? He was the one who had initiated this mess by involving his parents. He hadn't responded to her e-mail about the pregnancy; up until now she wasn't sure if he'd received it.

She touched his hand and motioned for him to come nearer. He bent his ear to her mouth. "Exactly why are your parents here?"

"To meet the mother of their grandchild," he answered without hesitation. "And, if you accept my proposal, their future daughter-in-law."

Reyna's jaw dropped at the same time Tyson dropped to his knee. A hush hovered over the room when he removed a diamond solitaire from his pocket.

"Reyna Mills, I love you. Will you marry me?"

"Is that all you got?" Leon said. "Man, I've got to work with you."

"Son, even I could have done better than that," the judge commented.

Everyone but Reyna poked fun at Tyson's lackluster proposal. It was perfect for her. Although simple, it offered the two things she desired most: love and commitment. Unfortunately, she couldn't accept, not yet, anyway.

She leaned forward. "Did you read the e-mail I sent you?" Reyna asked through clenched teeth, hoping no one else heard.

"Yes," Tyson answered emphatically.

"The whole e-mail?"

Tyson kissed her forehead. "Of course I read the entire message. In fact, I read the part where you admit you love me every night, before I go to bed."

Reyna's jaw fell once again. "Excuse us for a few minutes," she told the group. "I need to have a word with Tyson in private."

"I don't know why y'all need to talk in private," Mother Scott stated. "Seems to me, y'all done had too many private meetings," she said, nodding at Reyna's stomach.

"Mother," Pastor Drake warned, although he chuckled along with the rest of the group.

"Y'all know, I'm just giving y'all a hard time," Mother Scott admitted. "But we're not leaving right now." Mother Scott folded her arms. "We haven't eaten yet."

"Son, why don't you and Reyna go into her room and talk?" Jewel suggested.

"Thanks, Mom," Tyson said and stood to assist Reyna.

Reyna's head snapped from her mother to Tyson. "*Mom? Son?* Since when did you become so chummy?"

Jewel waved away Reyna's concern. "You know I've always liked Tyson. After he asked me for your hand in marriage, I couldn't help but adore him." Jewel looked contemplative. "I'm not sure why he asked my permission to marry you, considering he didn't find it necessary to ask my permission to knock you up."

Again, the room erupted with laughter, everyone joining in except Reyna. She grabbed Tyson's hand and stomped down the hallway. Had both Tyson and her mother lost their minds? They both knew there was a fifty-fifty chance that she was carrying Peyton's baby. And Mother Scott . . . what had happened to her keen discernment? Surely the Lord had revealed the odds to her.

"Tyson, what's going on?" she asked as soon as they stepped inside her old bedroom and closed the door. "Why did—" Tyson's kiss sucked the words from her mouth. She thought to resist, but he felt too good and it had been too long. She yielded and enjoyed the ride, with her back against the door.

"I've been waiting months to taste your lips again," he moaned once he finished feasting. "I missed you so much, sweetheart." He cupped her face and drank some more, then asked, "What day do you want to get married?"

"Why do you think I'm going to marry you?"

"You told me so, and I quote, 'I wanted to experience life with only you.'"

"Leave it to a lawyer to remember details." Reyna stepped away and walked over to the bed. She pointed to her abdomen. "I'm not exactly good marriage material at the moment. I have a lot of baggage."

"You also have potential, and I have big walk-in closets," he teased. "I'm not backing down."

"Tyson, I want to spend my life with you," she admitted. "But I won't hurt you further by lying to you." She paused and turned away. "Like I said in the e-mail, I don't know who the father of this baby is. I had sex with both of you within twenty-four hours. I want it to be you, really I do, but I just don't know. I can't do this to you."

Reyna closed her eyes and prayed for the strength to watch Tyson walk out of her life for good. Tyson was a good man. He didn't deserve the emotional trauma she'd dragged him through. If only she had realized his value sooner and hadn't been so stubborn.

She heard movement from behind, then felt Tyson's hands come around her waist and rest on her stomach.

"What you had with Peyton was animalistic. We made love," he said into her ear. "I love you, all of you. That includes the life that's growing inside you."

She spun around in his arms. She had to view his heart through those hazel eyes. The same love she saw the night they'd made love was there, but more intense. "What are you saying? You're willing to raise another man's child?"

"Let me explain something to you." He kissed her forehead. "When I was in college, I impregnated someone."

Her eyes widened. "Really? What happened to the baby?"

Tyson went on to explain the ordeal without revealing the woman's identity. "I hated myself, and up until recently, I didn't think myself worthy of another child."

"It was Paige, wasn't it?" she asked, guessing correctly.

"Yes," he answered honestly. "But the sexual part of our relationship ended with the pregnancy and subsequent abortion. We've remained friends over the years, but we both felt guilty about our selfish behavior. I think that's why we buried ourselves in our work. We had to overachieve, considering we used our future careers as an excuse not to keep the baby."

Reyna fingered a loose braid and pondered his words. "So what's the bottom line?"

"So what I'm saying is, you're it for me. You're the missing rib in my life. Are you perfect? No. Neither am I. Do you have baggage? Yes. So do I. At thirty-six, I'm just now learning how to give and receive unconditional love, but if you'll have me, I promise to love you with everything in me and raise the baby as my own. If the baby turns out to be mine—which I believe it will— then it's an added bonus. If Peyton's the father, then I'll adopt the baby. Either way, the baby you're carrying is mine."

Her fingers massaged his beard. "Oh, Tee, you're a perfect example of God's mercy and grace." She pulled his head down and kissed him. "You're going to make a great father. We'll take a DNA test as soon as possible."

He hugged her as close as humanly possible. "If that's what you want. The results won't make a difference to me. I'd rather wait until after the baby's born, when it's safer for both the mother and the baby."

"I know the results won't matter, but I owe you the truth. Remember, we can handle anything as long as we're honest with each other."

"Good. When can we get married?" He leaned in to kiss her, but she held his chin.

"Wait. First, I have to say something."

"Okay," he responded tentatively.

"I'm not marrying you because I need a father for my child or because I don't think I can do better. Not that you aren't a great catch. I'm not looking for love any longer, because I now love myself. I want to go back to school and eventually open my own practice. I don't want an arrangement. I want and deserve a real marriage, where we're friends, lovers, devoted only to each other in sickness and in health until death. You for me and me for you. It's okay to hide your emotions around our friends and family, but *I* want to know *all* of you. I want your heart bare and your emotions raw. I'll give you the same, and I promise to take good care of your heart. And you can't ever leave me, even when I make you mad, which I promise I'll try not to do more than once a week."

He smiled. "Deal. Anything else?"

"Oh yeah." She released his chin. "I love you, Tyson Fitzgerald Stokes." Her eyes misted with happy tears. God had given her the chance to express her feelings face-to-face with the man her heart yearned for.

"I love you more. Now, when will you marry me?" he asked again when their lips parted.

Reyna twisted her mouth. "I'll think about it."

By the time Tyson finished kissing her again, Reyna had called out a date and time.

"That's only two months from now. Why so soon?"

"I'm pregnant, but I don't want to *look* pregnant on my wedding day. And I'm wearing white. I'm not a virgin, but I am a new creature in Christ."

He nodded his approval. "Sounds good to me."

"Besides, I want to enjoy my wedding night before I get too big. Know what I mean?"

He winked. "I know exactly what you mean."

"That's enough talking. Reyna, go on and accept that pitiful proposal so we can eat. I'm hungry," Mother Scott fussed from the other side of the door.

Epilogue

Reyna held three-week-old Destiny Stokes in her arms while enjoying the movement of the rocking chair. Tyson had spared no expense when it came to decorating the nursery for their daughter, who entered the world kicking and screaming, feisty just like her mother.

Relief and joy bubbled in her heart when she beheld her brown-skinned daughter with hazel eyes—born alcohol free—for the first time. Reyna prayed every day that Destiny wasn't Peyton's child. With Tyson's eye color and her skin color, Destiny had to belong to Tyson.

Her husband didn't comment on the physical similarities, but at Reyna's insistence, he submitted to a paternity test, but only after Reyna agreed to allow him to sign the birth certificate. What he did express was his immediate love for their daughter. Like any new father, Tyson broadcast the news to anyone who'd listen. Everyone from the parking garage attendant to the gas station attendant knew Attorney Tyson Stokes was the proud father of a seven-pound, five-ounce baby girl.

Like her father, Destiny's maternal and paternal grandparents doted on her. Since her birth, Jewel had visited every morning, staying until noon to allow Reyna time to rest. After much prayer, the Stokes had fully accepted Reyna into their family. Tyson loved Reyna, and from what the Stokes could tell, Reyna reciprocated that love. Beverly Stokes had resigned from several charity boards to free up time to spend with the baby and Reyna on a regular basis. Judge Stokes hadn't made it official, but he contemplated reducing his court hours. Reyna and Tyson didn't doubt Destiny would address her grandfather as Grandpa Judge.

"I love you." The words came out muffled against Reyna's neck as Tyson knelt behind the rocking chair and kissed her on the neck.

"I love you more." Reyna tilted her head back to give him better access. "I didn't hear you come in. When did you get home?"

He lowered his head and briefly met her lips. "A few minutes ago. We won, but I'm glad the case is over. Now I can spend more time with my family." Little Destiny's bright eyes caught his attention. "Hey, sweetie. How's Daddy's baby girl doing?" The back of his right index finger stroked Destiny's cheek. That was when Reyna saw the envelope from Pace Laboratories tucked underneath his arm.

Reyna shifted little Destiny in her arms and pressed her against her bosom. Her heartbeat accelerated as she searched Tyson's face for a clue as to what the test revealed. She found none; Tyson was too busy talking to Destiny.

"The DNA results are back." Her voice quivered. "What does it say?"

Tyson ceased the baby talk and placed the envelope on Reyna's lap. "I don't know. I didn't open it."

"Why?" She squeezed Destiny tighter, as if to protect her.

Tyson stood and, with some resistance, removed the baby from Reyna's arms. After kissing her forehead, Tyson laid Destiny in the crib. He turned back to Reyna and placed his hands on her shoulders. "Sweetheart, there's no need to be afraid. I'm not going anywhere. Open it."

Reyna nodded but didn't speak. This was a defining moment. Their moment of truth. Could Tyson really accept her daughter if she proved not to be his? Would he abandon Destiny, like David Mills had abandoned her?

Her hands shook vigorously as she ripped the envelope open. Seconds later, a loud groan escaped Reyna's lips and tears cascaded down her cheeks.

"Well?"

She bowed her head. "You're . . ." The sob that was lodged in her throat broke forth, and she couldn't finish.

Tyson gently pried the paper from her shaky fingers and read the findings, then fell to his knees in front of her. He cupped her face with both hands and lifted her head, forcing her to look at him.

"Thank you for my daughter," he stated, then kissed her until her sobs turned into laughter.

Discussion Questions

1. Reyna was raised in the church and served in the church. However, she didn't have a good understanding of God or a solid relationship with Him. Is this common among churchgoers?

2. Pastor Jennings and Jewel were strict and rigid when it came to Christianity. Were you surprised by their past? Why or why not?

3. Reyna's "church only" upbringing and adult life left her naive. In your opinion, how important is it for Christians to have a balanced life?

4. Reyna experienced abandonment and neglect by her parents. Do you think that made her an easy target for manipulation?

5. Why do you think it was so easy for Reyna to dismiss Tyson's advances and good intentions and instead settle for an abusive relationship?

6. Tyson was a Christ follower, and yet he fell victim to sexual sin. Did his shortcomings surprise you? What do his actions after the event say about his character? Are accountability partners necessary in our Christian walk?

Discussion Questions

7. Reyna suffered emotionally after her father moved away. How important is it for blended families with small children to maintain a healthy relationship?

8. Peyton considered Reyna an easy target, describing her as needy. How important is it for women to feel good about themselves before entering into a relationship?

9. Mother Scott and First Lady Drake were prayer warriors and nurturers. Although at times their delivery was cold and blunt, their love was evident. Do you feel the modern church could benefit from more church mothers with their characteristics and personalities?

10. Reyna detested her mother, only to learn she'd traveled a path similar to Jewel's. Do you find that the traits that irritate you the most about others are ones you recognize in yourself?

11. Do you think Reyna will maintain her sobriety?

12. Who do you think is Destiny's biological father?

About the Author

A romantic at heart, Wanda B. Campbell uses relationships to demonstrate how the power of forgiveness and reconciliation can restore us back to God and one another. Wanda is a graduate of Western Career College. In addition to building a career in health care, she is currently pursuing her bachelor's degree in biblical studies. She currently resides in the San Francisco Bay Area with her husband of twenty-four years and two sons and enjoys spending time with her grandson.

She is an award-winning author of six Christian fiction novels. Visit the author's Web site, to learn more about her literary happenings @: www.wandabcampbell.com. Wanda loves hearing from readers. You can contact her at wbcampbell@prodigy.net.

Notes

Notes

Notes

ORDER FORM
URBAN BOOKS, LLC
78 E. Industry Ct
Deer Park, NY 11729

Name: (please print):_____

Address: _____

City/State: _____

Zip: _____

QTY	TITLES	PRICE
	3:57 A.M Timing Is Everything	$14.95
	A Man's Worth	$14.95
	A Woman's Worth	$14.95
	Abundant Rain	$14.95
	After The Feeling	$14.95
	Amaryllis	$14.95
	An Inconvenient Friend	$14.95
	Battle of Jericho	$14.95
	Be Careful What You Pray For	$14.95
	Beautiful Ugly	$14.95
	Been There Prayed That:	$14.95
	Before Redemption	$14.95

Shipping and handling-add $3.50 for 1st book, then $1.75 for each additional book.
Please send a check payable to:
Urban Books, LLC
Please allow 4-6 weeks for delivery

ORDER FORM
URBAN BOOKS, LLC
78 E. Industry Ct
Deer Park, NY 11729

Name: (please print): _____

Address: _____

City/State: _____

Zip: _____

QTY	TITLES	PRICE
	By the Grace of God	$14.95
	Confessions Of A Preachers Wife	$14.95
	Dance Into Destiny	$14.95
	Deliver Me From My Enemies	$14.95
	Desperate Decisions	$14.95
	Divorcing the Devil	$14.95
	Faith	$14.95
	First Comes Love	$14.95
	Flaws and All	$14.95
	Forgiven	$14.95
	Former Rain	$14.95
	Forsaken	$14.95

Shipping and handling-add $3.50 for 1st book, then $1.75 for each additional book.
Please send a check payable to:
Urban Books, LLC
Please allow 4-6 weeks for delivery

ORDER FORM
URBAN BOOKS, LLC
78 E. Industry Ct
Deer Park, NY 11729

Name: (please print):_____

Address: _____

City/State: _____

Zip: _____

QTY	TITLES	PRICE
	From Sinner To Saint	$14.95
	From The Extreme	$14.95
	God Is In Love With You	$14.95
	God Speaks To Me	$14.95
	Grace And Mercy	$14.95
	Guilty Of Love	$14.95
	Happily Ever Now	$14.95
	Heaven Bound	$14.95
	His Grace His Mercy	$14.95
	His Woman His Wife His Widow	$14.95
	Illusions	$14.95
	In Green Pastures	$14.95

Shipping and handling-add $3.50 for 1st book, then $1.75 for each additional book.

Please send a check payable to:

Urban Books, LLC

Please allow 4-6 weeks for delivery